Azma Dar

SPIDER

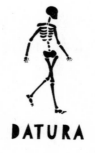

DATURA

DATURA BOOKS
An imprint of Watkins Media Ltd

Unit 11, Shepperton House
89 Shepperton Road
London N1 3DF
UK

daturabooks.com
twitter.com/daturabooks
Black Widow

A Datura Books paperback original, 2023

Cover by Alice Coleman
Edited by Ella Chappell and Robin Triggs
Set in Meridien

ISBN 978 1 91552 300 6
Ebook ISBN 978 1 91552 301 3

Printed and bound in the United Kingdom by TJ Books Limited.

9 8 7 6 5 4 3 2 1

For my Baji

PROLOGUE

The room where they keep the bodies is like a giant fridge, where people lie shelf upon shelf like frozen turkeys. I can't turn away from the thought of dressing them up with Christmas trimmings. I cough and slap a hand over my mouth to stop a crazed giggle escaping my lips. What is wrong with me? The fear and grief of the last few weeks, and the shock and dread of what I'm about to face have made me almost hysterical and out of control.

"Are you ready?" asks Inspector McKinley. Unable to speak, I nod. She reaches for my hand, but I brush her away as the doctor draws back the sheet. My skin begins to prickle, my breath quickens. The effects of the fire are horrific, but I can't tear my eyes away from him.

He looks nothing like the man I married on that winter's afternoon just a year ago. The sun had gleamed a mellow warmth from behind gun-metal clouds and a spiky fretwork of spindly branches. I'd worn jewels in my hair and a chiffon dress spangled with diamonds and pearls, white instead of the traditional red, just to make it clear to those inclined to judge me that I was still a pure, untarnished woman.

My husband had been a picture of calm; unwavering in his devotion to me. Tariq, with his dark, rosewood-coloured eyes that were both intense and sincere, and his endearing way of making the odd, small joke, then putting a finger to his lips

1

as he apologised for it. Despite all the doubt and suspicion, he'd been the single reason they'd finally admitted we made an elegant, luminous couple, an example of perseverance and faith.

A sob, and then I choke out the words, before I drop to my knees.

"It's him."

SOPHIE
One Month Earlier

They offered me a stunt double but I refused on the grounds of authenticity, even though I can't swim, and they've run out of life jackets. I'm standing somewhere over the Atlantic Ocean in the open door of a helicopter, blasted by wind and noise, staring at the cold, dark mass below. I'm about to ask for some kind of safety harness or a parachute at least, when the pilot walks over and pushes me roughly. This is how it feels, then. I've pushed a few people in my time, in different sorts of ways. I must say I'm quite enjoying plummeting towards the sea. When I hit the water seconds later, it's unexpectedly warm and soothing, and somehow, I'm perfectly capable of diving under to look for the enemy submarine.

"Surprise!" A familiar voice, but completely out of place in this context. Bond girls don't have children.

"Surprise!" says Zain again, and I feel his little hands on my shoulder, shaking me awake, and I leave my high-octane dream regretfully.

"Hello, darling," I say. I draw him up and sit him onto the bed with me, wrapping him in my arms, but he squirms and jumps off.

"I have to get the present," he says and picks up something from the chest of drawers. It's a sandwich on a plate, messily cut into squares. "I put marmalade in it."

"Ahhh, that's so lovely, thank you." The orange marmalade is Tariq's breakfast spread. I don't like it much, being a jammy girl myself, but I'll eat it just to keep Zain happy.

I know that he's gone to the extra effort because he wants me to tell him a waking up story, unusual for a rushed school morning. He's obsessed with *The Rhyming Rabbit* and has memorised most of the words. I put on a squeaky posh accent for the bunny and different silly voices for the other characters and he laughs gleefully.

When the story finishes, Zain goes to the bathroom, and I eat the sandwich in bed. Tariq left early, while I was still asleep. I glance around the room. It's not quite the gold and peacock blue boudoir of my dreams. Like many things in my life, it's a leftover from my husband's first marriage to Ruby. It's shabby chic, sickly saccharine, bordering on frumpy. A blur of distressed white wood, lace and pink paper roses. One wall is hung with sepia portraits of white women, none of whom have anything to do with Ruby, as she was Pakistani, and they are English Victorian ladies. But I've learned to keep quiet.

Zain comes back, dressed in his uniform. I brush his hair and tuck in his shirt, then tell him to go and eat breakfast. He likes making his own; to his five year-old mind the action of pouring milk over Coco Pops is cooking, just as the sandwich was.

I'm looking forward to my day. If all goes well, I might finally embark on the adventure I've been yearning for, an artistic journey that means almost everything to me.

I drive Zain to school, then go straight to Café Sprinkle on Great Horton Road near Bradford University. The place is popular with students and serves a Pakistani British fusion menu: chicken tikka shepherd's pie, masala chips, chilli chocolate fudge brownies. The décor is a dodgy synthesis of American diner meets Pakistani truck style. Colourful images of the kind found on Punjabi lorries, gaudy flowers and birds, are emblazoned across the walls, and customers are seated in round red booths with white piping. A jukebox in the corner is playing an Abrar hit, a Punjabi song about girls from Lahore having fun at a fairground. It's an eccentric mix but I like it, especially when it's bustling with students. It makes me feel young, trendy and intelligent too. I order a coffee and a rose and cardamom Danish pastry, then take the script out of my bag and smile.

It's not a leading role in a major movie, and I haven't even got the job yet, but it's *something* after all this time. An audition for a rice advert for an Asian satellite channel and I've only got two lines to say, but it's a solid opportunity at last. A chance for visibility. There'll be a small payment, but I'm not doing this for the money; I don't need to work. It's a mere steppingstone in my ambition to triumph as an actress.

It's eleven o'clock when I get the first phone call.

"Hello, sweetheart," says a familiar voice, full of overblown, honeyed charm. Suleiman. He's a distant relative of my ex-husband. I close my eyes. "How are you, my dear?"

"What do you want?" I say.

"Come on, you can be a bit more friendly than that."

"I'm very busy, Suleiman."

"Oh, if you insist!" he says. "I thought I'd give you a bit of advanced warning this time. I'm planning a little trip in the winter. I need everything to be sorted out before then. Unfortunately, my last investment was a disaster, so I'll have to make up for it."

"When?"

"Three months' time. The regular amount should do it. And I hope you don't need reminding – don't try anything silly. You know what'll happen…"

I cut him off. I don't need to hear the threats. It's a ghastly arrangement that I'm forced to keep to, and we both know I'll comply.

It might have been an impossible task to stick to the agreement without Tariq suspecting anything, if it hadn't been for all the different bank accounts we have. As well as our joint current and savings accounts, I have both an old personal and a savings account, from before any of my marriages, and a fund for Zain that Tariq's set up for his education. Tariq transfers money into my bank every month, a tidy sum that's more than I need for "housekeeping". I can move the money around as I need to and set some apart for these unheralded demands. So far, I've managed but I don't know how long it can go on for.

I'm determined not to let thoughts of Suleiman ruin my day and go back to what I was doing before he called. As I dip the pastry into the coffee and take a messy bite, I notice a woman, sitting a few tables away, staring at me. It's an impression, a feeling – her eyes are hidden behind large Hepburn sunglasses. She's wearing skinny-fit jeans and a denim jacket, and has long, dark hair. I want to ask her what she's looking at, but I can't make a scene; I'm Tariq's wife now, grateful that some of his reputation has rubbed off on me, helped me salvage any remnants of the good name I'd once enjoyed.

The telephone rings again, unknown number.

"What?" I snap, expecting Suleiman.

"Mrs Shah?" A woman's voice, low, professional. "This is Rachel from your husband's office. His PA."

I clear my throat and adopt a milder manner. "I know who you are," I say. "Is everything okay?"

"I was just wondering if you know where Tariq is today?"

"Sheffield," I reply. Was it Sheffield? I forget for a moment.

"Sheffield? Odd. He didn't mention it to me, and there's no record of it in the diary."

"I'm sure that's what he said last night. He said he was leaving early because he was going to Sheffield. For a meeting. A last-minute appointment? Perhaps he forgot to tell you." Tariq is a solicitor specialising in immigration law, and often takes meetings in other cities. When he has a lot on his mind, he sometimes forgets to tell *me* when he'll be out of town for the day.

My eyes return to the single page of script in my hand. *Nina holds up a plate of rice and sniffs it. She breathes in the aroma and smiles ecstatically.* Hmm. How do you sniff and breathe at the same time?

"Are you still there?" asks Rachel.

"Sorry. Oh, maybe try his mobile again? He might have been driving. You know how strict he is about that. If I hear from him, I'll pass on your message." I cut the call and go back to trying different accents on my killer lines.

Heaven's Own Basmati Rice
Very nice with special spice.

Beggars can't be choosers.

By five o'clock the pasta and salad for dinner are ready. Tariq is usually home by six, unless he's working late. The three of us eat together, then I put Zain to bed at eight, when Tariq and I have a relaxing evening, watching television, discussing the day, sometimes playing cards.

I change my clothes and brush my hair. Tariq says he likes a natural, make-up free face, but these days I feel like I need some help to cover my dark eye bags. Powdered and bronzed, I take out the script again and experiment with different poses and ways of saying my line in front of the mirror. Face turned up or down, with my eyes taking all the attention? Smile with lips cryptically closed or wide and happy? Look at the camera straight on, sideways, over my shoulder? I know the director will have his own ideas, but it's best to have my angles prepared.

I'm so absorbed in my rehearsal that I don't realise that it's almost seven o'clock and Tariq still hasn't returned. I feed Zain, then I call my husband. It goes straight to voicemail.

"Hi darling, just wondering when you'll be home," I say, after the beep.

After I tuck Zain into bed, I watch a programme about Grace

Kelly on Sky Arts. I'm spellbound by her beauty and her romance with the prince. Her tragic death brings a lump to my throat, but I reassure myself that she lives on through her work. I have similar, though more modest, aspirations for my own future.

I phone Tariq again, but it goes to voicemail. I eat my dinner because I don't want to spend the evening picking and nibbling. Then, spurred on by the documentary, I dig out a DVD of *Rear Window* and snuggle up on the sofa to enjoy the possibility of a husband murdering his wife. My favourite scene is when Grace Kelly breaks into the suspect's apartment, but I nod off long before I get there. When I wake up, it's past midnight and the television screen is blank.

I go to the conservatory and check the door into the garden. The fish tank hums companionably. I sit down for a moment and watch the silver dollars chase the neon guppies into their plastic castle. I'm angry now, my mind reaching back to the last time this happened. I accept it was partly my fault, then, but today is another story. I won't take any blame.

I phone Sameena, Tariq's sister-in-law from his first marriage, who lives in the Lake District. She answers on the fifth ring.

"Give Tariq the phone, please," I say, trying to keep my voice steady.

"Sophie? Tariq's not here. Is everything okay?" says Sameena.

"Don't lie to me, Sameena. Just put him on."

"I'm not lying. Why would I lie? Just tell me what's happened. Sophie?" She sounds genuinely concerned.

"He's been missing since this morning," I say. I take a breath. I must stay in control.

"What?"

"He didn't show up for work. Nobody's seen him all day and he still hasn't come home... I thought he might be with you."

"Well, he's not. I haven't spoken to him at all this week," says Sameena.

"I don't know who else to call," I say in a small voice.

"Listen, Sophie. Maybe his car's broken down and he's waiting for the AA. Maybe his phone's dead. I'd wait until morning before calling the police."

I make a cup of herbal tea, mandarin and orange blossom. It's tasteless really, just sweet-smelling warm water, but the hot liquid soothes me. I turn on my laptop and start Googling how to report a missing person. One link leads to another, *missing* changing to *murder*, *accident* to *death*. I slam the laptop shut. My hands are shaking.

It's 2.30am. I think of Amir. I can't call anyone else at this time of the night.

"Sophie?" He sounds alert, alarmed. "What's wrong? Is it Zain?"

"Zain's fine." I swallow and pause, and then I start crying. I tell him Tariq's missing, that I have no idea where he might be.

In the background I hear Amir's wife, drowsily asking him who's on the phone. He tells her to be quiet for a moment.

"I'll come over," says Amir.

"No," I say. "You don't need to. Get some sleep and come by first thing so you can take Zain to school. Is that okay? I'll leave for the police station as soon you arrive."

I stumble through another couple of hours, tidying up things that don't need to be tidied, staring at the clock, watching for the light to appear in the sky. I take a shower, change my clothes, and eat a digestive biscuit. Sameena's texted me four times during the night asking for news.

At six o'clock the doorbell rings, and I let Amir in. He's my ex-husband, so Islamically I should keep my distance, but I start to sob as I throw my arms around him.

PART ONE
AMIR AND SOPHIE

AMIR
2008

I'd known Sophie since we were children, but it never crossed my mind I'd end up marrying the small, serious kid who always looked at me with an air of disapproval. Whether I was grabbing the biggest slice of cake at a birthday party or undressing her Barbie dolls, from about five years old she'd watch my every move closely, her lips curved downwards. My mum banned me from playing with Sophie's toys when I kicked Big Mama, the giant My Little Pony, across the room, knocking over and smashing a vase.

But I did like my footie, so call it poetic justice or whatever, because years after the Big Mama incident, that's where I first got a crush on Sophie's friend, Kiran, at the girls' sixth form football final, Byron house against Shelley. Of course I'd seen her before with Sophie, but that was the day I really noticed Kiran, as she dribbled the ball in cute shorts, her black hair blazing red in the sun. Dazzling and perfectly formed, but crap at football, I thought she was the most beautiful thing in Bradford.

At first, we didn't do much apart from sit near each other at lunchtime and in the one lesson we shared, A-Level Chemistry. Kiran was doing Sociology and Biology, me, Maths and Business Studies. But it didn't matter. She was so bright and blooming and funny, and just so interested in me, that being around her for even a few minutes was like being on the loopiest rollercoaster I ever rode. I was used to being popular and flirted around a bit, but I'd never had a girlfriend, never met a girl who made my stomach go knotty. Kiran was kind and quietly confident and told me she loved cooking. I thought that might make my mum happy, when the time came. She was also religious, another good thing. Except that it was the wrong religion. Kiran was Sikh, me, a Muslim. Realistically, none of the mums and dads were going to be happy.

Understandably, we kept it a secret from them, and took Sophie along with us on our dates as a precaution. Kiran trusted her completely and asked her to act like a sort of guard dog, keeping watch at all times for any signs of danger. I felt a bit sorry for Sophie. It couldn't have been easy playing the permanent gooseberry, the *kebab me haddi*, as Mum would say, the bone in the kebab, but she carried out the duty without complaining.

SOPHIE
2008

Whilst I found the perfect love in Tariq, I first learned the definition of it when I became enamoured with Amir. His mother and mine were friends, having met at the health clinic and discovered that they were from the same town in Pakistan. When we were little, I didn't really think of him as anything other than a sticky, snot smeared brat who always ran the batteries out in our toys while he scandalously swigged Coke from a baby bottle he was too big for. Then, he used to bully me and, later, when we reached secondary school, he didn't notice me.

But it was in secondary school, when I was about fourteen, that I realised he'd cleaned up and stopped crying, and though he was still a little full of himself, he had the looks and swagger to get away with it.

Of course, I didn't even tell my closest friends about my quiet admiration. I was afraid they would think me unjustifiably vain, dreaming beyond my means. I wasn't unattractive or thick or geeky, but Amir was one of the most popular boys in my year, with his almost perfect face roughened up just enough by his wild, curly Italian footballer hair. He just wasn't going to notice me. Even worse was the thought that the boys or even Amir himself might hear about it once I confessed my feelings.

15

So, over the next few years, I kept quiet, acted indifferently, and loved him in silence. Then it came, unexpectedly. By then, we were both in college. I was sitting in the locker room at the end of lunch by myself, sorting out my books, when suddenly he was in front of me. A sudden burning sensation spread over me. Not an engulfing lust, but prickly nerves and a dread of saying something stupid and looking like an idiot.

"Hi Soph," he said. Soph. An endearment. Stay cool.

"Oh, hi. You all right?"

"How's it going? Cool dress." I was wearing a summery creation of peach lace.

"Thanks," I said.

"Ignore the idiots who said it looks like a nightie."

That wiped the happily ignorant smile off my face.

"Anyway, I wanted to ask you," he continued. Ask away, I thought, concentrating on turning the key in my locker, sealing the moment in my mind as the beginning of my great love story.

"That girl, your friend... Kiran is it?" The air slowly began to leak out of the romantic silver balloon I was wafting around in.

"What about her?" I asked.

"I... well... is she interested in going out, do you think?"

"She's not agoraphobic," I said, in an attempt to impress him with my wit and because it was all I had to comfort myself with.

"What does that mean?" he said, confused. I sighed.

"Never mind," I said. "I was trying to be funny."

"Oh, okay. So, what do you think? She hasn't got a boyfriend, has she?"

"No, she hasn't. She's not really that kind of girl." As I said it, I realised I might be unwittingly painting an unattractive picture of her, making her seem uptight and frigid instead of merely respectable and chaste. "But that's not for me to say, really. Who wants to know?"

Of course I was already pretty certain of the answer, but I

had a weak and straggly hope that it might be someone else. He tried and failed to look embarrassed.

"It's just me," he said.

"So why don't you tell her?"

"I'm worried about how she might react. Can't you talk to her first? Pave the way a bit?"

I said I would. Devastated as I was, I steeled myself into nurturing the heroic spirit of movies and fairy tales. It was, of course, a noble, selfless trait to have, but surely in the end it would also shine through and capture Amir's heart? For now, though, it meant I had to sacrifice my own love and happiness in the name of theirs.

The little hope that I'd had of Kiran not being interested in Amir soon dissipated when she rather over excitedly accepted his offer of having lunch in the college canteen.

"He just asked me out of the blue. I was in the library, standing in the queue with a pile of about seven books," she told me, at least three times. "I mean I'm not a wimp, but they were heavy–"

"And Amir saved the day by taking the weight of those crushing hardbacks into his manly arms," I finished off. "It was the most gentlemanly thing anyone's ever done for you." I was trying to be honourable, trying to douse my jealousy, but I couldn't help the catty remark. Envy wasn't good for the soul, but more importantly, it would give me away.

"You can mock all you want," said Kiran. "But it's true."

The lunches soon became a regular thing and progressed to dates out of college. Almost unbelievably, I was also invited along to these, and given the humiliating post of being the look-out. I hung around in the perimeters of parks or in the foyer of the cinema like a weirdo, to ensure there were no relatives following them. I spiced up the job by pretending I was an FBI agent. Imagining myself being tracked by a hired assassin was preferable to sulking over my unrequited love, and I reassured myself that at least this way I could keep an eye on their activities.

Although regular proximity to Amir had only increased my desire, I was oddly at ease with the situation. I just had to be patient. If my calculations were correct, relationships like this didn't last long, especially once people found out. Their days were numbered.

AMIR
2008

Some women like flowers or perfume or chocolate but for Kiran these were lazy, predictable choices. She demanded presents that had had some special effort put into them – a bunch of handpicked tulips or a CD of our favourite songs. Usually, she just wanted me to deliver a five-minute, sincere sounding lecture on how much she meant to me. This wasn't easy, but I did my best to keep her sweet, especially as she was always showering me with thoughtful little gifts. A scarf she bought but then embroidered my initials on to herself, a notebook she'd covered in pictures of my favourite biscuits, a quirky figure of a man playing cricket, made out of nuts and bolts and bent spoons that she'd bought from a craft stall in Leeds.

The Saturday she gave me the bracelet started off with the sun streaming through my bedroom window as I got dressed and slapped handfuls of Boss aftershave over my face. By the time I got to the lake, though, the sky was dark, and it was raining hard, and Kiran wasn't at our usual meeting place. It was too wet to hang around, and I trudged back the way I'd come. As I passed the café, I saw Kiran sitting at the window, waving to me, looking perfect in a fur trimmed hat and orange lipstick. I went in, shivery and miserable. Craving something warm and stodgy, I ordered a cup of tea and a portion of chips. Kiran was sipping on some blue juice.

"Did you bring any of those veggie pasties with you?" I asked. Kiran often made us picnics of various home baked goodies, pies, cakes and biscuits. Of course, I would have preferred chicken or meat myself, but she was a vegetarian.

"Is that all you think about, food?" said Kiran. "I can't cook and bring something every time. Mum will get suspicious."

The chips arrived quickly, and I attacked them hungrily. I could feel Kiran staring at me, maybe with disgust, but I didn't care. She didn't speak for about three minutes, the time it took for me to clean the plate, then opened her bag.

"I brought you something else," she said. "A surprise."

"What is it?" I said. "Brownies?"

She clicked her tongue in exasperation and closed her bag.

"Sorry," I said. "Only kidding. Show me."

She took out a small box, monogrammed with an A. I opened it. It was a bracelet made of wooden beads. In between the beads were dangly charms: a yellow button, a grey pearl, a minute shell.

"Hmm…" I said. "That's cute, but you know I don't wear jewellery. And it is a bit girly, with those bits hanging off it."

"I wouldn't expect you to, normally, but I customised this myself," she said. "The button's from the outfit I was wearing the first time we met, and that's the shell we found on that college trip to Scarborough."

"Oh yes…" I said, not recognising either.

"You don't remember any of them, do you?"

She was disappointed more than angry and I felt bad, not only because I had forgotten, but because to me the trinket was just… well, it was just a bit freaky.

"It's lovely," I lied.

"Can I put it on your wrist?" asked Kiran.

"Why don't you keep it?" I said.

She pursed her lips and looked away.

"I'm sorry," I said. "I didn't mean to hurt your feelings. It's really sweet. I love it."

"You obviously don't take this relationship as seriously as me," she said.

"Of course I do. Don't say that."

"Well, I don't know. How committed are you really?"

I hadn't thought of the future seriously. I daydreamed about it, but I knew that if my mum found out, it would be all over in an instant. She would never accept a girl who wasn't Muslim, and I never had any silly hopes that Kiran was going to convert to Islam. I wasn't sure how things were going to turn out for us. I just wanted to have some fun.

"Same as you, obviously," I said, hoping the vague reply would be enough.

"Really?" she said, eyes full of hope. "You mean you want to get married, too?"

"Yes, of course," I blurted out, in the shock of the moment, without thinking. I quickly tried to take my words back. "I mean it would be nice, but–" I stammered, but before I could get any further, Sophie appeared from nowhere, waving about frantically.

"Suki's here, looking for Kiran!" she said. "Hurry up, go now!"

"Oh my God!" said Kiran, in a kind of violent whisper. Her eyes were darting about in terror. She grabbed her coat and purse, sending coins and credit cards flying.

"I'll get them!" said Sophie, pushing Kiran towards the door, but it was too late. I could see Suki, her brother, striding across the grass and into the café, and he was inside the shop long before Kiran could get out and flee.

Mum knew, too, by the time I got home. I could tell from the way she was pummelling the chapatti dough.

Really my mum's a placid person, not one for hysterics or drama. I didn't realise this until Dad passed away three years ago from a sudden heart attack. After the first few days of shock and grief, she snapped into survival mode, learning to live life without the man who'd been with her for twenty-three years. She turned down financial help from the family and started a job cleaning houses instead, to make ends meet. A year later she started another little business, buying wholesale knitwear and selling it to friends and relatives, then branched out into towels, bed sheets and tablecloths. Soon she had a modest little enterprise going, enough to get us by. She encouraged me to be ambitious and do the best I could, hating the idea of me doing anything less because of what had happened to Dad. A deep closeness between us began to grow around that time, our bond strengthening out of tragedy.

I could understand why she was so mad. She was terrified I was going to ruin the life she'd worked so hard to give me.

"I'm sorry, Mum," I said. She slapped the sticky white ball in fury. "It just happened. It was... well, it was nothing, really."

I felt ashamed saying it. Kiran didn't deserve that. But what else could I do? I was fond of her, yeah, and I'd made her those flimsy promises, but hadn't I known all along that it would come to this? I could never resist my mother.

"I know it's not ideal, but she's a decent girl, Mum..." I hazarded. I was a feeble attempt, just to make myself feel better. At least I could tell myself I'd tried. Mum's eyes flashed at me. "Well... anyway, I won't see her if you don't want me to..." She picked up the dough and threw it into an empty ice cream box, slamming the lid down so hard the plastic cracked.

Mum imprisoned us both in the living room with *roti* and *aloo gosht*, and an Indian TV drama serial, its ear-blasting music filling the frozen, void like silence between us. When I tried to get up after dinner, saying I had an Economics assignment to do, her fingers clamped around my wrist, and she pulled me back onto the sofa without moving her eyes from the television. I had to endure another forty minutes of gaudy make-up and bad acting.

When it finally ended, Mum turned the volume down and turned to me.

"Speak," she said.

"I told you," I said. "I'm sorry."

"How long has this association been going on?"

"A few months."

"Haii!" She slapped her forehead. "Tell me the truth, Amir, don't lie. Is she in a dirty position?"

I tried to look puzzled.

"Have you made me into a *dadi*?" she asked.

"No, Mum, of course not!" I exclaimed, horrified. "We haven't done anything like that. There are no hidden grandchildren."

She closed her eyes and murmured a prayer.

"Thank God," she said. "Please, just promise to finish this now. Couldn't you think that I'm a widow?" She shed a tear and I patted her shoulder. "You're the only hope of my life, beta. I won't make you marry someone you don't like; you choose yourself. As long as she is one of us. Unless you want me to eat a box of Anadin or stand in the middle of Leeds Road and get squashed by a truck. Then you'll be looking at my bloated body in a metal drawer, sliding me in and out to show everyone." She was a placid woman, but it didn't stop her from doling out creative motherly threats from time to time.

"Stop it, Mum!"

I hugged her till she stopped crying, then she turned up the TV volume and we watched one of my all-time favourite Indian films, *Naseeb*, a story of murder and betrayal over a winning lottery ticket. A missing father identified by his three signet rings bearing various religious symbols. Best of all, a climatic fight scene in a revolving restaurant. It all worked out in the end, justice was served, and everyone was reunited.

The movie showed love that crossed boundaries of faith and overcame family feuds, and Mum sat there, cooing with approval.

I got the letter three days later. Of course I'd been thinking about Kiran, and how she was feeling, but I was hoping that, like me, she'd learn to think of those days as a sort of short, first love fun. If I'm honest, I was quite relieved; it seemed to be over. Deep down I'd been dreading the inevitable clash with the parents that I knew would come one day if we wanted them to accept our relationship. I didn't even have the courage to convince my own mother. How was I going to tackle Kiran's parents? Apart from that, I wasn't even sure I wanted to spend the rest of my life with her. I'd been excited by her catwalk looks and big personality at first, but recently I'd begun to feel I'd never be able to fulfil all her demands, give her non-stop proofs of my love. It was all too exhausting.

But now here was the envelope. It was addressed to me and written in neat capitals, but I knew it was her. Mum never even glanced at the mail. I'd dealt with it since Dad had passed away.

I opened it nervously, hoping it might be a loving goodbye.

My Darling,
Words can't describe the agony in my heart right now. I really feel it might be cracking in half. This might seem a bit extreme to you, but I have to be clear because at this point, we have no time to waste. Being apart from you has confirmed what I knew all along, that I love you more than anything. You're the star in my sky. More than that, you are my sky, moon, stars, sun. You are my world. I'll prove it to you, if you'll let me. Let's leave this city and start a new life. We'll be fresh, born again. My family will be furious, but I'll give them up for you, my angel.
All my heart,
Kiran

It made me dizzy just reading it. Once again, I was rocked at how much I'd become the centre of her world. She was ready to rebel against her parents, but it was different for me. I thought about Mum downstairs, pottering away peacefully, making tea and eating cream crackers. I'd never explained to Kiran what Mum and I meant to each other.

The letter touched something inside me, though. Mum had stamped out my infatuation for Kiran, made it look silly, unrealistic and wrong, but now I felt I owed her something, felt guilty for abandoning her like I had. It was because of me that she was so distraught. I couldn't run away with her, but I had to end things properly, say goodbye. It would be difficult, but it wasn't fair to chicken out. I was still weighing things up when the doorbell rang. I looked out of the window and saw Sophie and her mother, Aunty Resham. I went down and offered to make the tea, and seconds later Sophie followed me into the kitchen.

"I said you might need help," she said.

"Thanks," I muttered.

We put biscuits and a bowl of Indian snacks on a tray in silence.

"Did you get the letter?" she mumbled.

"Yes."

"And?"

"Tell her I'll be there."

"Are you sure? What about your mum?"

"Don't worry about her," I said. "Sophie, how is she?"

"She's okay."

"Did they…? What happened?"

"Nothing. Well, they didn't disown her or lock her up, if that's what you mean. But obviously they weren't happy about it."

"Amir!" Mum called from inside. "Get a move on! And bring some bread and butter too."

"Yes, Mum," I said. I gave Sophie the tray as I picked up the bread. "Tell Kiran to come to the lake tomorrow."

* * *

Late on Saturday afternoon I sneaked out when Mum was in the bathroom, knocking on the door to say goodbye, telling her I was going to see a mate. She grunted in reply, as she had a rule about not talking on the toilet.

The lake was sunny, the sky cast with a pinky gold light as the sun started to go down. I was almost wishing for the sky to turn gloomy and thunderous, add a risky, dangerous edge to the atmosphere.

I sat on a bench and practised what I was going to say to her. I'd just have to gently explain that maybe it was better to go our separate ways and one day we'd realise it was for the best. They were all clichéd lines, but I'd try and polish them with some worn-out charm. If necessary, I could blame it all on Mum and spout the classic Indian film line of how we owed our parents their happiness.

I waited an hour, then two, but Kiran never came. That was it, then. She must have had last-minute nerves. Either that or she'd been hijacked by her family, neither of which I could blame her for.

I didn't dare contact Kiran again. I'd just wait to see her at college on Monday. If she didn't come in, at least I'd get the story from Sophie.

SOPHIE
2008

It was okay, up to a point, Kiran's infatuation with Amir. Of course I understood it, given that I had fallen for his charms myself. But she didn't understand the unspoken principle, that for good Muslim boys a relationship with a woman from another religion was strictly "time pass". It might be caring, chatty, passionate, but in the end, it was just fun, fleeting and forbidden. In most cases they were pressurised into settling down with a good, parent-approved girl of a similar background. It was in this knowledge, that Kiran's hopes of marriage were ultimately doomed, that I was so tolerant of their continued dalliance.

I didn't exactly tell Suki about them myself. It simply came down to Kiran leaving one of her romantic gifts in my bedroom. She liked to show them to me before she gave them to Amir. Obviously I never told her how cloying and affected I found them. This time it was a notebook, with a suggestive poem written on the first page in curly calligraphy. She'd been trying to impress me with her handiwork, and I'd acted suitably touched, concealing my revulsion at both her liberal use of innuendo and the thought that it was intended for the object of my own affections. She forgot the book in my room, and all I had to do really, was leave it where she had left it, in plain sight on the chest of drawers. Later, when my brother Haroon was nosing around for a pair of nail clippers, he noticed it and picked it up. He was immediately engrossed.

"You saucy thing," he joked at first, but as he read further his face turned red, and he looked about to burst by the time he reached the end of it.

"*Besharam!*" he shouted. Shameless. He seemed unable to say anything else. I had to make him sit down before he went downstairs and told the whole house.

"It's not mine," I said. "Do you think I would do something like that?"

"You're lying."

"It's Kiran's." I told him everything and, as he played football with Kiran's brother, Suki, it wasn't long before Kiran's family found out too. Not long at all.

Ironically it was my brother that told me the news, the day after Kiran's intended meeting with Amir. I hadn't contacted Kiran, thinking that she'd rather be left alone to lick her wounds, and had assumed she hadn't got in touch with me for the same reason. It was understandable. But Haroon had the real story. Kiran hadn't phoned me because she'd taken an overdose of her mum's sleeping pills. When she hadn't appeared downstairs by lunchtime, her mother had gone up and found the door locked. Suki got a ladder and climbed in through the window and found her, lying in bed, still and cold. It was too late to do anything.

I was sick before I got to the bathroom, all over Mum's newly carpeted stairs. Fat tears dripped down my face, and, it seemed, out of my nose, as I went into the bathroom to wash away the regurgitated Weetabix. I'd wanted to remove Kiran from my path, but not like this. She was my friend, after all.

She might have been upset, furious with Amir, sulked or gone on a hunger strike in protest, run away to a hostel at worst. All of these I had envisaged when I told her that Amir wanted to break things off, but I'd never wanted her to *die*. How desperate must she have been? Poor, heartbroken Kiran. Her torment and love for Amir had been real. I didn't even want to imagine what her well-meaning parents were going through.

The more I went over it, though, the more my view began to change. It was tragic yes, but was I right to blame myself for it? Especially if, as I suspected, it had been a one-sided affair?

Kiran had outwitted me by getting her sister to post that letter to Amir, and had told me afterwards, because she wanted me to elicit a reply from him. When I'd then visited Amir, he'd said he would meet Kiran at the lake, but the moment's hesitation, the flicking of his eyes to the lounge where his mother sat cackling at the TV, and the dull, stunted vibrations emanating from him all signalled he didn't really mean it.

So, I'd told Kiran the truth, as I knew it to be. That Amir thought it best they never saw each other again.

Kiran was my friend, but I had to think long-term, consider everyone, especially her mum and dad. I fibbed, told a white lie, thinking that Kiran would be upset but recover, and Amir would deal with being stood up at the lake and might even be secretly relieved. Besides, what was I supposed to do? Amir hadn't elaborated on his plans, so I had no clue what he was up to. And I'd played matchmaker long enough now. Now that they were finally apart, I wasn't going to be instrumental in getting them back together. I'd made a mistake, I admit, but that didn't make it all my fault. I'd misjudged Kiran's reaction.

It was the first of the terrible things I did without meaning to, things that, in one way or another, led to the desperate circumstances I'm in now.

I'd acted with the best of intentions, for everybody. But still, Amir could never find out.

* * *

I wanted to possess Amir, of course, but I also wanted him to be happy with me, in particular with my behaviour towards his mother, Mumtaz. I'd realised how close he was to his mother now that he'd demonstrated his loyalty, in a roundabout way, by destroying a beautiful woman who had adored him. Yes, it had been partly because of me preventing their meeting, but I had only acted on the true, hidden emotions I had read in his face.

So I began to lay a bedrock for the seduction I was planning, by courting Amir's mother with frequent displays of my suitability as a perfect daughter-in-law. I accompanied my own mum on her visits to Mumtaz, with the excuse of needing to buy some towels and duvet covers from the little textiles shop she ran from the spare bedroom. Then I slowly started to awaken her bride-hunting instincts using other methods. I began tentatively, just by offering to make the tea myself. Before long I knew the exact kitchen cupboard locations of everything from screw pine essence to Ryvita and was offering Aunty Mumtaz regular head massages. It made my hands reek of mustard oil, but what were stinky palms in exchange for the love of my life?

The first time I saw Amir after Kiran died, I was left both dejected and hopeful. It was in the canteen, and he looked awful – ragged, messy, with a stubble and blotchy eyes. He noticed me and we glided across the room towards each other, a manoeuvre that would have been perfectly synchronised and deliciously romantic if we hadn't been coming together to commiserate over his dead girlfriend. He hugged me without hesitation, so surprising, welcome, and literally breathtaking. My parched being soaked up this downpour of unexpected affection. His long hair tickled my neck, and I took a long, silent draw of his scent, a clean, breezy fragrance with the faintest hint of spice. Had a touch of his mother's cooking become mingled with his aftershave? I didn't care. I was thirsty, rabid for more, but I gasped from the tightness of the squeeze, and he released me.

"I'm sorry, Soph," he said, through the tears. "It's just, you know how it feels." I nodded, taking in his new t-shirt. He must have thought nobody would notice, since it was plain grey and nondescript, but I knew every item of clothing he owned. He couldn't be completely destroyed. I'd seen the Indian films, full of heartbroken, wretched heroes, the appearance of whom Amir was emulating. They wandered around aimlessly, wailing out songs and sobbing like obsessed, lovestruck zombies. They certainly didn't have faculties that allowed them to spritz themselves with Calvin Klein aftershave or buy new Ralph Lauren polo shirts. As he babbled on about Kiran's virtues, a miniscule tendril of hope began to unfurl inside me.

AMIR
2008

I couldn't think why I hadn't noticed Sophie before. It wasn't that she was dowdy or plain. Far from it. Neither was she completely natural. Sophie, like Kiran, was always carefully groomed and made up. It was only because I'd been besotted by Kiran's sleek, sophisticated glamour, that I'd overlooked Sophie's soft, understated prettiness. It started off with reminiscences but fairly soon we had moved on to talking about other things over lunch, just normal things, films we'd both seen, places we wanted to visit, family gossip. It was a guiltily refreshing change from the intellectual, meaningful conversation I was used to having with Kiran.

Although I was interested in Sophie, I was careful not to come across as anything more than friends in public, especially at college. People were already whispering about me behind my back and giving me dirty looks in the corridors, probably because they held me responsible for Kiran's suicide. I didn't want to make it worse by showing them I was ready to move on.

Privately, I didn't think there was any point in stretching out my mourning, faking it, when in my heart I was ready for a new relationship. I did feel an odd twinge of guilt that it had happened so quickly, but I couldn't help it, and my relationship with Kiran had ended before her death.

At least this time, my conscience was clear regarding Mum. I hoped she wouldn't have too much of a problem with my choice this time.

There was some gentle resistance at the beginning. I asked Sophie if she wanted to see the latest Amir Khan film at the cinema. Sophie thought I wanted to take the mums with us and seemed puzzled when I explained I meant just the two of us.

"Why would you want to do that?" she asked.

"I like spending time with you," I said.

"So we can talk about Kiran?"

"Of course not!" I realised I had brushed this aside a bit too roughly. "I mean we can, if you want to, but I'd rather think about other things. Things you like. I haven't forgotten her, but I don't think it's healthy for either of us to dwell on that."

"If you're sure."

"We've got too much to look forward to."

SOPHIE
2009

Six months after that first cinema trip, Amir took me out for a birthday dinner at a Turkish restaurant. Our relationship was still a secret, so we chose somewhere out of town, like we did for all our dates, where we were unlikely to be spotted by a busybody "aunty". It was a dark, intimate, charcoal-scented space, lit with onion-shaped mosaic lanterns glinting in a spectrum of jewel like colours. We ordered mezze and Amir's meaty favourite, the mixed grill, then he handed me a small gold gift bag.

I was hoping there would be something in there that would seal the unspoken commitment that I felt we'd made to each other. Compared to my friends' parents, mine were fairly easy-going. There were to be no discos, drinking or dates, but we were able to go out with friends at the weekends, and for the most part we stuck to the rules. I was confident my parents would approve of Amir, once he actually did suggest marriage. I didn't bring the subject up myself. I was afraid of repeating Kiran's mistake and scaring him off, but I was also worried that I couldn't keep Mum and Dad from finding out for long.

I felt childishly excited as I took the bag from Amir, and it must have shown. He was gazing at me, a smile on his face.

There was a short cylindrical object inside, the box size used for items of jewellery, wrapped in gold spotted cream tissue and tied with metallic ribbon. My heart began to beat at an abrupt, jaunty pace. I couldn't believe my wish was about to be finally granted.

"Oh my goodness, Amir," I said.

"I hope you like it," he said. "Open it, then!"

I took a quick breath and unwrapped it, tearing the delicate paper where it was stuck down with too much Sellotape. But there was no plush velvet box under the triple layers of tissue. Instead, it was a dull, cold tin, a scented candle. It was so unexpected that I almost dropped it.

"Oh!" I said.

"Isn't that your favourite?" said Amir. "Pina colada. I know, we have the halal mocktail version, but you're not going to drink it, are you?" He laughed.

I wanted to cry. I gulped and covered my eyes with one hand.

"Soph, what's up?" said Amir.

"Nothing," I said. "Thank you."

"You're welcome. Ooh, here come the starters." The waitress set down plates of hummus and other dips, olives, pastries and a basket of bread. "Here, take your special order. Your cheesy borek." He pushed cigarette shaped rolls towards me.

I'd been so looking forward to this evening, but now I didn't feel like eating anything. I broke a piece off and forced myself to swallow it. I was angry at myself, more than Amir. Why had I built up such lofty hopes, lost myself in fairy story imaginings? I was stupid, stupid –

"Stupid," I muttered.

"Sorry?" said Amir.

"Oh. Nothing."

"I didn't tell you what my mum did the other day. She bought three pairs of sandals, same design in different colours. Gold, silver and bronze. She couldn't decide which one she liked best. But bargain price, apparently." He tore up a piece of bread and dipped it in yogurt. I stared at my plate. "What's wrong?"

"Just feeling a bit... it's hot in here." I was dizzy now, and my temples were throbbing.

"Have a drink. Shall I get some more ice?" He gestured to the waitress and said something to her quietly. I closed my eyes. I felt his hand on mine. "Have some water, Soph."

"I'll be okay in a minute." I waited a moment, then opened my eyes and took a sip of water. The room seemed to grow darker. "Have the lights turned off or am I imagining it?"

"Yes, they're dimming the lights. You're not blacking out."

I was feeling disoriented, confused. And now a crackling, fizzing star was floating towards me, and happy birthday music was playing. The waitress placed a pink cake with a hissing sparkler stuck in it on the table. People on the other tables started to clap.

"I was going to save this till the end, but I thought you might need a bit of sugar."

"You went to so much effort for me," I said, and I was moved by his thoughtfulness. "But I'm not sure if I can eat any right now."

"Don't eat it, darling," said Amir. "But just take a proper look at it."

"Yeah, it's really pretty—" I began, then my eye fell on the piped lettering. The "i" in "Sophie" was dotted with a gold circle. "Is that...?"

The dizziness cleared and I was laughing and crying at the same time as Amir picked up the ring, a simple diamond solitaire, and put it on my finger, smearing it with buttercream, even before he asked the question.

"Want to get married?"

SOPHIE
2011

As I'd expected, my parents were delighted with my choice. Amir's mother was happy, too. She spoke to Mum, and we were formally engaged. Mum was furious at my deceptions but gave in a little when Dad reminded her of how they had met themselves, on a PIA flight from Karachi to Lahore where he was a passenger, and she was an air hostess. They'd broken family conventions by falling in love and getting married.

Unlike me, my mother was a slim, slight woman, with short hair, a "feathery" crop that she chose for practicality rather than vanity. She couldn't stand the effort required to style and care for anything longer. It suited her, a simple frame for her beautiful grey eyes and finely boned face that belied her steel. She was sharp witted and strong willed and didn't take nonsense from anyone.

Dad was the softer of the two. Mum might try and discipline us, but Dad was both ultimately in charge and the one to bend the rules. Things that Mum refused us, like video games, new trainers, trips and holidays, Dad gave in to, after just a polite request. There wasn't even any need for begging or pleading up. He was ready to indulge us, thrived on it. He was earning a good living as an accountant and could afford to. In short, I was allowed to do what I wanted.

It was a long engagement. We waited another two years, so

I could finish my college course and Amir could settle into a job and save some money.

When the time came, Dad wanted to invite all his and Mum's plentiful brothers and sisters, along with all their children and grandchildren, as well as "close friends" (the GP, the friendly librarian, all the neighbours). Amir's mum was bringing a hundred people along with her in the *baraat*, or the groom's party, making the final number of guests 580. But Mum and Dad were willing to pay for the best, so I wasn't complaining. None of us knew then that I'd be doing this more than once. I booked a plush hotel and made sure every last detail was perfect. I had tall vases filled with fresh lilies and roses by all the entrances, goldfish in bowls on the tables, and a six-tier *real* cake sculpted out of violet coloured chocolate. There were no just-for-effect dummy layers in my wedding gateau.

To top it all off, I gave them a heart-rending *ruksati*, a bride's farewell to remember. In reality, I couldn't be happier to be leaving Mum and Dad to be with Amir, and would have been fine with a quick hug, but instead I clung to Dad like a leech and wailed, just verging on screaming, and feigned dizziness. Everyone looked worried, but apart from my parents, they were all secretly enjoying the moment of high drama I'd provided for them. It was the most fun they'd have all year.

I'd persuaded Amir to mark our marriage with a new home. Their old house had become mortgage-free when Amir's dad died a few years ago. Amir only needed a few thousand pounds to make the purchase of a brand-new, four-bedroom semi on a modern development a fairly straightforward process. There were several green spaces in the "village" – children's play areas, a miniature forest, and a picnic place with a little lake.

Of course Amir's mum, Mumtaz, had been reluctant to give up her shabby old place at first, protesting that she had memories sealed in its walls and locked in the cupboards, but relented easily enough when she saw the new kitchen. When it came to choosing between ageing sentiments under peeling wallpaper and slick gadgets beneath smooth, glossy units, there was no contest. Add to that my bribe that the new house would have much more space to accommodate the horde of grandchildren that would be sure to arrive imminently, and the old lady was putty in my hands.

Amir and his mother moved in three weeks before the wedding to settle in and get ready to welcome me. I didn't visit during that time. I was busy with my own preparations, and both our families were entertaining guests who had come especially for the festivities.

We stayed in a hotel on the wedding night, and the next morning I allowed myself to feel and behave like a silly, frivolous girl, going home holding hands to open all our presents. They were all piled up on and around the coffee table, and Mumtaz's relatives sat in a circle around the room. Those without seats sat on the floor. My mum and dad were also there, Mum with a notebook to jot down who had given what, so she could return the favour in the coming years. An eye for an eye. A kettle for a kettle. Or a kettle for a toaster, for variety.

As expected, there was an assortment of kitchen gadgets, as well as clocks, crystal vases, dessert bowls, and a plant stand shaped like an elephant.

"Why don't you take one of these home, Mum?" I said, handing her one of the kettles. Hers had blown up last week.

"We'll see later," said Mum. "How much money did Mrs Malik give you?"

"Thirty," I said. "It'll look nice in your kitchen." Mum frowned at me and too late, I realised why she was hesitating. By offering her the kettle, I had just given an open invitation to everyone else to take whatever they fancied. One of the aunties shuffled across the room and picked up a gold carriage clock decorated with butterflies.

"*Bari sohni eh,*" she said. "Extremely attractive. It will match my dining room showcase back in Multan. I collect china insects. Do you mind if I take it?"

"Haa, go ahead," said Mumtaz. I didn't like the clock, but I was shocked.

"What are they going to do with a hundred clocks. Go tick tock tick tock?" said Mumtaz, laughing uproariously. "Anything else you like?"

"Maybe you can open the rest of the presents later, Sophie?" said Mum.

"No, let's get it over with!" said Mumtaz.

So, it went on, a marketplace made of my wedding presents. Eventually we got to the last few things, which I'd asked for specifically from my friends, including the bread bin and tea and coffee canisters.

"We won't be needing these," said Mumtaz breezily. "I've already bought some. Wooden bread bin and beige tins. Didn't you see?" I hadn't been in the kitchen yet. I was still enjoying being pampered as new bride, being waited on hand and foot since I arrived.

"But I ordered these especially," I said. The bread bin I'd chosen was black with LE PAIN emblazoned across it in classic silver italics, and it had matching canisters for sugar, tea and coffee. They were beautiful, carefully chosen as a striking accent to our pristine white kitchen.

"So did I. From Argos. Very smart. They've got a picture of a bunch of fruit on them. Peach and grapes, plus corn ears. Harvest range."

I hated the ugly Harvest range, a brown, outdated, countrified design.

"You can decide later, Sophie," soothed Dad.

"It's okay," said Mumtaz. "I'll be the one to sacrifice. I'll throw my autumnal collection in the bin."

"You don't have to do that," I said, though it was too late. I'd got what I wanted but had been made to look like an arch-villain on my first day.

* * *

Amir was wonderful in those early days. Cheeky, attentive, smitten completely, and I drank in every moment with him. We didn't have enough money saved for a honeymoon, but Amir promised to take me somewhere as soon as we did. Instead, we made the best of Bradford. We ate out, went to the cinema, took long walks in local beauty spots like Haworth and Bolton Abbey, with its shallow, rock-strewn river that you could wade right across, and secret hidden waterfall.

After a couple of weeks Amir went back to work, and during the day I was left alone with his mother. I did what I could to be a model daughter-in-law, pressing her legs, doing all the housework and even offering to cook, but she wouldn't let me anywhere near the cooker. She was happy for me to slave around doing all the other thankless tasks, but the stove, which allowed for some artistry and could be appreciated by others, was her domain entirely. Who admired the way you polished a table or hoovered up a cobweb? It seemed to me that by having sole power over my husband's stomach, she still held supreme control over his heart.

I complained to Amir. It was an agreement we'd made early on, to air our grievances to each other openly, not suppress them to fester and explode lethally later.

"Darling, what's the problem?" said Amir, nuzzling my shoulder. "You don't even like cooking. Just let Mum get on with it."

"But I'd like to make something for you to eat," I said. "You love your food."

"Hmmmm. I like kebabs. Made by Mum. Just kidding. Why don't you just concentrate on looking beautiful... then I can eat you, how about that?"

* * *

The realisation of a true, lifelong love is a powerful moment. In between the beginning of my first obsession, Amir, and the time of the actual wedding, I discovered my other love, my vocation.

Some of my own old college friends were into theatre, and a few weeks before the wedding, they persuaded me to go with them to see a small production of a play from India. Of course I knew Asian actors must do theatre too, but I usually associated them with the popular Bollywood films. I watched films avidly, even though ninety-five percent of them were complete rubbish. The number of British or American films featuring Asian characters that I could think of could be counted on one hand.

I was mesmerised by the play, the raw immediacy of it, real actors doing proper acting. It was the story of a woman driven mad by her nit-picking husband. We talked about it all the way home and by the time I went to bed I'd decided I was going to be an actress. It was what I'd been longing for – something that I'd be bursting with inspiration to do every day. The process of expressing an idea creatively, the wealth of stories yet to discover, and ultimately, being appreciated for executing it all with brilliance. It made me tremble with excitement to imagine it, unlike the hairdressing job I'd tried and quickly got bored of.

There wasn't much time for me to enrol on a course with the impending wedding, and it seemed fitting to me that my two dreams should be intertwined, with the culmination of one woven into the inception of the other. The wedding was in July and the course started in September. It all tessellated perfectly.

I didn't tell Amir about my ambitions. I thought it would be a wonderful little surprise for him, his wife announcing her plan to add some glamour to his life. He would lap up the opportunity to be seen on my arm once I "arrived".

I got into the habit of doing the housework in a couple of hours, then devoting the rest of the day to reading plays and film scripts in preparation. I pictured myself as Maggie the Cat, Scarlett O'Hara, Rose from Titanic.

The course was just a short one, nothing too long, expensive or serious, just enough for me to try it out, a warmup, at an acting school in Leeds. Once I'd settled in, introduced myself to the acting community, I'd take whatever steps were necessary to progress to the top. For now, all I had to do was tell my husband.

Amir didn't really have a sweet tooth. He disliked biscuits (too crumbly) and chocolate (a woman's sin), but he was partial to Victoria sponge sandwiched with chopped tinned pineapple and slathered in freshly whipped cream. Baking was the one area in which I had the upper hand. My mother-in-law hated measuring scales and was baffled by the oven. She couldn't work out how to turn it on, and temperatures confused her. I didn't enlighten her. I was scared that I'd lose my superiority in even this last little talent if she worked out the difference between Celsius and gas mark.

On the day I was going to make the announcement, I baked the cake in the morning, once Mumtaz was out of the kitchen. She'd cooked one of Amir's least favourite meals, daal and plain boiled rice. This was an advantage. Amir was a wholehearted carnivore, ravenous lover of steaks, chops and any curry with meat in it. For the most part his mum indulged his greedy appetite, but occasionally she made him eat daal, telling him the mushy lentils would help cleanse his digestive system and stop it from getting clogged with greasy residue. The dish was tempered with a *tarka* of fried garlic and chillies. Its distinctive aroma always put Amir in a sour mood as soon as he opened the door.

At five fifteen every day I went upstairs to beautify myself. I wanted him to breathe me in the moment he clapped eyes on me, for the sight of me to melt his worries, the weariness of the day. It was an ancient ritual, which had stood firm through the ages and worked just as well in the modern day. It was simply making an effort for your mate, keeping him happy, stopping him from straying.

I splashed on some Chanel No 5, put on some simple pearls and went downstairs. Mumtaz made a sound of approval. I made a little chit-chat about the television, willing her to stay in a good mood, then went into the kitchen. The daal sat in a fat pot on the cooker, dull, yellow flecked with vibrant green coriander. I knew it was awful of me, but my heart cackled at the thought of Amir turning up his nose. I cut up the tinned pineapple and sandwiched the two layers of sponge with it, spread a thick layer of vanilla scented cream over the top and sides, decorated it with luscious, sliced strawberries, then sprinkled it all with flaky almonds and icing sugar.

At nine minutes past six, Amir's keys turned in the lock. I cleared the space around the cake, so it was a glorious spectacle. He came in and slid his hands around me, smelt my perfume. I thought if we could be frozen like that forever, I would be happy. Instead, I wriggled.

"Your mum might walk in," I said.

"So?" said Amir. "It's all legal."

"She's made your favourite."

"I know." He pretended to make a grumpy face, then smiled. "But this makes up for it."

"Me or the sponge?"

"Cake's good too but no comparison." I squealed as he bit my ear.

"How about we get the daal over and done with and then take the dessert upstairs for an early night?" I suggested, and he laughed wickedly in reply.

My mother-in-law usually left us to it at dinner time. She ate her meals in the living room, in front of the television, but I liked eating at the table. That was the way it had been in my own home, and I loved dressing the table and laying out the food, even though I hadn't cooked it most of the time. There was beauty in the form of spoons and plates, a jar of flowers,

a few tealights, and I liked to make our reunion after a day
spent apart special. That day, however, I kept it deliberately
plain, no candles or flowers, just to emphasise the drabness of
the dinner, so my dessert would look even more magnificent
in contrast. I was tempted to go a step further and raid my
mother-in-law's hoard for some frightful brown crockery, but
I couldn't bring myself to do the ugly deed.

We got through the meal quickly, me not really listening to
Amir complaining about some spat at the office as I mentally
rehearsed my announcement. Upstairs, I put the plates of cake
on the bed. My strategy was to spring my news on him while
he was still immersed in the pudding, but to my annoyance,
he suggested we liven things up by taking the cake under the
covers. I wouldn't have minded another time, but I needed to
be thinking clearly when I broached my subject, and that was
going to be impossible if I was having cream and crumbs licked
off me. I pointed out that my crisp white bed linen would be
ruined by airborne blobs of passionate jam, and he grumpily
agreed to eat first in a civilised manner. He was soon wolfing it
down, making appreciative noises.

"Well, I've got a surprise for you," I began. He paused mid-
glace cherry.

"Oh my God," he said. "So soon… Oh Sophie, you've made
me the happiest man!" He held out his hand, but I batted it
away as gently as I could.

"No, darling, not that," I said. He'd expressed his hasty desire
to have mini Amirs crawling around him lots of times, and
before I'd been infected by my acting bug, I'd gladly agreed.
That had been before the wedding, but things were different
now. I had a real goal for myself, one that required dedication,
patience and talent. Children were readily producible. A quick
little tumble and voila! A pleasant evening for Amir, at least
eighteen years of exhaustion for me – beginning with the
vile symptoms of pregnancy and the agony of birth, followed
by endless tears, sleepless nights, feeding and washing and

waiting on them hand and foot. Plodding and scraping through
life wrapped in chains. Of course, I knew the beautiful side of
motherhood would overshadow all this, but for the moment
I wasn't interested. I'd discreetly been on the Pill since we got
married, without telling anyone.

Amir's face wrinkled in disappointment, and he got stuck
back into his pudding, nibbling at an almond flake in an
irritatingly dainty way.

"It can be a bit boring at home by myself, so I thought I
would do something with my time," I said.

"You've got Mum," he said. "If you're bored go shopping.
Iron in bulk."

I liked to iron my clothes on a daily basis, all our outfits for
the day nice and fresh. His mother preferred doing a three-
hour marathon session on a Wednesday afternoon. But that
was beside the point. It was a blatantly outrageous suggestion,
as though any of those mundane tasks were a fulfilling way to
spend a life.

"No, Amir, I meant a course," I said, patiently.

"Bookkeeping?"

I sighed, struggling to keep cool.

"Not bookkeeping," I said. "Something much more original."

"Nail art?"

"Why don't you let me finish?"

"Sorry. Come and cuddle up and tell me all about it."

"Let's talk first." His face fell and he opened his mouth to
speak but I carried on before he could come up with any more
distractions.

"It's an acting course," I said.

"Acting what?"

"What do you mean, acting what? Theatre, movies,
television. You know, the stuff you watch all the time."

"You want to be an actress." He smiled the easy grin I loved,
but I was inflamed by its sight now.

"Why are you laughing?" I fumed quietly.

"I thought that was the expected reaction to a joke."

"Don't try to be funny. It's not a joke."

"What else then? You want me to be serious about such a silly idea? Real people don't become actresses. It's a fantasy hobby for people with leisurely lives, no responsibilities, idle money lying around. You've got a mother-in-law and a home to look after." He handed me the empty plate, then slid under the duvet and turned onto his side. "It would be good if you changed the hand towels in the bathrooms once in a while."

I couldn't believe what I was hearing.

"It starts on Thursday," I said.

"Ring them up and cancel," he said. "What will people think if they hear? Mum's not going to like it. Come on, I need a back rub after eating all that. Gas is stuck." He attempted to burp, and I closed my eyes.

"I need to go to the bathroom," I said. I went into the en suite and stayed there, thinking, until I could hear him snoring, lost in the sleep of the ignorant. I loved Amir but this unexpected reaction wasn't acceptable. I was entitled to my dreams, and the world I was creating for myself wasn't just the whimsical fantasy of a lazy stargazer, spinning impossible candyfloss scenarios that dissolved in seconds. It was an unshakeable aim of substance that I was intent on reaching, and I couldn't allow Amir to stop me.

I bent over and hobbled forward, muttering, "It can't be, it can't be!" I gazed into the distance and showed a range of expressions on my face: love, sorrow, childish joy, all memories from a distant past.

I was portraying an eighty year-old farmer's wife, reunited with her long-lost friend after fifty years. The challenge was to depict her emotions using a maximum of three words. As I ended my little scene by raising my hands to the heavens, the rest of the acting class started clapping and giving me encouraging praise. I'd never felt so exhilarated in my life.

Adrenaline and confidence were coursing through my body, but adversely, I also felt shy and eager to please.

It was my first acting class. Amir thought I was at yoga. The class was taking place in the assembly hall of a local primary school. Not exactly the professional studio I'd been imagining but it didn't matter. It was easy for my mind to transform it into a Hollywood rehearsal room, the ropes and ladder hanging from the climbing frame part of the set of the new film I was in, and me there practising my next scene with Matt Damon.

"Before you all go," said Craig, the teacher, at the end of the class. "I have some exciting news. I know we're only at the beginning of the course, but some of you might want to audition for this." He held up a black and white printed sheet. "A company from India are shooting a film in London and they're over here scouting for new talent. All the details are on here. Please take one as you go out, and well done, everyone!"

I put on my coat and picked up a sheet. "Have you got what it takes to impress world-famous director Chunky Chaudhary?" A wild, glowing ember of a thought began to ignite inside me. Perhaps I could become the next Katrina Kaif, the English-born star who was now a sensation in Bollywood.

I lingered until the other students had left before speaking to Craig.

"I was wondering if you could give me any feedback on how I did?" I asked. "You can be honest; I can take it."

"Really good for a first day," said Craig. "Have you done any acting before?"

"Never. Do you think I have potential?"

"Definitely. All the trembling and limping you did; it was a great physical performance. And you should definitely audition for the film."

The ember became a flame, then, and I went home with a cosy glow of achievement inside me, a fire that I had to keep burning with sincerity and care, away from Amir and his mother, no matter what it took.

AMIR
2011

At first I was surprised. Sophie had always been the voice of sense in my life, telling it how it was in her straight, poker faced but funny way.

Acting. It was weird, totally out of character. I didn't like the idea at all and nipped it in the bud. My property business was still growing and relied on word of mouth from the community. I couldn't afford to lose customers because of their disapproval of my wife's whims.

To make it up to her I suggested a holiday in Bali. I thought about making it a surprise, but it was a long time to wait, and as it was compensation for Sophie sacrificing her acting ambitions, I thought it was better to get my little token of appreciation in early. I picked up some brochures on the way home and wrapped them up. A compromise surprise.

She looked unimpressed at the package.

"What's this?" she said. "I already ordered a subscription to *Cosmo*, remember?"

"Did you?" I said. "Anyway, it's not *Cosmo*." She unwrapped it.

"Is this a joke?" she said. "Did you clear out the waiting area at work?" Sometimes the sarcasm was way too much.

"Yeah, then I went out and bought wrapping paper," I said. "Even I'm not that much of an advanced prankster. Do you want to go or not?"

She tried supressing a smile, but it broke out, lighting up her face, and the small effort that I'd made was more than worth it.

Uncle Suleiman was Dad's cousin's sister-in-law's husband. As nobody could be bothered to work his exact relationship to us, Suleiman had been upgraded out of vagueness and given the dubious status of *"chacha"*, literally meaning "father's younger brother". He was a bit of a shady figure as we were growing up, a man spoken about in tones of rage or suspicious whispers. There would be times when he visited, sometimes bringing us extravagant presents, shirts for Dad and *salwar kameez* material for Mum, posh battery-operated toys for me. Other times all he brought was an uneasy mood, and these stays usually involved him and Mum and Dad shutting themselves in the dining room and screaming at each other. In between visits there would be long periods when no one spoke to him. The prime example of this was when he left Aunty Deeba and their twin daughters for his hairdresser, fifteen years ago. The hairdresser dumped him eight months later and he wangled his way back into Aunty Deeba's life, only to leave her again for a rich widow. Another ostracism followed.

Now here he was in my office, wearing a silver suit under a black trench coat instead of his usual sloppy trousers and illustrated jumpers. He even sometimes wore Christmas pudding knits in May.

"Aladdin Park," he said, fiddling with the lock on his briefcase. "Bloody codes. 559 something."

"Isn't that the adventure playground place in Karachi?" I said.

"That's the one. Very good. See, even you've heard of it, and you haven't been to Pakistan for... how long?"

"Eleven years."

"Haa, eleven years, see? And you still remember it. This is

a brilliant investment opportunity, *puttar*. Forget Defence or Clifton. Aladdin Park is the area to put your money in."

"It's not really for me, Uncle."

"Where does your mum stay when she goes to Pakistan?" said Suleiman. "Just with the relatives, getting passed round and round like... green chutney."

"Everyone loves to have her. They fight over it."

"Hmm. Maybe at first. But after three months even close family lose the enthusiasm. In the end your own home is your own home. Don't you think it would be nice for her to have a... widow pad of her own?"

I knew Mum had complained about having to move house five times during a two-week holiday to please relatives, and at the same time not outstay her welcome with any one member of the family. At £22,000 for a two-bedroom flat, with only an £8,000 deposit, it was a good deal. The remaining balance could be paid in affordable instalments. A bit too easily, I let Uncle Suleiman talk me into it and he safely tucked a cheque for what should have been Sophie's holiday money into his briefcase.

It was very ill advised, but it was, well... a justified impulse. I had very valid reasons. I was doing something that Mum would really value, and it wasn't a bad thing for me and Sophie either. There would surely be trips to Karachi for us, too, and what better place to stay than our own luxury apartment? I had no idea how Sophie was going to react to the news that her idyllic Indian Ocean holiday had been dropped for a piece of real estate in Pakistan. I only had two thousand pounds left, but I put that away for a rainy day. I had to soften the blow and went for the simple solution. I knew I had good taste when it came to ladies' jewels and Sophie herself had approved of my choices in the past. I went to a Pakistani shop that did high quality imitation gold jewellery and bought her a bangle inlaid with pearls and turquoise. I picked up a bunch of pale pink roses, then gritted my teeth as I plucked up the courage to confess.

Still, it seemed like Sophie had an advantage over me when it came to who was putting more effort into our marriage. She'd given up the acting, and now I'd snatched away her holiday. To top it all off, when I got home, she'd made a roast chicken with my favourite Yorkshire puddings. Even Mum was at the table with us, in honour of the special dinner.

"What's wrong, darling?" said Sophie. "Don't worry. I've made Bisto for your Yorkies. I sacrificed my standards for your enjoyment."

The first time she'd made a roast she'd made homemade gravy, but I had, childishly, I'll admit, demanded a boat of Bisto. She'd tried to convince me to at least taste it, but I'd insisted on my packaged sauce, which had stood by me tastily for twenty-five years. It must have taken some willpower on her part to give in, especially as when I secretly tried the homemade gravy later, it was delicious.

I'd handed Sophie the flowers when I came in, but left the bangle in my briefcase for later, until after dinner. Suddenly I felt a pang of regret, an unexplained sadness. I'd always thought she wanted to be a stay-at-home mother. She'd never mentioned any great ambitions to have a career, until this silly acting idea. We'd talked about having a baby straight away, and I'd presumed that it would just happen. But maybe I was completely wrong. Maybe she was one of those quiet adventurers, those with a thousand dreams they never told anyone about. And now I'd put an end to any chance of her being able to see much of the world any time in the near future. I promised myself that I would talk to her about other possibilities.

Mum made a few appreciative noises about the food, then shuffled into the lounge, leaving us to clear up. I sat at the table, piling up the plates while Sophie took things through into the kitchen. I was intending to drop the bomb of bad news upstairs – the bedroom felt like safer ground. Sophie returned from the kitchen carrying a bag.

"What do you think?" she said, whipping out a slinky summer dress, and handing me the bag. "For the holiday. I sent the passports off too."

I looked in the bag and took out a man's t-shirt. It was going to be much worse if I postponed the truth till later.

"Err..." I said. It was all I could manage. I gave her a guilty smile.

"What's wrong?" she said.

"Well... I'm really sorry..."

"I don't think I want to hear this..." She turned to walk away, but I grabbed her hand.

"It's just that an investment opportunity came up," I said. "It was too good to pass up." She snatched her hand and the t-shirt away.

"Investment? Investment? You cancelled our honeymoon for an investment? What is it?"

"It's a flat," I said. She thought about this for a second.

"Okay. Property development. You'll make a profit then. It means we can still go."

"Well, no. It's in Karachi. A little holiday pad for Mum."

"What? You've given up our holiday so she can go swanning around in Pakistan?"

She was jabbing at me with her finger as she screamed. I wasn't going to put up with that.

"What's wrong with you?" I said. "Sophie! Stop it!" I pushed her slightly. It was honestly a defensive reaction; I thought she was going to poke my eye out, but it took her by surprise, and she fell back on to a chair. Mum came running in with a frightened face. Sophie started crying.

"Oh my God, Amir, what have you done?" said Mum. "Have you gone mad?" She put her arms around Sophie, tried to quieten her.

"I didn't do anything," I said.

"This isn't nothing!" said Mum.

"I cancelled the holiday."

"What? Why?"

"I put a deposit down on a flat. For you, in Pakistan."

"What for? I don't want a flat in Pakistan!"

"I thought you'd be pleased."

"You should have asked me first. Get a refund. We don't need it."

"I can't. It's not refundable."

She asked me which company it was, and I told her about Uncle Suleiman.

"He sent his regards," I said. "He even said he'll come and visit you once you've been to Pakistan to see the flat, to get some feedback." Mum glared at me, and I thought she might give me a thump or two but instead she slapped her own forehead.

"How could you have given your halal, hard-earned money to that corrupt conman, Amir?" she shouted. I tried to explain but she stormed out, still ranting about my stupidity and Suleiman's immoral character. I turned to Sophie and began to apologise but she shook her head and also left the room.

Sophie was still sniffing when I got into bed. She was lying down, facing away from me.

"I'm sorry," I said. I dropped the velvet box containing the gold bangle over her shoulder. I turned away and closed my eyes. A few minutes later I heard the hinges of the box opening and then it snapped shut.

I fell asleep, praying that there was some truth in what they said about learning about each other and growing together through time. I certainly didn't understand the Sophie I'd seen today.

SOPHIE
2011

Days later, Mumtaz booked her PIA flight to Karachi. When I asked Amir how much it cost, he said it was only five hundred and she was paying for it from her widow's allowance. Hmm. At least he wasn't contributing to his mother's holiday after ruining mine.

I was angry and hurt by Amir letting me down, but it now gave me justification for the secrets I had been keeping from him. If he could make his own decisions regarding our future, choose what he thought was beneficial, I could do the same. I wasn't committing acts of betrayal. I was trying to steer our life towards success with my covert endeavours. The acting lessons. The job applications for small roles, even voluntary ones, just to get experience. And, on a different note, but still hidden from Amir, taking the Pill. He had no idea. He thought it was just destiny that nothing had happened yet, and I let him go on believing it. If he started talking about going to the doctor to investigate why it was taking so long, I'd just stop taking it and let nature take its course. I controlled what happened to my body, not him.

I let Amir make it up to me with his peace offering of a gold bangle. It was exquisite, I'll give him that. I was heartbroken, betrayed, but I couldn't help it. It wasn't just the jewellery. There was a magic about him that I couldn't resist. Silly things.

His odd manner of pursing his lips in an apologetic smile, or the way he rung his hands when he was sorry, a naughty boy getting told off. Or just his grin. They were ingrained somewhere deep inside me, as though I'd known them forever, flitting, chimerical memories from an unreadable place. I gave in because I needed him in order to exist. And because by giving in I was storing up good deeds, ammunition for future battles.

Mumtaz was packed and ready for her holiday. Her overstuffed suitcases were filled with requests from relatives – everything from peanut butter and Mars bars to shower gel and pop socks. Amir loaded them into the car and we drove her to Manchester airport. I gave her a jolly, warm farewell. I wanted to forget everything, and I was looking forward to having the house to ourselves for the first time. Although he didn't mention his intentions, I could feel Amir's frisky energy on the way home as he sang along to the radio and cracked silly jokes.

I was expecting him to leap on me as soon as we got in through the front door, but instead he hung up his coat and disappeared into the downstairs loo. I went into the living room and arranged myself artfully on the sofa, the top three buttons of my dress undone. He came in and started looking through the pile of mail on the sideboard.

"Any chance of a cup of tea?" he asked, without even a glance in my direction. I didn't understand it.

"Sure you don't want a massage instead?" I offered.

"Tea will do, thanks. And a couple of digestives, if there are any."

I made the bloody tea, and some hot chocolate for myself while I was at it. We drank in silence, while he watched the television like a robot. Then he put his hand in his pocket and threw a packet of pills on to the coffee table.

It was a moment from a nightmare, a slow shutter still that intensified every flicker of movement and atom of emotion.

"I didn't know how to tell you," I stammered.

"Do you know what an idiot I felt when I found it?" he said. "All this time I've been longing for that baby, and you've been murdering all my hopes behind my back!"

"I'm sorry, darling!" I begged. I promised I'd do whatever he wanted me to. I needed him to calm down, to trust me again, not suspect me of anything else. It wouldn't do for him to discover any more of my secrets.

AMIR
2011

Sophie had a habit of misplacing things. I was only looking for the Sellotape to fix Mum's luggage tags, not spying on her, when I went through the drawer and found the Pill supply. All my hopes were squashed by a girly pink packet. I was mad, but at her lie, not at the fact that it was what she wanted.

I could read her well enough to know she was skittish from her flirty actions in the car. I played along, joking and messing around. Her face was a picture when we got home and I asked for the tea while she was busy draping herself over the sofa, and even better when I conjured the tablets up out of thin air.

"I'm sorry I didn't know how to tell you," she babbled. I was furious but I wanted to avoid an argument.

"You should have told me how you felt," I said. "I just thought we wanted the same thing. It's what we talked about."

"You're obsessed with it," said Sophie. "What could I do?"

"I want you to be able to talk to me, Soph. Truthfully. You've got a right to decide what you want." I held out the packet, but she didn't take it.

"No. Throw it away. I know what I want. I want to make you happy."

SOPHIE
2011

It was a drizzly October afternoon, the most exciting day of my life, apart from my wedding day, perhaps. The day of the audition. The acting had been going well and Craig was pleased with my progress. It was difficult not having anyone to share my small successes with. I didn't tell any of my friends. I couldn't risk any of them letting something slip, and neither did I want to tarnish our image of the perfect couple, show them I was a wife who hid things from her husband. A wife who lied.

A Google search on Chunky (real name Harilal) told me he was in the textiles industry, not exactly a multi-millionaire, but comfortably wealthy. Hula Hoop Productions was his latest venture, with his brother Dobby (real name Dalbir), and although he had no formal training as a film director, he thought his "observations" on his friends' film sets were enough to qualify him for the role. It wasn't highly promising news, but it was a foot in the door, and that was all I wanted for now.

I arrived at the class early to prepare for the audition. Craig had given us a monologue to rehearse from the script in progress, entitled *Monty and the Ghost*. I wasn't really nervous. I hadn't heard of Chunky until recently, so it wasn't as though he was someone I was especially in awe of.

Chunky appeared an hour and a half late, with an entourage of secretaries and assistants. He was in his late fifties, with dyed black hair and moustache, silver glasses and jowls that gave him a perpetually disgusted expression. He was chunky, and it was emphasised by his royal blue silk shirt and white trousers.

"Please, Mr Craig, I can only give you half an hour," he growled as he sat down to watch us. A girl wearing headphones scribbled down on a clipboard as we performed.

Since participating in the classes I'd developed a belief in myself and I was confident as I climbed up the steps to the stage, but still my palms began to sweat a little. I took deep breaths and felt calm as I began the monologue. It was a supporting actor role. The character, a haunted villager.

"Believe me or believe me not," I began in a low tone and Cornish accent, my own little touch. I paused for effect, then increased my volume as the speech progressed. "It's an hour after midnight you'll see 'em. The one-legged bandit carrying his headless cat under his arm, walking along thump, thump…"

I didn't make any mistakes, and although Chunky wasn't giving anything away, the audience seemed appreciative. I took a bow before walking off the stage, smiling, feeling a sense of joy and power.

"He was impressed," said Craig, when we were packing up the chairs after Chunky had left. "I guess we'll find out soon enough."

For the next five days I trudged about the house doing the usual tedious tasks, cutting corners on hoovering and cleaning, overlooking hard to reach cobwebs and pretending there was nothing under the rug. I cooked all manner of *chat patte* foods, spicy, finger licking, meaty snacks that Amir loved, then spent the rest of the time watching classic films to learn my craft – *Sophie's Choice, Erin Brockovich, Thelma and Louise.*

On Friday afternoon, Craig rang me.

"I tried my best to convince Chunky, but he only wanted

two people from our group," he said. "So, I'm afraid most of you are going to be disappointed."

"Oh well, thanks for letting me know," I said, trying not to sound too upset. "Would you mind keeping me on your email list in case anything else comes up? So, who did get a part, then?"

"Well... I did. And so did you."

"What?" I was incredulous. A proper acting job. My persistence had paid off.

"He's gone back to India for now," said Craig. "He'll be back in a few months to shoot the film."

"A few months?"

"Don't worry, I'll keep in touch with updates. You won't miss anything."

I wasn't worried about missing anything out of forgetfulness. My situation might be very different in a few months' time. In the morning I had taken a pregnancy test. Result: positive.

I wrapped and disposed of each piece of evidence carefully, making sure that all the bits of the test were put into a carrier bag and then a black bag with other rubbish and thrown outside into the wheelie bin straight away. I wasn't going to make the same mistake again. Amir wasn't going to discover anything I didn't want him to.

Mumtaz was due back in another ten days after her extra-long long-haul holiday. I knew I had to do whatever I needed to before she returned, not only because it would be easier practically without her around. I was also afraid of the uncanny knack old Pakistani women had of sensing these things, sniffing out pregnancies like a hound tracked his prey. I was focused solely on my career, especially now that my talent had been noted and I had a definite project to look forward to. It was easier to think of it as disease that I was going to cleanse myself of, a harmful, decaying thing, instead of what it really was, a tiny bud about to burst with life. I couldn't let myself be influenced by Amir's sentimentalities. Still, I could taste the bile in my throat as I rang the clinic to book the appointment. They told me to come in four days' time for midday and I would be finished by late afternoon.

I waited till Amir was asleep that night before checking the pile of things I needed to take with me. A towel, a change of clothes, slippers, toiletries. It wasn't a hospital bag for new mums. I wasn't going to be bringing anything back with me.

The last few days had been good. Almost perfect. Amir believed that all I wanted was his happiness, and of course I did. I just needed it to be compatible with Chunky's movie. I'd decided it would be best to keep it to myself for now and at least wait until I knew which part I'd got. If it was small, I might get away with excuses like shopping when I was shooting, but if the schedule was busy, I could just tell him I had some other kind of "normal" temporary job, then give him the sensational surprise when it was all finished and the film was released.

I'd made Amir boiled eggs for breakfast, and he was being especially attentive to me.

"You're an angel, you know that?" He hugged me close, pure and easy, as I mumbled a protestation against the halo, he was crowning me with.

"Let's go out for dinner tonight," he said.

"Not tonight... I'll be tired by the time you get back," I said.

"Well don't work so hard. Go back to bed now, relax all day, no need to cook, take a break from the housework. You'll be refreshed by the evening."

"Can't we just get a takeaway?"

"I thought it would be nice to get out of the house. But it's up to you. I'm just your slave, you know that. Let me know what you decide."

He went, leaving me stroking my cheek where his stubble had scraped it.

* * *

My heart was unsteady and loud as I sat in the waiting room at the clinic, watching the grim faces of the two other women, my mind a battlefield of one desire against another, aspirations pitted against loyalty and love. A life of success and fame, art and beauty, fighting the instinctive tenderness I was already feeling for the life inside me. Amir and I, too, had been so content recently that I was beginning to feel guilty about such a huge betrayal of his trust. I also couldn't help thinking how perfect it would be to complete his happiness with the gift of a child.

The nurse called me in.

AMIR
2011

Sophie decided to go out after all. I was pleased. I wanted her to be a pampered, cherished woman. I dreaded becoming one of those men who slipped into boring routines for the rest of their lives once they'd got the girl, no thrills or romance. I'd stuffed up with the holiday. The least I could do was take her out to dinner now and again. We ordered chickpea chaat and fried tilapia for starters and were sipping on mango lassis when she told me.

It was the promise of a dream, and the start of the nightmare.

SOPHIE
2012

Handwash was the worst. Just one whiff and it would set me off. Amir threw away all the pumps and replaced them with bars of plain old Imperial Leather. I normally hated that stuffy old smell, reminiscent of my childhood, but it was just what I needed in my sickly condition. I couldn't bear anything that tried to be sensuous, floral or zingy. It was the same with Amir's aftershave too. I couldn't stand for him to be near me after he'd splashed himself with Kouros.

Mumtaz was full of remedies for abating the sickness – orange barley water, jelly beans, Strepsils, lemon slices. She even suggested I nibble on a piece of chalk.

The house had four bedrooms, so there was plenty of space for the nursery, but even as I mulled over wallpaper samples and bedding designs, I felt Mumtaz's overly possessive tentacles unfurling towards me, undulating in anticipation, ready to wrap themselves around the child once it arrived.

Although for the first few months the baby would sleep in our bedroom, I wanted to move it into the nursery fairly soon after, so it could learn good sleep habits.

"No need for a nursery," said Mumtaz. "He'll sleep in my room. He needs someone in the night – see, even the doctors say it." She held up a baby safety leaflet that had fallen out of my maternity goody bag.

"It's fine for it to be in its own room after a few months," I said.

"What if it cries?"

"We've got a high-tech monitor, so we'll be able to hear everything."

"You don't even wake up with those infernal sounding mobile alarms," she said. "How are a little lamb's whimpers going to rouse you?"

"Anyway, he'll sleep easy enough when you plug him up with a dummy."

"I'm not going to get one of those ugly things," said Mumtaz. "They make children look like bulldogs."

She was quiet on the sleeping arrangements subject after that, but it didn't matter. We both knew there was nothing to stop her from creeping into the nursery at night whenever she wanted, especially as it would be in the room next to hers, and Amir and I slept on the top floor.

Mumtaz tried to involve herself in everything. She selected pushchairs from her beloved Argos catalogue, and I made a note of them, but later told her they were all out of stock. She hadn't yet mastered the skill of typing the WiFi code into her mobile and was terrified of catching cancer from the laptop, so she had no internet access. She wouldn't be checking up on stock levels any time soon.

Then there was the debate on names. I liked short, cool names, easy to pronounce – Isa, Zaki, Rayaan. Mumtaz chose ones more suited to a middle-aged Pakistan uncle with a curly moustache and rubber flip flops, than an innocent newborn – Delawar, Jamsher, Shahnawaz. She was positive it was a boy (she was able to predict this from the shape of my body) and refused to even discuss girls' names.

It felt like the control over my baby's future was being pulled out of my hands. I had to keep hold of it somehow.

The months went by and finally I received an email asking me to come to the first day of shooting, which was taking place in a supermarket in Leeds. There was still no information about my role in the film, but there was an outline of the story – a ludicrous tale about an Indian heart surgeon running a dance academy in a haunted English country mansion. I assumed they would give us our parts on the day. Perhaps that was how Chunky worked.

The shoot was scheduled for two weeks before my due date and I was worried. I didn't know how many days I'd be needed for. I asked Craig to contact the company to find out, but he got no reply. All I could do was turn up and see what happened.

I told Amir and Mumtaz I was going for a pre-birth blood test. Of course it was of my own invention, but they knew nothing about the patient-midwife calendar apart from what I told them.

A small section of the supermarket had been closed off, and there was a fresh, fizzy energy in the air when I arrived, and I knew I could easily become addicted to it. People were chattering and laughing, sharing stories of previous work and the latest industry gossip, exchanging numbers or business cards, promising to put good words in for each other. I felt shy and conscious of both my inexperience and my bulgy physical state but listened eagerly to everything they were saying. I wanted to become like them and this was the day I was taking my first step on that path. Focussing on them also distracted me from the period-like pains I'd been having for the last two or three hours. Braxton Hicks, I thought.

Craig came in a few minutes later, but before we had a chance to talk, Chunky appeared, dressed in a leopard print shirt and several gold lockets, and everyone quietened down. He looked us over, then had a mumbled conversation with his assistant.

"Jay, where is Jay?" he said. Someone told him Jay was at lunch. "Get him someone, please. Right, you three, to the freezer section. Ice cream, pizza, chips, I'll let you choose. And you, lady." He pointed at me. "Diapers, please."

"What about a script?" I asked. "When will we get that?" Chunky rolled his eyes impatiently.

"What are you talking about, lady?" he said. "This is a crowd scene. No speaking parts."

"What? You've called me, a heavily pregnant woman, all the way over for a crowd scene?"

"*Bas, bas!* Enough! We don't know anything about that!" It was true, he didn't know, so I kept quiet. I was fuming at having been misled, but it was better than nothing. Seeing me calm down, Chunky nodded at me and said, "Okay, I'll upgrade you, because of this authenticity. Girls, get her a trolley and take her to baby section."

There was a lot of waiting around and by the time we were ready to shoot the scene, two hours later, the pain I'd been feeling had steadily increased. It was as though I was clenched in the fist of a giant, rings of pain crushing my abdomen and thighs. It wasn't only stronger now, but more frequent and the episodes were lasting longer. There was no way these were practice cramps. I knew I was in labour.

There was no way of predicting how long it would go on for before the baby was born. I'd heard it could take as long as twenty-four hours. For now, it was bearable with heavy breathing and walking around, away from everyone else. All I needed to do was get through another hour or so and finish the filming, then I could go to hospital. I couldn't lose the rare opportunity that had come my way. Just another hour or so of shooting to get through and I would have my first real acting credit. I was timing the pains closely, so I could somehow try and get back to do my scene between contractions.

The main character, Jay, was lingering over choosing between cotton wool balls and pleats, while I stood a little way behind with Craig, looking at rompers. I was determined to say something, so I uttered a line of dialogue that I'd made up.

"Cut the chat," shouted Chunky into a handheld loudspeaker. "Shut up and look at the wet wipes."

I was about to protest, but the agony squeezed me, seven minutes earlier than expected, and I doubled up.

"What's she doing?" said Chunky. "Look, I know you're keen, but just do what you're told. I don't want any acting."

"I don't think she's acting," said Craig. "She's not that good. Are you okay, hun?"

"Just get on with it," I said. "I need to leave." I no longer cared about dialogue or method or any of it, as long as I got my name on the cast list. Chunky had other ideas.

"Are you saying she's gone into labour?" he said, suddenly excited. "This is the cinematic gold. Any chances we can shoot when the pains are coming? Jay's a doctor, he will help you. We'll give you a 'Special thanks to…' at the end."

I wasn't looking my best, I was sure my expressions would be quite unbecoming, and it was going to be more than a little embarrassing, but the temptation of making screen history plus the appreciative mention was irresistible. I gave into the bribe.

They missed the next two contractions as the cameraman had disappeared off for a toilet break. When he started filming on the third one, I could hardly stand. I grabbed a swivel chair from behind a checkout and sat down, bent over, rocking back and forth, shaking my legs, knocking my knees together, doing anything I could do get through it.

"Should I ring for an ambulance?" muttered Craig, the only person who seemed to be treating the situation as real, whilst Jay dabbed at my face with a dry flannel. It was all I could do not to slap him.

"Jay, tell her she's doing really well," said Chunky.

It was only on hearing those stereotypical birth partner words that I realised that Amir should have been saying them. In the excitement of the shoot and the horror of labour I had forgotten to phone him.

"Call my husband," I panted to Craig, once Chunky finally stopped the camera rolling.

"I don't have his number."

I threw my mobile at him, not caring about smashing the screen. I was due for an upgrade.

"Look under Amir Husband," I said. Amir had put this title in case of these very emergencies, in case I was unconscious or flustered, so a stranger could easily find who to contact.

"Weirdo," said Chunky. "Real life *Memento*."

As Craig began to swipe through the contacts slowly, I felt the intense need to go to the toilet, and I realised it was all too late.

"Call the ambulance," I shouted, whacking Chunky with a bag of Pampers as he tried to position himself behind the tripod, no doubt thinking that the bloody, gruesome highlight demanded his own personal attention. Craig asked one of the Tesco staff members if there was a private room I could go to, and she led me away from the cameras, my body pulsating with waves of unbearable pain.

An hour later, on a sofa in the Tesco staff room, Amir and I clutched each other, as the paramedic took our silent, still son away. Amir was sobbing. I sat quietly, my mind and body both exhausted and in shock. What had I done? I was an insane, greedy woman obsessed with a crap film that was never going see the light of day. How could I have done it? Sacrificed my child? Then, seconds later, we heard the baby scream.

"Don't worry, he's fine," said the paramedic. "He was just being a bit anti-social." She placed him in my arms, still waxy and slippery under the towel he was wrapped in, a squishy, dark-haired, red-faced boy, a tiny bit of me and Amir. I started crying, not from joy or pain, but pure guilt, in a moment of absolute truth. My own self-centredness had led to this, endangering the most precious, priceless things in my life. I thanked God again and again, still feeling sick from thinking that our son had died because of me.

"I'm sorry," I blubbered, and Amir stroked my face and told me to hush, it could wait.

I confessed all later, and Amir endearingly told me it was okay, admitting that maybe he should have just let me do the acting in the first place. There would have been no need for all the secrecy.

Those first few days should have been scary, but all I could feel was an overwhelming sense of peace. I was surprised at how easily it all came to me – the practical tasks of changing and feeding, and the primal, intense, response to my son's every demand.

I quickly decided on a name so there wouldn't have to be any discussion with Mumtaz on the subject. A beautiful time in our life was beginning. I chose Zain, a name I had always liked, that meant beauty and grace, to symbolise the much-needed joy that he'd brought us.

AMIR
2012

I forgave her. Holding my son in my arms, there was nothing else I could do. We'd had a few silly upsets, but he was going to give us a bright new start.

We never mentioned it again. We'd both made mistakes, and I resolved to overlook everything, not to keep harping back to it. And neither did we talk specifically of this second chance. It was just a feeling conveyed at different moments. Sinking, silent looks, bubbles of laughter at the adorable antics of our son, our fingers touching, lingering.

I was sad, though, to see Sophie struggling to find the same peace with Mum. They had petty arguments all the time. Swaddling or sleeping bag, bibs or tissues, the right way to burp a baby. They didn't agree on anything. Mum wasn't without her faults. She tactlessly chose Zain's four-month birthday to announce she was semi retiring from cooking, and Sophie could finally take over "eighty-five percent" responsibility of the kitchen. This cunningly left her a bit of leeway to go back and make herself spicy impulse binges when she fancied them. Otherwise, the kitchen was Sophie's, and Mum would handle the babysitting. To be fair, Sophie tried her best, but it upset even me when I saw her, on the few occasions I was home early or at the weekend, forcing herself to finish the deep frying whilst battling the urge to pick up a crying Zain, leaving him to be soothed by Mum with a dummy dipped in Gripe Water.

They complained to me separately, niggling and pecking at me constantly, like those nibbling little fish used in fashionable pedicures. The prospect of it loomed miserably over me every evening as I drove home.

One night I came home late, after a frustrating day at the office. A couple of house sales had fallen through, and a client was threatening to sue me for not mentioning a bungalow was situated behind a smelly recycling centre.

The place was in a mess. Mum was in bed with the flu, and Sophie was nattering away on the phone. Zain was lying under his baby gym, surrounded by an earthquake of toys, mashed carrot smeared over his face. I went into the kitchen, hoping to find some form of dinner, a juicy chicken leg maybe. Even the dreaded daal would have done. Instead, I found a grizzled jacket potato withering away in the microwave, and a can of beans dumped on the worktop, half opened with the tin cutter still stuck in the top, blotches of sauce dripping down the sides. I would usually come home and flop down on the sofa while Mum or Sophie finished laying out the meal, but tonight I stayed in the kitchen, picking up spoons and forks and kitchen towel scraps, wiping jellified fat and crumbs off the surfaces. All this chaos and she hadn't even cooked anything.

If I'm honest, I wasn't what they call domesticated, not in those days. But seeing the stacks of plates and bowls in the sink, even I couldn't ignore them. I picked up a sponge and squirted on a slick of washing up liquid.

Sophie was in the doorway, glaring at me.

"What are you doing?" she said.

"Just helping you out a bit," I said. "Looks like you've had a tough day."

"I have. Zain's had a bad tummy since he woke up. He's been crying all day."

"Is he okay?"

"You're not trying to help. You're trying to show me up."

"Did you take him to the doctor?"

"Trying to look like the perfect husband. Making me look like a useless wife."

"Don't be silly, Sophie. There's no one here. Who am I going to impress?"

"There's no one here now, but I know you. Next time we're with friends and the topic of bossy wives comes up, you'll say you wash dishes. Just because you've done it once in three years. You can say it and it won't be a lie."

"You're being delusional. I didn't even think of that." I dropped the sponge back into the sink and wiped my hands. "I was just trying to help." Then, utterly stupidly, "God knows you need it."

She screamed then and flung a baby bottle at the wall. I was shocked, frightened but enraged too. With all my self-restraint I kept my mouth shut. It would do no good to argue more now. I was thinking of Zain, of Mum asleep upstairs. I walked out and went to McDonald's.

SOPHIE
2012

We'd had squabbles before, but I'd never seen that rage on his face. I cowered as he stormed out. Yes, I threw the bottle, but it was just the pressure of the day spent walking around with a wailing baby getting to me.

It should have been a time woven with precious, gossamer moments; it was what you lived for: a beautiful baby and perfect home. But it was marred by our petty disputes, childish disagreements erupting into horrible rows. I tried my best, but Amir was moody and fractious, and at times I also found it hard to take his lack of empathy with me. I didn't have many friends in those days. My college friends had mostly moved away. I wasn't a natural loner, I enjoyed company, having a busy social circle, but I hadn't made many new friends after we got married, apart from Craig, my acting tutor, and Rizwana, a woman I met at the baby immunisation clinic. It just hadn't occurred to me. I'd thought I'd only ever need Amir. But it was a deceptive fallacy – the idea of a soulmate, a connection embedded deep in hearts, blood, marrow, that crackled and burned between you like so much lightning. By the time I realised this it was too late – I was stuck at home day and night with Zain.

Mumtaz had cleverly manipulated the structure of the household to suit her. I wouldn't have minded her looking after him – she was his grandmother and they were natural instincts, but when I couldn't quieten his crying fits and she could, my heart sank.

One sultry night Zain was more unsettled than usual. The nursery was uncomfortably warm and even though I opened the window the air was thick and still, with no breeze at all. After an hour of crying and being walked around on my shoulder he eventually fell asleep. I laid him down in the cot carefully, held my breath, waited, and when he didn't stir, I crept stealthily from the room. I went upstairs and fell into my own bed, exhausted. I only wanted to close my eyes and rest for a few minutes, stay awake in case Zain started crying again, but I fell into a deep sleep immediately.

When I woke up again, suddenly, almost three hours had passed. Amir was still asleep, lying on his back, mouth open, otter-like. I got up and went to the bathroom and splashed my face with cold water, then brushed my teeth. I wanted to fall straight back into bed, but I knew I should go down and check on Zain first.

His cot was empty. I stared for a moment, confused. Had I taken him into our bed? Was I still dreaming? No, I was awake, and Zain should be here in the nursery. I gasped and looked desperately under the thin blanket, patting it down wildly as if the baby had somehow wriggled under the flat sheet. I cried out and ran down the corridor towards Mumtaz's room, calling out for her. The door was open, the room dark. I switched on the light. There was nobody there.

"Amir!" I shouted, as I ran down the stairs. I flung open all the doors to the rooms, flipping on the lights, but there was nobody there. Amir hadn't appeared. I knew he was probably still in his stupor. I sat down on the armchair in the lounge, my head bowed and clasped in my hands, trying to think with a clear head. Mumtaz was gone too. What had got into the mind of the old woman? Had she taken my boy in a fit of craziness? Or had they both been kidnapped by a madman? Terrifying thoughts burst and vibrated in my brain. The curtain at the French doors moved slowly with a gentle waft of wind, and I realised the door was open. Another shard of fear pierced through me. I ran to the door, pulling open the curtain and stepped out into the night, ready to search every inch of the Earth for my son.

The garden was dark with a soft graphite sootiness. It backed onto a deserted yard, and the lack of streetlights, along with the cherry tree and several rose bushes made it shadowy and delusive. I was peering towards the end of the garden when something caught my attention. As my eyes grew accustomed to the darkness a figure began to form, standing, holding something. Was it my baby? I gasped but the sound was lost in the low rumble of a car in the distance. I was unsure of how to approach the phantom. I wasn't a good runner, and I couldn't risk them seeing me and sprinting off out through the back gate, if indeed they had Zain. Equally I was frightened they might attack me. Having run out thoughtlessly in my desperation to find him, I hadn't brought any sort of weapon with me, and now there was no time to go back and arm myself. All I could do was creep up and attempt to surprise the figure.

Heart thudding at an incredible rate, my body slippery with sweat and fear, I took small steps towards the end of the garden as quickly and quietly as I could. The figure moved suddenly, lifting the thing it was holding, putting it over its shoulder. I was close enough to see a tiny face. Zain!

"Oi!" I shouted, springing towards them, and the figure turned. It was Mumtaz.

"Mum!" I said.

"What is it?" she whispered angrily.

"What are you doing out here?"

"Speak softly!" she said. "He was crying, and it was too hot inside, so I brought him out here. Such a warm night. Look how peaceful he is now."

"Give him to me!" I said. "Why did you bring him out here? I thought… I thought… something had happened."

"Calm down, Sophie. There's no need to be like that. He was upset and you didn't wake up. I thought I'd let you get some sleep."

I took the baby from her and took him up, past the nursery and up into my own room without another word. Then I sat on the bed and cried.

I began to get all sorts of outlandish thoughts after that, imagining that Mumtaz might do anything, whisk my baby away or get rid of me in her obsession with him. I was scared to let Zain out of my sight, but of course this wasn't possible. Amir told me that my fears were unfounded, and maybe they were, but in my tense, nervous state they were lodged firmly in my mind.

My only respite was the local mother and baby group, but even that I only went to every three weeks or so, after baby weighing. Zain was a podgy boy, and I didn't like the health visitor's suggestions that he go on a diet. Apparently, I was supposed to dilute the formula and give him only one rusk instead of two for breakfast. I tried it once, but he had a fit when the reduced calorie meal finished and the Farley's box on the worktop was out of his grabbing range.

The centre had organised a mother and baby trip to the cinema, and my friend Rizwana suggested I go with her. I leapt at the chance. It had been ages since Amir and I had been. It was a morning show, so those with school-age children could be back well before three o'clock.

It was a sunny day and I decided to walk rather than take the car. The town centre wasn't far, a fifteen-minute walk. I unfolded the pushchair and parked it against the front door to hold it open. I quickly went upstairs to get Zain, who was in the cot. I'd just stepped out of my room when Mumtaz appeared in the hallway.

"Where are you off to?" she said.

"Just going to see a film," I said.

"Why don't you just leave him at home? He's been a bit sneezy the last few days. You go and enjoy yourself." She moved to block my way down the stairs.

"I'm taking him with me. And we're getting late. Please move out of the way."

"He's got a cough. Don't argue with me."

"He's my baby. I know what's best for him." I waited for a moment, but she just stood there. "Look, I don't want to upset you. You're an old woman now. I know you get bored, and you need something to do, but sticking your nose into my business isn't the answer."

"What? He's my grandson! He is my business!"

"You're not a normal granny. You're obsessed! But you can't dominate us anymore."

"Badtameez!" she shouted, giving me a sharp slap on the cheek. "Amir will hear about this. Now get lost if you want to but give my grandson to me." She went for him then, with a rugby snatch worthy of a Premiership player. But I reacted despite the sting on my face, or perhaps because of it, dodging the tackle, turning and elbowing her away.

I didn't mean to use much strength. It was an act of protection, purely defensive, but it was enough to knock her hard. Her eyes widened in surprise as she toppled back. I glanced down at Zain to check him for a split second but looked up instantly when I heard the thud. Mumtaz had hit the wall and lost her balance, and was flying down the stairs, wildly lashing out, trying to grab anything to stop her fall. I cried out and ran forward, scrabbling at the air to try and get hold of her, but she landed at the bottom, her head hitting first the post and then the corner of the wall with a crack. I screamed and went down the stairs as fast as I could. Mumtaz was lying at the bottom, motionless. Dark blood was slowly seeping out into her hair and into the carpet, making a thick, gloopy orb around her head. Horrified, I crouched down, still holding Zain in one arm. I touched her hesitantly on the shoulder, my hand shaking, but recoiled when I felt the warm wetness of her blood on my fingertips.

"Mum," I whispered. "Mum, open your eyes. Are you okay?"

"I don't think so," said a voice. I looked up and saw Amir's uncle, Suleiman, standing there. He'd obviously walked in through the open door.

"Check her," I said. "Call the ambulance. Quickly, please, just dial 999." I thrust my phone into his hand.

"Wait," he said. He kneeled beside her and lifted her wrist, checking for a pulse, before placing two fingers on her neck to make sure. "I think she's gone."

"What?" I said. "She can't be!" My mouth began to fill with saliva, and I thought I was going to vomit. I gulped it down and started panting.

"What happened?"

Mind scrambling, I garbled a story. "I was in the bathroom. I heard her fall. She… she must have tripped."

"I heard everything," he said. "Saw it."

I got hysterical then.

"I'm sorry, I'm sorry, I'm sorry," I bleated. "I didn't mean anything. I pushed her by accident. Oh my God! She's dead. I've killed her… I didn't mean to hurt her. I was just trying to protect Zain; we were getting late. I just wanted to take him for a walk."

"Cinema. You were taking him to the cinema," said Suleiman. I nodded. My phone began ringing. It was Rizwana, probably wondering where I was. I cut it off.

"Let's call the ambulance," I said. I put the baby into the pushchair. It had been moved and the front door was shut. Steadying myself with a hand on the wall, I looked at the mobile, my mind blank, confused about how to go about calling emergency services. I looked dumbly at Suleiman.

"Who shall I ask for?" I said. "Police or doctor?"

"Put it away," he said. "I wouldn't recommend doing that yet." He propelled me towards the living room and sat me down on the sofa. "Calm down first."

He was right. I closed my eyes and breathed slowly.

"Do you know how this looks?" said Suleiman. "It's a nasty fall, with only your word for what happened. How will anyone believe you did it innocently, that you weren't trying to bump the old woman off?"

"No! It was an accident! I didn't do it on purpose!"

"You're not exactly the dutiful daughter, are you? I heard you even played that song on your wedding, *Sass kutni*." He was referring to a humorous bhangra number, about a girl who wants to beat up her husband's interfering mother.

"What are you talking about?" I said. "It's just a stupid song!"

"Not stupid. Heera was the best bhangra band that ever lived. Arguably. Anyway, it wasn't a wise move."

"Lots of people play that song. They don't mean it!"

"They don't have a dead mother-in-law on the stairs."

"It was an accident; you know it was."

"Of course it was," he said. "But look what happened. Do you think the police are going to believe you?"

"Please please please," I said. "Get me a lawyer. Tell me what to do." Suleiman nodded and patted me on the shoulder.

"The only way out of it is this," said Suleiman. "You need another witness. Me. I'm just an odd random relative, why would we plot something together? I'll say I saw her fall. Her foot got caught in her trousers and she tripped over, down the stairs and crash, straight into the wall. Understand?"

I stared at him.

"Yes," I said.

"Good," he said. "But our accounts have to be the same. Or they'll never believe us, and you know what that means.

Hurry, we have to call for help now otherwise we'll have to explain the delay."

We went over the story again to make sure all the details matched, then we phoned for an ambulance.

AMIR
2012

I was completely unprepared for the shock of Mum's death, coming at me like cannon fire in the dead of night. My mother, my guide, my friend, telling me off or sharing a silly joke from her armchair one minute, and the next, slipped and smashed into a place that was out of my reach. The police said it was unlucky, a freak accident. Suleiman saw her tripping over her *shalwar*. She was always complaining that the tailor sewed her trousers too long for her. Three or four times they'd got tangled in the wheels of the supermarket trolley. I had half a mind to sue the tailor, but what would be the point? Mum wasn't coming back. The only thing that slightly softened the pain was the doctors telling me that it must have been quick. The way she'd always wanted it, something that she'd prayed for, to be spared any long and humiliating illness that made her a burden on me or anyone else.

Sophie surprised me during that time. She seemed nearly as devastated as me – a few times I found her crying by herself when she thought there was nobody around – but she was strong, brought me to my senses, pulled me through those mechanical days. I went through them automatically, eating and sleeping at the right times without tasting or feeling refreshed. It was like being haunted by Mum. I wasn't seeing a ghost or hearing whispers. I suppose I was spooked out by her absence. In the morning I'd come down expecting to see her at the breakfast bar drinking tea and eating crackers, her Asian radio station playing softly in the background. I'd knock her bedroom door before going to bed to say goodnight, then open it and be greeted by a cold, empty room smelling of stale air. A couple of times I went in and lay down on her bed. The linen was still scented with the talcum powder and tea rose perfume she'd loved, and I hugged and sobbed into the pillow, as though it could take me to her or come alive and cuddle me back.

Gradually, though, the sharpness of grief began to wear down, as things went back to a sort of normal. I started work again, the visitors stopped coming to pay condolences, and we trudged on, one person short, filling gaps with old stories and memories and the raw grit of the present.

It was a nice surprise the first time she turned up at my office, Zain looking adorable in little boater hat, fat thighs poking out of a summer romper. Sophie, not so good. Her eyes had been smudged charcoal dusty (without make-up) for the last few weeks, and the dark lipstick made her mouth look mean. She was putting on weight and her jeans looked lumpy. I felt awful for noticing these things, but they just glared badly under the unforgiving tube lights.

I took Sophie into my room, leaving Zain with the girls cooing over him outside.

"This is unexpected," I said. "Is everything okay?"

"I just thought you might need me," she said. "I wanted to check if you were okay."

"'Course I am. It's good to be back."

"Well. That's good. Do you want me to stay for a little while? Keep you company? We could go for a coffee maybe?"

"You've got ten minutes. I've got a client to see. Not enough time for a coffee, sorry."

Her faced flushed black.

"Don't fob me off like that," she said. "'You've got ten minutes.' I'm not some office junior. I'm your wife."

"Darling, I'm sorry, I didn't mean it like that. Let's have coffee here. I'll get someone to make it for us."

"Leave it. I don't want any now. I'll go."

"No, stay a few minutes longer. I said I'm sorry. Anyway, Zain seems to be having fun with his new aunties." He was a friendly baby, didn't cry with strangers.

"I didn't realise you worked with so many girls," said Sophie.

"Like you said, office juniors. Some of them are just here for experience."

It didn't stop, after that. Sometimes she'd bring lunch, other times it was some obscure form that needed signing or she was simply "just passing by". Zain was a common excuse. He was missing me, or did I think he had a temperature? She began ticking with rage when I suggested it would have been easier to check it with a thermometer at home.

It was distracting, irritating, interrupted my flow, even made me a bit panicky. I began to dread the double doors opening to reveal her portly figure pushing through with the pram, but I was powerless to stop it.

SOPHIE
2012

I certainly didn't visit Amir that first time to keep an eye on him; I was worried about him. He'd been back at work for only a couple of days, and I thought he might still be feeling a bit depressed. I knew he'd be over the moon to see Zain in the office, have an opportunity to show him off to all his colleagues.

He obviously wasn't depressed. He was leaning on one of the girls' desks, laughing his head off at some senseless joke. He straightened up when I went in, with a look of guilty shock, then faked delight at seeing me. I wasn't fooled.

Once I realised the kind of unsuitable atmosphere he was in, I started making a point of going in at least twice a week, just to monitor the situation, make them all aware that if any hanky-panky went on, I'd be the first to pick up on it. And anyway, I thought it was a nice thing to do. It had been so blissful after Mumtaz went. Not blissful that she was dead, of course, but in the sense that the tragedy really did bring us truly together.

I was still guilt-ridden by what had happened even though I knew it wasn't my fault. Any mother would have reacted in the same way. She'd tried to snatch Zain out of my hands. But, however much I tried to convince myself that it was purely an accident, I was still traumatised by the memory of her falling

86

back, her eyes widening with the realisation that she was about to go flying through the air, and the disgusting crack as her head hit the wall.

I forced myself to think practically, told myself I was acting in the best interests of everyone involved. I'd been very distressed when Kiran died, but I hadn't lost my head, and keeping quiet about my part in that unfortunate affair had proved beneficial for all. Amir had a loving family now and even Mumtaz had enjoyed the blessing of a grandson. It was just such a great shame she hadn't given herself any boundaries when it came to him, though, or she'd still be alive.

There was no way I could risk Amir knowing the truth about the accident. I knew he loved and trusted me, but the arguments he'd witnessed between Mumtaz, and I might make him think I was trying to cover up a deliberate, murderous action. I couldn't do it to Zain, put him in the danger of his mother ending up in jail. Even if he did believe me, surely those whispers of doubt and suspicion would linger? It would be the end of our relationship, in all the ways that mattered. It was far, far better that Amir stayed in the happy delusion that his mother had fallen after getting knotted up in her too long trousers.

Mumtaz had been dead two months when Suleiman returned. He'd been at the house amongst the rest of the family, for the funeral and two or three days after, but I hadn't spoken to him alone.

It was the day after Amir had gone back to the estate agency when he paid me a visit. I was relieved. Here was the only person in the world to whom I could express the fears I had canned up inside. My conspirator, my protector.

"Thank God you came," I said, when Suleiman was comfortable, curled up with a mug of tea and a plate of scones, laying back on the sofa like a sultan.

"I wanted to see you earlier," he said. "But I knew Amir was still at home. What's the matter with you? You look rough. A bit messy if I might say so."

I wasn't sure if he was trying to be sympathetic or critical. Either way, I wasn't happy at the remark.

"I'm just tired," I said. "Why? What part of me looks messy? The hair? Or my skin? Do I look old? I haven't been using my usual face cream, maybe that's why."

"Don't worry," he said. "You look fine. As long as it's not because you've been spending too much time fretting and agonising over our little secret."

"Well, not agonising exactly, but it does cross my mind now and again."

"Why? You know what they found," said Suleiman. "The head injuries were consistent with what we told them. She fell down the stairs. The truth. You have to remember, Sophie, we've done nothing wrong. All we did was make things easier for everyone, avoided unnecessary fuss. Do you think dear Mumtaz would be happy putting Amir through all of that?"

I shook my head.

"Good," he said. "So really we were only carrying out poor Bhabi's own wishes."

"I suppose so," I said.

"That's my girl." He sliced a scone in half and spread a thick layer of butter and jam on it and took a large bite. "I like these with clotted cream but never mind. I made a good witness, didn't I? We even made page two of the *Bradford Beagle*. 'Ill-fitted outfit ends in tragic tumble'."

"Let's change the subject," I said. "I don't want to think about it."

"Fine." We were quiet for a minute or so, and I shut my eyes tightly to get rid of the image summoned up by the newspaper headline. When I opened them, Suleiman was staring at me. Then he leaned over and brushed my hair off my face, tucking it behind my ear. I flinched.

"Lovely hair," he said. "Messy, but lovely. I can see a shade of red in there, when the light shines on it."

"You should probably go," I said. "Amir pops in sometimes

when he's out doing viewings. You don't want him to find you here."

"True, but really, it's not like we're doing anything… *illicit*, is it?"

"What are you talking about, Uncle?"

"Oh! I'm not your uncle. I'm not even Amir's real uncle. In fact, I can't even remember how we're related. Anyway, there's something you can help me with."

I was unnerved by his weird behaviour, but still naively thought he might have clothes that needed darning or dinners he wanted cooking. We were never quite sure what his domestic arrangements were at any one time.

"I'm thinking of visiting Japan next month," he said. "I have some business interests over there."

Cat sitting? Sightseeing advice? Nothing so complicated.

"I'm running a couple of thousand pounds short. The tickets are quite expensive this time of year."

And it all clicked into place beautifully. Dressed in the slick chic garb of oriental travel, presented irresistibly over the cosiest fireside cuppa, whispered endearingly like the confidences between lifelong friends, it was just that ugly old thing, blackmail.

Like I said, Amir had no idea what I had done for him. What I was doing for him. I had a bit of money still in the bank from the lump sum my parents had given me on our wedding. I transferred two and a half thousand pounds into Suleiman's account. I didn't care, if it meant hanging on to my husband.

Innocent explanations. Amir was full of them. But I knew what he was like. That short attention span. How could I forget how quickly he transferred his affections from the newly deceased Kiran to me? I dreaded the moment when it would happen again. Surrounded by all those frothy girls, Mel and Manjeet, Yasmin and Bunty, Mikado-thin and Mr Sheen glossy, it was all too easy to see.

I tried keeping an eye on his phone, the gadget guilty of a thousand sins of the modern age. It was the easiest and most obvious way to catch a cheat but depended on him being somewhat dense and not deleting incriminating communications. I sneaked it out of his pocket when he was in the bathroom or checked in the middle of the night when he was asleep. There were no photos of other women, that much was clear. I was pleased to see my own on his home page, with a few more in the album, along with lots of Zain. There were, however, several WhatsApp chats I wasn't happy with. Nothing dirty or even too flirty, but they had a tone that was too giggly for my liking. Mostly they were work related, reminders for the next day, but one of them concerned a mystery gift.

MEL: *Thanks for the presents, they're perfect...*
                    AMIR: *Ur welcome, glad you liked them*
MEL: *You have great taste; I never would have guessed lol*
                    AMIR: *LOL what r u trying to say*
                    AMIR: *I look like I've got bad taste?*
MEL: *Nooooooo u know I didn't mean that*

I confronted Amir with it over breakfast.

"Why are you chatting to all these women on WhatsApp?" I asked.

"What women?" he said. "I hardly even use WhatsApp. And how do you know? Have you been checking my phone or something?"

"I just turned the alarm off this morning and there were messages on there. Even if I did, I'm your wife. What does it matter, unless you've got something to hide?"

"That's not the point. You can read whatever's on there because you won't find anything. The point is you don't trust me. You went behind my back. You were spying on me."

I was quiet for a moment.

"So?" I said.

"So what?"

"Why are you having all these conversations with other women? You never bother writing more than three words whenever I text you."

"It's just work stuff, nothing interesting. Necessary stuff."

"Chats about your good taste and sexy presents? That's necessary work stuff?"

"My God, Sophie, stop this. Yeah, it was work. It was just a bunch of flowers and a subscription to *Hello!* magazine. It was from all of us, not just me."

"So why did she say you're the one with the good taste if it was from all of you?"

"Because I ordered them. Stop being so paranoid."

"Why did you order them? Why not get one of the other girls to do it? And she put that face with the hearts in his eyes."

Amir slammed his mug down into the sink, cracking the handle, and strode out of the house. Oddly this was what it took for me to believe him.

AMIR
2013

Mrs Badshah was a landlady and a regular client of ours. Her husband owned a restaurant and she dealt with their rental properties. She already had three flats on our books and had just finished developing a house, a mid-terrace with a cellar converted into a kitchen and a luxury en-suite attic bedroom. We viewed the house and then I took her for a coffee to finalise the details.

In her own eyes at least, Mrs Badshah was a very glamorous woman, with a permed fringe, thick white make-up, and hefty false eyelashes that looked like brooms. She was wearing a transparent red kaftan over a white t-shirt and shiny black leggings, and her nails sparkled with tiny rubies. When I went to order the coffees, she pouted her lips and took a selfie in front of a life-size cardboard cut-out of soap opera star Pat Butcher holding the menu. Pat had never actually visited the café, but the owner Mr Javed was a fan, and his son was apparently a whizz with Photoshop.

"Right, I don't want any too big families," said Mrs Badshah, when I was back at the table with the drinks. "Max two kids, over five years old. And no pregnant women. That means there'll be a baby at some point soon. Not acceptable. And no grandparents. Leads to in-law fights. Not having any plates thrown at my expensive wallpapers. Especially ones full of *karahi* chicken."

"But it's a five-bedroom house," I said. "Of course, your potential tenants are going to be big families."

"I'm not having any *junglees* running around my beautiful house. It cost me a fortune to get it all done up like that."

"It's going to be difficult."

"Well, then at least get references. I'm leaving it in your good hands." She put her hand on my wrist and leaned over with a smile. "I know I can trust you."

"I'll have a cappuccino too, please, Amir."

I jumped and looked up. Sophie was standing there, holding Zain.

"Sophie!" I yanked my hand away from Mrs Badshah and stood up. "What are you doing here?"

"I was going to have an innocent cup of coffee, unlike some," she said.

"This is my wife, Sophie," I said. "Sophie, this one of our clients, Mrs Badshah. She's just refurbished a house near here."

"*Badshah* means king," said Mrs Badshah. "But I'm the rental queen." She threw back her head and laughed indulgently.

"That's a title with a nice cheap ring to it," said Sophie.

"Sophie!" I said. "She's just joking." Thank God Mrs Badshah was still at the tail end of her chortle and hadn't heard the comment. "Sophie, why don't you get us a table and order some food, and we'll have lunch once our meeting is over. We won't be long." I steered her gently away.

"Don't push me, Amir!" snapped Sophie.

"Ooh!" said Mrs Badshah. "Temper, temper!"

"You shut up and keep out of it! Old cow."

"Sophie!" I said. People were looking now. "Go and sit in the car."

"Look at her! Face painted like a drag queen, pawing at my husband! I saw what you were doing!" Mrs Badshah was on her feet now.

"Jealous little bitch," she said. "I see what he means now, when he calls you plain and worn out."

"What?" I said. The woman was lying. "I never said anything like that." Sophie glared at me, then charged off, knocking Pat Butcher over. The room was still for a minute, then Mr Javed hurried over and picked her up.

"I'm really sorry," I mumbled. "She's not herself…"

"No need," said Mrs Badshah.

"Thank you… Thanks for understanding. I really want to apologise. It was completely unacceptable."

"Like I said, no need. We won't be doing any more business together."

"No, please…" But she'd already put on her puffa-jacket and picked up her handbag.

"Last word," she said. "You need to put her on a dog lead."

SOPHIE
2013

I was fuming. All I wanted from Amir was faithfulness. I'd sacrificed everything for this man. I accepted that it was common for women to put their careers on hold when they had children and I was happy to devote myself to my husband and son. But I was also aware of time passing, and in the entertainment industry, looks and youth were essential, and I felt that I was putting more at risk than most. Every day I wondered if a tiny fleck of my beauty was fading, if every dust mote in sunlight carried away another lost chance at success. What would be left by the time I finally reached the stage or stood in front of a camera?

Amir's flirting wasn't only disloyal, it also gave credence to my feelings of inadequacy, adding to the pressure already building in my head. If my own husband didn't like how I looked and preferred the company of other women, what was the rest of the world going to think?

The payment I'd made to Suleiman, too, had been for Amir's sake. For so much of my life, I had centred everything around him.

However, I knew I should have dealt with the situation differently. I should have given Amir a chance to explain. The old bat wasn't his type, and why would he go after someone like her when he had all those girls in the office to choose from? I knew I'd have to eat humble pie otherwise things could get out of control.

I'd expected him to be furious when he came home that night, but he walked in slowly, hunched and defeated instead of striding in, ready for battle. He didn't look at me as he sat down next to where Zain was lying in his baby swing.

"I'm so sorry, Amir," I said. "I don't know why I did it. I went mad. It was unforgivable." He looked up, surprised, then nodded. He didn't talk to me again for the rest of the evening, took his dinner into the study that he used as a PlayStation room. The next morning, though, he was humming at breakfast and grabbed my hand when I gave him his cup of tea. Normally I didn't bother making his tea if we weren't talking, but I was trying to make amends.

"I'm sorry too," he said. "I shouldn't have let her hold my hand."

"She was stroking it," I said.

"I know... I was just thinking about what she was saying."

"She was suggesting something, was she?"

"It was nothing like that, Sophie! What's the point if you won't let me speak?"

"Sorry."

"It was just about the tenancy. She was coming out with all sorts of un-doable ideas. Look, let's just forget it, shall we?"

I nodded and curled my arm around his neck.

"But Soph," he said. "Please don't do it again."

Looking messy, as Suleiman had put it, wasn't going to help me. The incident with the Badshah woman taught me two things. I really did need to keep a closer eye on Amir, and I had to step up my game. I didn't believe Amir had made the comment about me looking plain and worn out. We'd had our quarrels, but as far as I knew, he'd never breathed a word against me to anyone else. A couple of weeks after the argument, I got Mum to babysit Zain and went to the salon for a facial and a haircut, and whatever faddish new treatment I could find. Already I felt a hundred times better, the buffing and polishing sloughing away more than just ancient skin cells. I was often too tired to look after myself properly but that was going to change. Neglecting my appearance wasn't good for my relationship or my career.

I phoned Amir at the office.

"Hello, gorgeous," I said. I was Siamese smooth, purring like a Persian Blue. Give him something a little bit different, a bit of cheek, not the usual request for bread and milk on the way home. I could feel Amir sit up and pay attention. I told him I'd arranged for Zain to stay with Mum overnight, so we could have a special dinner and a romantic, intimate evening. As I'd hoped, he suggested we go out, and leave the romantic and intimate part till later.

I started getting ready at about four. I took out a long turquoise chiffon dress and wore my hair down so Amir could appreciate the freshly cut layers. The dress didn't fit as perfectly as I'd hoped, with a couple of little bulges here and there. Lotus bloom perfumed and smoky eyed, I was ready by half past six and sat down to watch *Come Dine with Me* till Amir got home.

Two hours later and still no date. The usual awful thoughts ran through my head, but I told myself it must be traffic, some office emergency, a last-minute viewing, a vital sale. I tried phoning him but there was no answer. 9 o'clock.

It was twenty past nine when the key rattled and Amir came in, yawning lazily in a loud, exaggerated way. I felt sick. He was too relaxed. Not sorry, not nervous. My anger rose instantly, making me almost pant.

"Finally decided to make an entrance?" I shouted, even before he got in through the living room door. He froze.

"Oh my God, I am so sorry, darling! I meant to call you. There was so much going on… I feel terrible."

"Where have you been then? What was going on?"

"It was Manj. She was in a bad state, having these awful stomach cramps, almost screaming in agony."

"You were helping her with period pain?"

"Don't be silly, Sophie! I took her to hospital. It turned out to be appendicitis."

"Why did you have to take her? Why couldn't one of the other girls do it? Or her family?"

"One of the girls came with us. But they wouldn't have managed without my help; she could hardly walk."

I took a deep breath, but it didn't work. The frustration came boiling, erupting out.

"Oh, so you were carrying her in your arms, were you? So bloody heroic. Probably didn't want to put her down."

"Stop it, Sophie."

"And why did you have to stay there for three hours? You could have left her there with Bubbles or whatever the other little minx is called. Or I suppose she was in your lap while you sat in the waiting room?" I put on an irritating, high-pitched voice. "Oh Amir! Please don't leave me in this big scary hospital all by myself!"

"Shut up, Sophie, just stop it! Have a bit of sympathy for someone else for once!"

"What are you saying? Huh? You saying I'm selfish?"

I was trembling, sweating with rage. Roaring, I picked up a china vase and flung it at the wall, and it shattered almost musically, a deep, crashing bass mixed with gentler, tinkly notes. Seeing Amir's face cloud over, I knew he was livid. I launched myself at him in self-defence before he could even open his mouth, clawing and scratching, managing to gouge a few bits of flesh off his face. He pushed me off and began walking away.

"That's it! Go out like usual!" I screamed. "You coward!" He stopped and turned.

"What do you want, Sophie? I'm warning you, don't push me."

"*You're* warning *me*?"

"Yeah, I am."

"Always late, always somewhere else, with Manj or Bunty or that cheap slapper you pretended was a landlady!"

"Shut up and calm down." His voice was tight, every word hard and clear, like a little hailstone. "I forgot to call you and I'm sorry, but it was an emergency, and you don't need to behave like this."

"You're not sorry," I said, driving a fist into his chest. He stepped away, backwards.

"Don't, Sophie."

"What are you going to do, coward? Hit me back? I don't believe anything you say. All your lies." He stopped.

"There's no point then, is there? If you don't believe me?" he said. "I don't know what's happened to you, but I can't take this anymore." He paused for a split second. "I divorce you."

"What?" My blood chilled. "No! Wait! Don't say anything else. Stop stop stop stop!" I charged at him again, this time armed with a cushion to cover his mouth before he could utter those horrific, irrevocable words, but he gave me a shove and spat them out.

"I divorce you." And finally, once more. "I divorce you."

SOPHIE
Present Day

Amir pats me awkwardly on the back and sits me down.

"I'll take care of Zain," he says. "Or do you want me to come with you to the police station?" I assure him I'll be fine and ask him to phone my parents to tell them what's going on. I kiss Zain's sleepy little hand, then pick up my keys and head out, praying under my breath.

Friday morning seems to be a popular time for crime. A pair of drunken middle-aged women and a man boasting about smashing his neighbour's ugly water feature are being taken into cells, and there's a report of a burglary at the home of a Pakistani family.

"It's wedding season," says the woman walking me to the interview room. "Burglars know there's loads of gold lying around. You've probably got some too, haven't you?"

"Yes, but we keep it in the safe in the bank," I say. She nods approvingly.

"Can I get you a cup of tea or coffee?" I decline the offer and she leaves, telling me that someone will be here shortly. It's a beige room with a desk and two chairs, a painting of a brown mansion on the wall, and a tower of cardboard boxes in the corner.

A few seconds later the door opens, and a policeman comes in and sits down with a notebook. He introduces himself as Sergeant Willis and takes down my name and address and asks me why I'm here, humming at the end of every sentence.

"When was the last time you saw him, hmmm?" he asks.

"Yesterday morning, when he left for work," I say.

"Right. So, you gave him your usual goodbye peck on the cheek, hmmm? Waved him away from the front door?"

"No… he left early. I was still in bed."

"But you saw him leave?"

"Well, no, I didn't see him actually leave. But his car was gone, so he must have done, mustn't he?"

"I'm just trying to get an accurate picture of what happened, hmmm?" He smiles patiently.

"I think he said goodbye. I think I heard him picking up his keys from the dressing table."

Sergeant Willis writes in his notepad. "And how was his mood, night before last? Was he acting strange? Did he say anything unusual?"

"No, nothing strange," I say. "Everything was normal. He came home, had dinner, watched a bit of telly, went to bed."

"You didn't have an argument or anything like that? A disagreement of any sort?"

It's the question I've been waiting for and I'm prepared. I pass over it smoothly, without any tell-tale flickers of alarm in my expression.

"No, nothing like that happened," I say.

"That's good to hear," he says. "And is there anything missing, hmmm? Any clothes? His passport? Any luggage gone walkabout? Suitcases, trolleys, that sort of thing?"

"No. I don't know. I don't know where he keeps his passport. I didn't notice any suitcases missing. They're in the garage. I haven't looked."

"And how did he normally travel to work?"

"He drove."

"So, the car's missing too?"

"Yes. It's a black Mercedes. I can't remember the registration number, but I can check and tell you later."

He makes a few more notes, then promises to get on to it straight away. He tells me not to worry and says he'll ring me later.

He does ring me later but has nothing to tell me. They've made the basic enquiries at the hospitals, are looking out for Tariq's car and keeping an eye on his bank account. I check the suitcases and look through the clothes in his wardrobe. Nothing seems unusual. Nothing is missing. It seems as though Tariq has disappeared into thin air.

I can't say how the days stretch on, endless and unbearable. I do everything a loving wife should in my position. I ring the few friends we have, Tariq's colleagues, Ruby's family. I don't have contact details for any of Tariq's old friends, but I get some numbers from his friend, Jimmy, and ring them, too. I post messages on Facebook and Twitter. Nobody can tell me anything. I park my car near the places he used to go to regularly – the gym, his office, the supermarket, the petrol station, and watch. I'm good at that, watching people without them knowing. I hang around the town centre and stare into crowds. Tariq means star and I search for my single, gleaming star in a sky of millions and fail.

After all this time, those years of hopelessness, I'd finally, in Tariq, captured the essence of happiness, the tranquillity I needed in my life. I can't describe the agony.

SOPHIE

I speak to the police again, but they've had no more luck than I have. There's also a shift in their attitude. Apparently, some missing persons choose to disappear themselves. Being a grown, successful, mentally stable man, Tariq isn't particularly vulnerable, so it's unlikely that they'll pursue his case much further. The thought of them never finding him makes me feel cast adrift too, floating without purpose or destination.

I've been wandering the streets but perhaps it's time to look inwards. The one place I haven't searched is in Tariq's study. The police didn't find anything useful, but I might come across something they didn't notice, something that will give me the answers I want.

I've never spent more than five minutes in the study and that was just to do the hoovering. After we got married, I tried popping into the room while Tariq was working a couple of times, just for a chat, but he was uncommunicative, absorbed in reading notes, so I left him to it. He only went in there when he needed to, and I understood it meant it must be important. He didn't need disturbances.

It's a warm, woody room, with a big mahogany desk and a pair of bookshelves on either side of a brick fireplace. I sit on the black leather swivel chair and spin around on it slowly as I wait for inspiration, as though what remains of Tariq's spirit will nudge me towards a sign.

I look through the desk drawers. They're filled with folders and notebooks, boxes of staples and paper clips. Everything is immaculately neat and organised. I flip through a couple of notebooks, but they make no sense to me. They seem to be work related, written in some sort of coded shorthand – probably only decipherable by Tariq himself. There isn't anything in this clinical filing system that can help me.

I'm about to turn away when I notice there's an extra drawer above the others. It's thinner than the rest, only a couple of inches thick, and has no handle. Instead, there's an indentation at the top to pull it out, and I open it. It's organised into sections, each one containing more stationery – pens, paper clips, stamps. On the side there's a small photo album, one of those slide in ones. As I expect, it's full of pictures of his son, Ayaan, but as I get to the last few pages, I'm surprised to find my own face looking up at me. My eyes blur as I bring the book to my heart. It's a silent but heart wrenching gesture of our love. Concrete proof that it wasn't just my imagination, that we did have something true before things began to turn sour. I can't help it. I break down, cry uncontrollably.

I gather myself together a couple of minutes later. This isn't what I came here for. Putting the album on the desk so I can take it with me, I get up and move on to the shelves. Apart from books on law, there's a collection of atlases and a section devoted to crime fiction. My taste leans towards rom-coms and biographies, but Tariq enjoyed mysteries and spy thrillers. I pull out odd titles and glance at the blurbs. *The Day of the Jackal*, *Tinker Tailor Soldier Spy*, *Red Dragon*. I remember Tariq telling me the latter is about a genius cannibal, and I shiver and push it back into its slot in the shelf. I break into a sweat as I think of someone who read these gory novels falling prey to a gruesome fate himself and imagine Tariq boiling in a cauldron of human soup.

I grab an illustrated atlas that's lying on the desk for distraction and sit back on the chair. There's a finely etched vintage map with gold details on the cover, and I open it with high expectations of more sumptuous images, but my heart darkens as I see the inscription on the first page, written in a calligraphic hand.

May our adventures be infinite my love

Ruby, Ruby, Ruby! Would I never escape her? I'd been touched by my own pictures in the drawer but was Ruby's book taking pride of place by being on top of the desk where he could see it at all times? Had Tariq been thinking of embarking on an everlasting adventure, of going to meet his wife in another world while he was with me? I flip through the book. Ruby has put stickers on several pages, ridiculous, glittery Hello Kitty faces, presumably on the places they've visited together – Paris, Brussels, Johannesburg, Istanbul, Florida, Marrakech. I had so many hopes for our life together, adventures Tariq and I were going to have, but we never had the chance. I feel destroyed, but more than that I feel hatred. I smash the book on to the table and stumble out of the room, taking the album with me. I don't regret anything that I've done.

SOPHIE

Ayaan has been living with Sameena for the last few months following an incident that... well, I'd rather forget about now. I've asked Sameena many times if she knows where Tariq is, but I've heard nothing. Now I've had a new thought. It's Ayaan's birthday. If Tariq is still alive, I'm certain he'll be with his son today.

I've arranged for Mum to take care of Zain, and I set out early. It'll take me just under two hours to reach Sameena's house in the Lake District. It's a radiant Saturday and the air is clear and fresh. I drive with the windows open and play some happy, romantic Bollywood songs from the 90s, Kumar Sanu at his best. Despite my sorrow, the breeze and the music fill me with freedom and the hope I need. I'm moving closer to Tariq; I can sense it in my soul.

I haven't told Sameena I'm coming. I don't want to warn her, give her a chance to cover up if she's hiding anything. I find the house easily enough, a swanky, pale brick barn conversion set in open green hills. The house I share with Tariq is nice, but this is more my style, modern with lots of big windows. I make some mental design notes for the future. Perhaps I'll be able to afford something like this one day? But now I must concentrate on the mission I've set myself. There's only one other car outside the house. Evidently there's no birthday party going on, then.

Sameena answers the door almost immediately, and she's plainly shocked to see me.

"Sophie. This is a surprise," she says after a frozen moment.

"Can I come in?" I say. "Or is it a bad time?" She looks over her shoulder into the house.

"I was just… yes… yes, of course. Come in." She gives me a brief, awkward hug, then leads me through a large, open-plan living area, into a cosier room furnished with comfortable, squashy sofas and lots of tropical looking plants. Toys are scattered in one corner, spilling out of a wooden crate, bricks, cars, ponies and dolls. She has a son and a daughter of her own.

"Sorry about all the mess," she says, picking up colouring pencils off an armchair. "Have a seat, please." I think about it for a second. Should I talk to her or just insist on searching the house? I sit down.

"Where are the children?" I ask.

"Upstairs. On the PlayStation, I think. I'll go and call Ayaan down for you."

"No rush. Let's have a chat first."

"You should have told me you were coming to wish him happy birthday," she says, glancing at the gift bag I've brought with me.

"I know, but I didn't want to you to go to any trouble."

"It's not any trouble, Sophie. After everything that's happened. I just feel so helpless. But how are you coping? Have you heard anything at all from Tariq? Any news?" she says.

"Nothing. What about you? He didn't call Ayaan today?" I ask.

"No," she says. "I would have told you."

"What do you think has happened to him, Sameena? Do you think he's… Surely if he was okay, he would have phoned Ayaan to say happy birthday?"

"I don't know, Sophie. I'm sure he's fine, somewhere, there

must be some explanation. All we can do is pray for his safe return."

I hide my face in my hands and start crying. It's partly genuine. Of course I am grief-stricken at the whole situation, but right now my mind is elsewhere, scheming, calculating, and I have to use all my thespian skills to muster up the realistic weeping. It's a good job I've been practising. I'm not sure if Sameena is lying to me. I'm hoping she'll offer me a drink to replace all the tears I'm shedding, so I can search the room, or better still, go through her mobile, which is lying on the coffee table, but Sameena does nothing. I presume she must be watching, but my eyes are closed. Then she moves across and pats my shoulder.

"Come on, Sophie," she says. "Please don't cry."

"Water," I mutter.

"I'll get you some. Or would you like some tea? Might calm you down a bit."

"Yes." I sniff and give a tight little smile. "Tea would be nice."

She goes into the kitchen, and I can't believe my luck – she's left her mobile behind. I seize my chance and snatch it. Unbelievably, there's no screen lock. It's a different phone to mine and it takes me a few moments to work out how to get into the call list. I scroll down looking for Tariq's name but there's nothing. I go to her WhatsApp and look through the messages, keeping an eye out for any weird names that could be my husband, when I spot a Prof T. Is this her cheesy petname for Tariq? I open the conversation but only manage to read the last message before I hear Sameena coming back and quickly put the phone on the table.

Prof T: *See you at 4, usual place, xx*

Sameena pauses at the door with the tray and looks at me, but I give her a disarming smile and she sets the food on to the coffee table, picking up the mobile as she sits down. She's brought birthday cake to have with the tea.

"Looks delicious," I say.

"I hope so. I baked it myself," she says.

"I'm sorry," I say. "I'm trying to be strong, but sometimes it gets to me."

"It's understandable. I can't imagine what it must be like."

"I'm just… getting through the days, that's all."

"How's Zain coping? You should have brought him along too. He could have played with the children."

"Yes, I thought of that, but it's a long drive and he gets bored in the car. He's with my mum. She spoils him rotten, you know, typical granny," I say, and we both laugh. "Sameena, please, think back, can you remember anything Tariq said that might give us a clue?"

"I don't know, Sophie. Look, all I can say is don't give up hope. Trust in Allah. It's hard to believe but everything will be alright, Insha Allah."

"I'm trying, Sameena, it's all I have." I sigh and take a bite of the cake. It is delicious, moist and chocolatey and not too rich. I think of my next move as I take a sip of tea. "Most importantly, how's Ayaan been? How has he taken it?"

"It's tough for him, of course, but we try to keep him happy. He loves being with Adam and Laila, and he's doing well at school."

"Thank you, Sameena, for everything you do for him."

"There's nothing to thank me for. After Ruby…" She doesn't say any more. I can see her pain and change the subject after a suitable pause.

"Shall I go and see the birthday boy, then?" I ask.

"I'll give him a shout," says Sameena.

"No problem, I'll go up and see him."

She hesitates, but then nods and walks out of the room. I follow her up the spiral staircase located in the main living space.

"Ayaan, sweetheart, Aunty Sophie's here to see you," says Sameena.

* * *

Ayaan's grown in the few months since I last saw him. I hug him, and to my surprise, he lets me. I'm moved. He's a piece of my husband, my only live, breathing connection to him.

"Happy birthday, darling," I say, handing him the bag.

He rips the dinosaur wrapping paper off his presents excitedly. I bought them in a rush, but I remembered his obsession with T-Rex and managed to find a robotic version at half price, along with a colouring set.

I'm content to just sit on the floor and watch as Ayaan shows the gifts to his cousins. I ask him about his school and friends, and he seems happy, all things considered.

The room is bright and busy. There's a bed shaped like a racing car, school paintings pinned on the wall, a canvas wigwam in the corner, a small shelf heaving with books. There's a pile of new toys on the floor, some still wrapped in plastic. I stare at them. A Buzz Lightyear jigsaw puzzle, a Transformers car/robot, Lego Police Command Centre. Sameena stands by, tapping away on her mobile but I feel her observing me. After a few minutes she tells them to wash up and go down for lunch.

"Well, it's nice you're here; you can have lunch with us," she says. I recognise the sentiment behind this invitation. She feels obliged to give it as there's only so long she can delay lunch for the children but thinks it won't be accepted.

"That would be lovely," I say in my sweetest voice. She hides her shock well.

"Great," she says, moving towards the door.

"I'll just use the bathroom first, if that's okay?" I say.

She pauses for a suspicious second but then directs me towards the end of the hall to the family bathroom and stays there till I shut the door. Surely she's not going to stand guard till I go out again? I keep my eyes on the gap under the door, like they do in the movies, to judge whether there's an intruder on the other side. I feel like a woman in jeopardy, which, to a degree I am. The strip along the floor is dense, shadowy, but then, to my surprise, the method works. The darkness scatters and there is movement. She must have gone. I press my ear against the door but can't hear anything. I wait a couple of minutes, distracting myself by silently nosing about in the bathroom cabinet, which is full of luxurious creams and scrubs. Hmm, well, Sameena does have good skin. I make a mental note of the brands as I open one and rub it on my cheeks. It's rich and smooth and delicately perfumed. I might buy one myself if it will help my skin look dewy and lush on the big screen, when the time comes.

I hope I've given her enough time to get bored of waiting and go downstairs, but just in case she is lingering down the corridor I flush the toilet and wash my hands to keep up the pretence. I open the door quietly and listen. She's downstairs, talking to the children and rattling dishes.

I work methodically, starting at the end furthest from the staircase, opening each door to do a speedy assessment. Three of the rooms belong to the children, including the one we were just in, Ayaan's bedroom. There's nobody in them now, and I don't think there's any point in searching them. I doubt Tariq's hiding under one of the beds.

Next there's a perfectly styled guest room that looks like it's out of a show home, and finally there's Sameena's room, softer, more casual, but still well designed, with a neutral palette and lots of exposed brick.

If there's anything to find it will be in here. I go to the desk by the window, which takes up the whole wall, providing a spectacular, panoramic view of fields and woodland. The desk is covered in an unruly mixture of letters, notebooks, children's drawings and odd bits of jewellery. It will take me too long to sit here and read all these things. I pick up a diary and leaf through it. After school clubs, scribbled recipes, dentist's appointments. I consider stealing it so I can have a more thorough look, but I doubt it'll have anything interesting in it. Besides she'll miss it immediately if she relies on it so much. I put it down. What am I doing? What did I expect to find? Tariq to be tucked up in bed in the guest room? There's nobody up here.

The door opens and Sameena is glaring at me.

"What are you doing?" she says.

"I… splendid views, just beautiful," I say, springing to my feet. "The door was open, and I couldn't resist. I'm a country gal at heart. Sorry, I should have asked first."

"The door was closed." She holds it open now and gestures with her head for me to leave the room.

Downstairs, I make my excuses and tell her I won't stay for lunch.

It's already half past two by the time I leave. There's still time till Sameena's meeting with Prof T. Something is going on. Why was she so jumpy and nervous around me? I suppose it could be because of what Tariq has told her about me in the past, but she's a grown woman. What am I going to do to her?

But there's more. That pile of presents in Ayaan's bedroom. Lego Police Command Centre. I remember Tariq on his laptop a few months ago when I passed him his coffee, looking at the same toy online, comparing prices on different websites. He'd even laughed and told me not to tell Ayaan as it was going to be a surprise for Eid. In the end he'd bought him a new bike, but could he have bought it now, for Ayaan's birthday, instead? He must be the person Sameena is meeting this afternoon.

There's only one road leading out of Sameena's property, so I drive a bit further down, then park in a side road where I can see her if she goes past, and fifteen minutes later, she does. I follow, keeping my distance. These are narrow country lanes, fast and empty, where it's easy to spot other cars. On the other hand, it's not unusual for the same car to follow you for some time, as there are long stretches of road where there's nowhere else to go.

Eventually we reach a village shopping area, a few quaint, boutique shops, in an old cobbled high street. There's a bookseller, an antiques shop, an old-fashioned confectioner's with tins of fudge and pear drops in the window. Sameena parks the car and goes into a café, the three children in tow. I was right. It must be a birthday celebration. I get out of the car and go and stand by the window of the shop. How can I go in without being seen, and looking foolish and paranoid? I won't be able to spy on them clearly through the window.

I'll just go in and buy a coffee. It's not that strange, it's the first place I can stop to get one after leaving her house and can be explained if necessary. I hope it won't come to that. One look is all it will take. I murmur a prayer and enter the shop.

I walk up to the counter and look at the display of gateaux and pastries. There's a mirror on the wall behind the till. Perfect. I scan the café and see them, a vibrant, laughing family. There's a man with a beanie on, facing away from me, his hair dark like Tariq's, his build similar. I wait and stare, my heart thumping. He turns and calls the waitress and then looks towards me, at the mirror next to the menu. I look down.

It's not Tariq. It's just Sameena's husband, Tom. He's a graphic designer – not a professor or academic of any sort. It's obviously just a nauseating nickname.

I don't bother with the cappuccino.

I collect Zain from Mum's and then pick up some filet of fish meals from the McDonald's drive thru, even though Zain's already had his dinner. Mum packed some biryani for me too, but the mood I'm in is febrile and dangerous, and will only be doused with a pillowy bap and lots of chips.

We eat in the kitchen at the breakfast bar. Zain gives up halfway through the burger and goes upstairs to play with his toys for ten minutes before bed, and I'm finishing off his leftovers when my mobile rings. I roll my eyes. It's Faraz.

"I hope I'm not disturbing you," he says. "I just wanted to make sure you're okay. I heard what happened."

"I'm fine, thank you," I say. "It's nice of you to think of me."

"I think of you a lot. I mean, I've been worried about you since this happened."

"It's Tariq you should be worried about. Please pray that he comes home safely."

"Of course, such a good man, so polite. He will come back to you soon, Insha Allah."

"How do you know that?"

"I'm just saying a dua, wishing you well."

"But how do you know he's polite?"

"I heard it around, he's well known. Anyway, please let me know if you need anything. I'm always here for you." He puts the phone down.

I don't believe him. Faraz is my second ex-husband and, as far as I know, he's never met Tariq.

PART TWO
SOPHIE AND FARAZ

FARAZ
2014

When I told people I'd come to England to study, they often assumed I was one of those fake students who enrolled on learning ESOL courses at suspicious colleges and kept renewing their membership every six months for ten years. But I was the real deal. I was doing a business degree at university.

My father had a stable business manufacturing ceiling fans and a nice home in Lahore, a grand but small mansion, flower garden, one Jeep, one Toyota, one Yamaha, three servants, cook, driver. But I had a good brain and an ambition to make it even bigger. Most of all, I had a passion for England.

Nobody's really ever understood how strong my feelings are. Yes, like others, I came also for the excitement, for the thrills and the shine and the beautiful girls. But there's no other place like it. The history and glamour and art and splendour are cool in one way, cosy in another. My second favourite things were the famous landmarks, the Big Ben, the British Museum, the London Wheel. My top favourite thing – well it sounds a bit rude putting it like that – was, is, always will be, Her Royal Highness, Her Majesty the Queen. In Pakistan my family thought I was *paagal*, crazy, when I put her poster in my room. In England everyone also thought I was completely bananas. But for me she represents supreme grace, poise, a true lady, a lady with morals and manners from a chivalrous bygone day, a vanishing world.

England was all those things, and more, and it welcomed me, as it had many others, like a big, warm, cushiony mom. I hearted England. So I settled in Leeds, leaving my parents behind in Lahore, and began studying Business and Marketing at the university.

A few years ago, my *nikaah* had been performed with Muskaan, my second cousin, in a very simple ceremony. We were officially married in the Islamic way, but she stayed with her family. We were still young, in our late teens, and we didn't live together as husband and wife. The *ruksati*, the bride leaving for her husband's home, would follow later, with a bigger wedding reception. Some families adopt this custom as a sort of more definite engagement, a way of confirming the bond between a couple before they're ready to live together, for whatever reason. In our case, it had firstly been our young age. Now, I wanted to study abroad before I committed myself fully to marriage.

At the time of the *nikaah*, I'd had no definite plans for foreign study. I'd gone along with my parents' wishes. Muskaan was a nice girl, pretty and well educated. I'd had no real objection.

Now I was in the UK, we had regular Skype chats, when, mostly, Muskaan showed me all her latest shopping. The wedding was going to be in Pakistan, in about eighteen months' time, and she was already making preparations. She would also ask me about the procedures we had to go through to arrange her visa for England, and my head would begin to ache.

I really didn't want to think about it. I had slowly realised it wasn't going to be straightforward at all. Immigration laws were always getting tighter, with new rules and requirements being set up to trip you up and catch you out. That wasn't going to happen to me. I had gone through too many years tapping on calculators like a madman and sitting through weary lectures to lose everything so easily. No. There was too much I still wanted to achieve. The businesses I was going to set up. The marketing agency. The fast food chain. The car washing empire.

There were only a few ways in which I could guarantee a longer stay in the UK. Firstly, I could claim political asylum. It would be an outright lie, and that was out of the question for me.

Secondly, I could start up a new business, but I had to prove I had £50,000 for investment. This, also, was impossible. Although my father was a successful man, there certainly wasn't that kind of money lying around. I knew if I asked him, he would borrow it, but I didn't want him to go through the humiliation of begging or have the worry of paying it back hanging over him.

The last method of staying in the UK was to marry a British woman. There were drawbacks, but it was definitely the more appealing option. The biggest hurdle in this case was, of course, Muskaan, who was at that time intoxicated with wedding spirit and hitting the bazaars at full throttle.

It was partly why my friends advised me to do a marriage of convenience, a paper marriage. There were plenty of women who would do it for the money, eight or nine thousand, to include mutually agreed backstory and staged photos. And when my passport was safely stamped with my indefinite leave to remain, we would get a quiet divorce. Muskaan would understand it was all an act, there was no love or even any physical contact except what we would do for the pictures. Muskaan and I could have our proper wedding later and she could join me over here.

But I couldn't do it. The idea turned my stomach. I hated any type of lying or dishonesty, and the thought of treating the sacred ritual of marriage in such a sly and underhand way was unbearable. I didn't want to hurt Muskaan, but if she respected me, she would understand that I couldn't build our relationship on lies and deceit. It went against my principles to buy an illegal wife. If I had to marry again to stay in England,

I would do it properly. If Muskaan was happy with me taking a second wife, it would be perfect, otherwise we would have to go our separate ways. I couldn't return to Pakistan just to be with her. I would resent giving up my dreams forever. As the day of my visa expiry crept nearer, I knew I had to find my bride quickly.

My father understood. He'd struggled himself in the early days and knew you had to make sacrifices for success sometimes.

"Do what you have to, son," he said, when I spoke to him on Skype and told him I intended to get married in England, to a British born lady, unknown at present. "Just don't bring shame on us."

Mother was a different story. She shouted and wept and threw a date stone at the webcam. What other more shameful thing could I do? This was the worst. Breaking a vow, a marriage, and the porcelain heart of a pure and chaste young woman. Muskaan would be inconsolable. The name Muskaan meant smile. Her smiles would be strictly limited after my infamy.

"There's no need to tell her," I said. "Keep it quiet until I know for sure what's happening. You don't want to upset her for no reason if nothing happens."

Mother grudgingly agreed to this, in fact made me promise to keep my lips sealed. There was no need for anyone to know about the heinous act I was about to commit. They would all find out in good time. You never knew – it might not work out the way I wanted it, she added slyly.

So, I tentatively started to put out the feelers. I didn't know many people apart from other students and my flatmates. To find a partner through the old-fashioned route, one really needed a reliable aunty network. The aunties wanted nothing better than to set up a union of two lonely hearts. There were rumours of them placing bets on who could arrange the longest lasting marriage.

However, my friends advised me not to waste time with this

traditional word of mouth method, warning me I'd be out of the door once the girl's parents realised what my immigration status was. They knew because of their own experiences. One of them had turned up to the introduction meeting to find a police car waiting for him and had driven off past the house into the night. I thought it was hopelessly tragic but romantic at the same time. Another had managed to get into the house of his potential but failed when the girl had asked him to sing her favourite hymn to prove his Englishness.

The safest option, they said, was the paper marriage.

But I pressed on with my quest. I managed, with the help of some crocodile tears, to convince a friend's mother that I was a decent but desperate man, and she set up a meeting for me with her sister's niece-in-law. It was a disaster. The girl had a list of demands to be met after marriage – a visit to an "international" restaurant at least once a week, no beards, honeymoon in Malaysia. Plus, I had to do the housework. I left feeling like I'd escaped from a prison sentence.

It's truly a technological age, our lives ruled by the internet, and it was to this master of our destinies I turned to in my hour of need. I opened an account with MuslimMrandMrs. com, took a flattering selfie and uploaded my profile. I ignored the terms and conditions clause that said you needed to have permanent UK residency to register. They had no means of checking yet. I could do the explaining later, when I found the perfect, understanding lady. I wasn't looking for the beautiful dream girl of my silly teenage years. This wasn't just a marriage of convenience – I intended to see it through properly, and I wanted an honest, trustworthy woman, a reliable presence to stand by me through a lifetime.

Once I'd registered on the website it was like the floodgates opening. The surprising thing was that even I received lots of messages. It wasn't just me enquiring after them. I politely turned down four and decided to reply to the three that sounded most appealing.

Aminah - pearlofyorkshire

Age-27. Never been married, lives in Leeds
Occupation: financial consultant.
Looking for husband aged 25-35 years.
Minimum education: A Levels.
Minimum height: 5ft 10.
Must be fun-loving, honest, enjoy outdoor activities such as cycling, walking, tennis, rowing. No time wasters please.

Mariya - mariya21

Age 33. Based in Ealing, London.
Occupation: cardiologist.
Enjoys reading, film, travel, stand-up comedy (as audience member not entertainer!! LOL)
Looking for someone professional, not necessarily in medicine, with GSOH and similar interests. Age 35-50.

Sophie - easternrose

Age 27. Divorced. Single mother.
I was previously a hair and beauty consultant but I'm now spending time looking after my son.
Aspiring actress.
Varied interests, film, books, dining out.
Looking for life partner not just a husband, someone to share my highs and lows, the special moments and the sad ones, someone to love, cherish and trust with my heart.

SOPHIE
2014

I sneaked into the room I was sharing with Zain and switched on the laptop. A secret hum began to buzz inside me as I saw that I had three new messages, a whirring of hope that something would happen to put an end to the bleakness of my life.

I'd moved back in with my parents and brother after the divorce. I'd applied for a council house, but the waiting list was endless. *The divorce.* It didn't bear thinking about. Both mine and Zain's lives shattered by Amir's callousness. I'd pleaded with him to take the words back, pretend the whole thing had never happened. But he was adamant. If nothing else he wasn't a liar, he said, and how could he lie before God?

I wasn't completely penniless. Amir set up a generous fund for Zain, and even a reasonable allowance for me, just until I sorted myself out. He put the house up for sale and promised to give me my share. Now the rage of the moment was over, I supposed this was what they called amicable.

The first two or three months passed by in a depressing but peaceful way. As a newly divorced woman, I was required, Islamically, to spend the first three months at home. While Zain whiled away his time being pampered by his grandparents, I lay in my room mulling and weeping over my fate, my great love vanished in a boom of tempers. For so many years all I'd wanted was to be loved by Amir, and when it had happened, I'd felt delirious, invincible. There were so many perfect moments. That first breathless hug in college, our wedding, lavish in itself but flawless because of him, the birth of our son, and just his smiles, his touch, his face. Without Amir I was a plundered, wretched woman with nothing of value left in my life.

But no, that wasn't true. Although I craved love, I wouldn't allow myself to be defined by a man. I had Zain, who was the by far the most precious gift I'd ever been given. I still had my dreams. And Amir's absence meant I now had freedom to pursue them. Gradually the melancholy began to clear, my mind uncloud, the path ahead illuminate. I would become an actress, and I would find a true, lasting love, even if it meant Amir had to be replaced.

From the way Mum talked, it seemed that the thought of finding me a husband hadn't crossed her mind. She was only concerned about me looking after Zain as best as I could, giving him all my time and love. As if I could do anything less.

It was simple to put my plan into operation without anyone finding out. I had my own laptop so there wasn't any chance of anyone searching through the history. I registered on MuslimMrandMrs.com and uploaded my details.

The first messages arrived within a few hours. Enquiries from accountants, businessmen, small time singers, students, a teacher. I first made a long list, going purely on their looks. Then I read their profiles and narrowed it down to three.

Yunus - princeofpakistan

Age 37. Live in Hull.

Qualified accountant.

Enjoy dining out, especially Chinese and Thai food, and light sports, nothing too extreme.

Would like a queen to share my kingdom with. Genuine ladies with a royal commitment only please.

Raza - spicyguru

Age 29. I am London based.

Chartered accountant.

5ft 10, muscular physique (achieved through many dedicated hours in the gym).

Looking for a beautiful lady with nice eyes and fair complexion to be my running mate. Pakistani/Kashmiri preferred but not essential.

Faraz - faraz123

Age 28. Live in Leeds.

5ft 9.

Enjoy all sports, especially cricket and carom board.

I am looking for a sensitive lady for a real relationship who will have good understanding with me. Looks not important but a caring person is important for me.

Spicyguru was the best looking but the more I glanced at his unpleasant username and pompous profile, the more I was put off by it. After a couple of minutes of thinking it over, I deleted his message, too. This left Faraz123 and princeofPakistan . I read back over what they had sent me.

Dear easternrose,

Hope you're good. Liked your profile on here and think we might be a good match for each other. Have been on here a while now and have had fair share of teasers and time wasters, so hoping you're neither! How do you want to do this? Emailing, chat or just cut to the chase and meet up? We can do it just the two of us, meet for chai shai, or go really old school and go to your house or you come to mine, with the families, whichever suits you, I'm cool with all of the above.

So yeah, anyway, we both know what we're in to basically, do you want to expand on that? I really like your pic, I hope you don't mind me saying so. Not trying to be a creep! So you like dining out? Any favourite restaurants?

Also just wondering what the situation was with your son that you've mentioned? Fine with it really, but just wanted to be clear on circumstances.

I hope to hear from you soon,
Regards,
Yunus

Dear easternrose,

Salaam and kindest regards. Thanking you in advance for reading my message and taking time for this. I very much like your details on this site, and hoping we can develop something good, InshaAllah.

To give some more details about my own self, I am studying a Media and Marketing degree at Leeds University, and I hope to go on to good and successful business so I can support my family to be.

My requirements are simple for my life partner. Honest, trustworthy, loyal. I don't care about fashions and lipsticks or highly qualified and money. If we can hit it off that will be great.

So I hope you can reply and I really look forward to that day.

Best regards,
Faraz

I decided to send the same message to both of them, in order to give them an even playing field.

Salaam, and thank you for your message. I would like to continue at the moment just communicating by email, if that's okay with you. I feel it may be a little too early to meet up yet.

I think it's best also to clarify the situation with my son. He is three years old and lives with me. I have no plans to change this should I decide to remarry in the future. I hope you understand this.

What else would you like to know about me? You know about my interests, though I don't really have time for them at the moment. What else do I like? Blue skies, yellow flowers, the summer, pineapples, coconuts, aloo chane, Rahat Fateh Ali Khan, the Bourne films but also old Hollywood. I like visiting Pakistan though I haven't been for many years. What about you?

I have to admit that I am sad sometimes at what life has thrown at me but I want to change things for the better. I think this healing process will start with a strong and loving partner.

I hope this gives you an idea of what I'm looking for and if things are meant to be we will meet soon.

Best wishes,
Sophie

I sent the message and turned off the computer. I was about to go out when Rizwana called me. She was probably ringing to update me with some family gossip, since we had several mutual relatives.

"Really sorry to hear what's happened," she said.

"What news? Has somebody died?" I asked, worried.

"You mean you don't know?" she said, then her tone changed. "Oh, I shouldn't have said anything. It's nothing." She often did this, dropped a hint of something, then pretended she hadn't meant to.

"Just tell me, Rizwana," I said.

"It's about Amir."

I gasped. "What about him? Tell me!"

"He's given his aunts permission to find him a new wife."

I felt like someone had punched the air out of me, then a rage erupted instantly inside me. It only made me more desperate to do what I'd been doing since moving to Mum's, after my weekly supermarket trip. I'd convinced Mum this counted as a "necessary" outing, so I was allowed out under my divorcee's curfew.

The For Sale sign made my stomach turn a little. It was inconceivable that only four months ago we were a happy little family, edging our way towards the dreams we had made for ourselves. I wasn't ready to let the memory go. I couldn't explain it, even to myself. I'd made a very conscious decision to move forward, and I wanted to see this as a bright and joyous surge ahead. But Amir had been the heart of me for so long, years before he even knew, and I couldn't just erase him from my life.

It was just getting dark, and I parked across the road under a tree, from where I had a clear view into the living room, especially good as Amir was a lazy sod who never bothered to draw the curtains. From there I could see him, just sitting watching television, usually with a doner kebab or chicken burger. Sometimes, if I was lucky, he'd break the routine and get the weights out and do a bit of exercise, but whatever, I didn't care, I was content just to watch him doing nothing and let the sight seep into me.

FARAZ
2014

The first date was in Café Sprinkle, a *desi* style coffee shop near Bradford University. It was a fashionable place, covered in pictures of Pakistani lorries and buses. I supposed they were meant to make one feel nostalgic and homesick. They did conjure up memories of home, but ones I would rather forget, of rattling along at an insanely breakneck speed, in those smelly, squashy vehicles, of the noisy, tuneful horns and grimy black dust. No thank you. Please give me a civilised double decker any day.

I arrived early. I'd made the effort to get a haircut in the morning and really felt smart after my coiffing.

She was a bit rounder than I'd expected, softer looking, more weary, but still pretty. More loveable and cuddly, I thought. It had crossed my mind that she might bring her little boy along, but she came alone. I didn't mind the idea of being a stepfather. He was only a small boy, not old enough to rebel against me. It gave me a warm feeling, actually. It was nice that I'd be helping her, giving her support at a lonely and vulnerable time. After all that's what the Muslims of old did, help widowed and divorced ladies by marrying them. I hope this angle would have a positive effect on my mother too.

Sophie ordered a latte and a piece of chocolate fudge cake. I took this as a good sign. She must feel at least halfway comfortable with me. I knew ladies generally didn't partake of fatty treats in public.

"So… have you been doing this long?" she asked.

"Not at all," I said. "This is my first. You are my first." She smiled. It was adorable.

"I suppose we should be clear on what we're looking for. Marriage, friendship, flirtation?"

"Please, Sophie *jee*. Only marriage for me. Nothing else. No flings."

"I should start with the most important thing. You know about my son?"

"Yes, of course. I know it won't be easy to adjust, especially for him. But I would make all efforts from my side."

A breath escaped her then.

"That's very good of you. Thank you," she said. "You don't have any children yourself, do you? Or been married before?"

I denied it. It didn't really count, I thought, the business with Muskaan. It would make a very bad impression at this stage. Let her get to know me better and then she could judge.

She offered to tell me anything I wanted to know about her first marriage, but I had nothing to ask, so she gave me a potted history herself. She told me about the beatings and the other women. The details made me shudder. When I couldn't bear to hear any more about that monstrous ex-husband, I told her to please try and forget it, and we talked about other things. My business plans, our families (mine edited, admittedly), the best shopping areas in Leeds, my immigration status, and holiday ambitions, which – uncannily – matched (Egypt). Then came the million-dollar question.

"What are your views on the Royals?" I asked, trying to hide my tension. What if she was an anti-monarchist?

"Waste of space," she said, rolling her eyes. I winced. "They use taxpayer's money to go on holidays and attend parties. I mean what else do they actually *do*?"

Oh dear. And things had been going so well. I cleared my throat.

"That's a bit unkind, if I may say so," I said. "They do an enormous amount of charity work, to begin with."

Sophie looked at me blankly. "Oh, you actually like them?" she said.

"I have too much respect for them, yes." I sighed, not sure if this difference of opinion was too much to ignore. "If you really hate them, it might be a deal-breaker for me."

Her mouth dropped open, but then she gathered herself.

"I don't hate them," she said. "If I'm honest, I quite like Kate and I was a huge fan of Princess Diana. I only said those things without thinking. The thing is, I had a traumatic experience many years ago."

"Really? Would you like to share it with me?"

"I used to have a cat, but sadly it... well it got run over. It was on the day of Prince Edward's wedding. Since then, any mention of the Windsors reminds me of that tragic accident."

I breathed a sigh of relief. Her heart-rending story explained her comments.

"Thank you for understanding," she said. "It's silly, really. Maybe you can help me overcome it."

I would try my best. Sophie was attractive, affable, easy to talk to, and had a magnetic laugh that made you laugh with her. By the end of the evening there was a flush in my heart, a hope that this might work out, and I couldn't wait to see her again.

SOPHIE
2015

"I'm not going to support you on this," said my mother. "I'm sorry, but I have to do what's best for Zain."

Two months after that first meeting in the café, Faraz had taken me to the Tropical Gardens in Leeds, where he'd hidden an emerald and ruby ring in the petals of a giant lotus and asked me to marry him. I was shocked, humbled and yes, delighted at the speed of it all. He was thoughtful, chatty and attentive. "Decent". That's how the oldies would describe him. Very decent boy. He had hopes for greater things and would soon begin to create a small world for himself.

I didn't enquire into the exact figures of his bank balance, but he told me his parents in Pakistan were well off and were paying for his postgraduate degree at Leeds. I assumed they must be wealthy. University fees weren't cheap, especially for foreign students. His financial background seemed sound enough for him to start building his business within the next two years and give me a chance to work on my showreel too. I'd told him about my goals, and he was encouraging, excited even. It was a welcome change to have some support.

I couldn't pretend there was a flare of immediate passion, but he certainly wasn't disagreeable. He had a nice face and an aura of benevolence about him. Maybe he was slightly on the stubby side, but nothing a few hours a week in the gym wouldn't fix. On the whole, Faraz was better than anything I could have hoped for so soon after the break-up with Amir, and love might slowly flower between us. At the very least Amir would be forced to pay attention. He would see I wasn't his pathetic cast off. That I was something worth missing.

"I always think of Zain first," I said to Mum. "That's why I'm doing this. Don't you think he needs a father figure? A role model?"

"He's got Amir for that. Amir's a good father. There's no need for him to be excluded from Zain's life. You should arrange for them to see each other more often instead of just at the weekends."

I bristled. I could neither understand nor bear it when she sang Amir's praises, when she knew what he'd done to me.

"For God's sake, Mum! When are you going to see that Amir's not the angel you think he is?"

"I know what Amir is, Sophie, and I know you," said Mum.

"What's that supposed to mean?"

"Don't speak to me like that, Sophie."

I drew a deep breath. I couldn't lose my temper if I wanted to get through this.

"The point is, Saint Amir's not a permanent fixture in Zain's life, is he?" I said.

"What's going on?" asked Dad, walking into the room. "More problems with Amir?"

"Do you know what she wants to do, Isaac?" said my mother. "She wants to get married to a boy here on a student visa. Someone she's picked up off the internet!" My father's eyes popped out for a moment as he registered this.

I'd anticipated Mum's reaction to the news, but I was hoping Dad would be more supportive.

"Out of the question," he said.

"Why?" I said.

"You're not marrying him. Full stop."

"Why not? What's wrong with him? You haven't even met him yet. He's a very well- mannered and honest man."

"I'm sure he is but he's not for us."

"Why, because he's from Pakistan? Or because I found him on a marriage website?"

"Well, now you mention it, yes, all of the above. But they aren't my main reasons."

"You know it's a kind of racism, don't you? And it's rich coming from you! You came over from Pakistan yourself!"

"That's enough! That was different. We were honest young men, trying our best for our families. But we never lied or swindled anyone. The young Pakistanis coming over these days are nothing but con artists. They put on smooth masks, tell sob stories and girls swoon over them. They get their visas and off they go, leaving the poor girls in a mess. It's happened so many times in our own family. Even you know that." It was true. It was a problem that had been especially common in the 1990s, when at least two of my cousins had been tricked into marriage just for immigration purposes. Both men had wives and children back in Pakistan.

"He's not like that," I said.

"I don't care. And anyway, that's not my main reason for saying no. It's far too soon for you to be marrying again. You need to let things settle down."

I didn't reply. Instead, I refused to eat for the next four meals, and it worked like magic. My mother didn't relent, but my father was soon outside my bedroom door with a McDonald's fish meal, offering to walk me down the aisle.

So, three weeks later, without Mum's blessing, we were married. We had a civil ceremony at a registry office on a Friday morning, followed by the *nikaah* at the mosque in the afternoon, and a quiet dinner later at a restaurant. I wore a coppery dress this time, a striking design even though it was just something off the peg from an Asian bridal boutique. The bride should stand out from the other guests, even when it's a modest event. The only guests were my parents and brother with his wife, and a few of Faraz's friends, who happily took a flurry of photographs that we could use for his visa application. We did our best to look natural and deeply in love, so the Home Office wouldn't wrongly accuse us of having undergone a scam marriage for money and immigration purposes.

I'd asked the restaurant to hang a banner and copper and pink balloons, and we had a simple cake adorned with fresh flowers. Well, until Faraz stuck a chubby Pakistani couple made out of fondant on the top when I wasn't looking. It ruined the whole look, but he said he made it himself after watching an Instagram tutorial, so I let the sugary newlyweds be. I didn't want to begin our life together by hurting his feelings.

After the restaurant we went to Mum's house. Faraz had been sharing a flat with friends, so Mum had grudgingly agreed to let us stay with her for a few days until we sorted out our own place. We were going to leave for a long honeymoon weekend in the Lake District, and stopped off at Mum's to collect our luggage, and to do a last-minute check on Zain.

Faraz insisted we take a few more pictures at home and asked my brother to take a couple of "candid shots" – both of us laughing on the sofa with cups of tea, and me crouching down as Zain whispered something in my ear. The latter was an absolutely natural moment, unplanned, but I heard Faraz muttering approvingly.

"Just like Lady Diana on her wedding day," he said, referring to the famous photograph. "Comforting the bridesmaids." It was an added bonus, adding credibility to my newly invented role as a Diana fan. Although the cat story had been a fib, the Diana part wasn't completely untrue. I had always admired her style.

We moved on to more styled poses, and were standing by the living room window, gazing at each other, my arms looped around Faraz's neck, his around my waist, when Amir walked in.

I wasn't surprised. He'd stayed away from the wedding, but I'd known he was coming to collect Zain. Still, seeing him in front of me while I was entwined with another man felt unnatural, criminal. I froze for a moment as we stared at each other, until Faraz patted me on the hip, and whispered, "Say cheese, darling."

I remembered then that the alluring man in the doorway had tossed me out like a screwed-up scrap into a trash can. Faraz, though, had restored me, raised me up, given me a sense of value. I turned away from Amir and smiled seductively at Faraz, drawing him in closer so our foreheads were touching. Faraz's grip tightened around my waist.

"Oh!" he said, with a half gasp half laugh.

"Congratulations, Sophie," said Amir, when the photo had been taken. "Faraz. May Allah bless you with a very happy life together."

"And your good name is?" said Faraz, extending his hand.

"This is Amir," I said.

Faraz hesitated but finished off the handshake and nodded.

"Is Zain ready?" asked Amir.

"He just went up to choose which teddy he's taking," I said. "I'll get him. I'll be back in a minute, darling." I stroked Faraz's face tenderly and gave him another slow, private smile. It was an excessive, flagrant display of affection, with a double edge, intended for more than just Faraz's benefit.

I shut out the encounter with Amir, not wanting it to smudge my weekend with its tangle of confusing emotions.

The drive up to the Lake District was surreal. The newness of "us" was still too much to take in, and the car seemed to be humming with the electricity of our nerves. We talked like usual, and occasionally our fingers brushed against each other, but I think Faraz refrained from anything else because he wanted the honeymoon night to be faultless. And it was. Faraz carried me over the threshold of the heady, lily-scented hotel bedroom, whispering I was his princess, his queen, his majesty. A bit silly, I thought, but sweet too, in a way, and he was sweet, respectful and gentle. It was heavenly, lying in his arms after all those desolate months, creaking with loneliness and anger.

When I awoke in the morning, it felt like a slightly suspenseful scene from a movie. *New bride wakes up to find bed empty and hears the sound of a shower running in the background.* A lovely man, a serene setting, but a hint of (invented) mystery in the background, it was all just gorgeous. Did my dramatic soul need that sliver of peril to ruin it, or, even, perfect it? Of course it didn't, but I just enjoyed imagining it.

Then, from Faraz's side of the bed, his phone buzzed.

FARAZ
2015

How could I have been such a jerk? I told myself I'll tell her early on, but things had moved much faster than I expected. I wanted to tell her at the third meeting, a trip to the cinema, but the mood had been so light and ravishing, and Sophie had so much enthusiasm for the film that I didn't want to spoil the atmosphere. The next time we met I proposed, and that was a precision rehearsed event, with no room for errors. After that there were a few snatched little meetings of the organisational kind, and before I knew it, we were married.

I came out of the pine-scented shower with pristine dreams for the future in my heart and a respectable towel wrapped around my waist. I thought it was too early in our relationship to surprise her with anything other than that, especially in the dazzling morning sunlight.

Sophie was on the phone, still lying in bed wearing a delicious black nightie. I could hear an animated voice on the other side. Probably her mother, I thought, checking to see that everything had gone smoothly. It had gone smoothly, alright, and I smiled as I fiddled with the tea tray, trying to waste time in case Sophie decided to extend our lazy lie-in. But she didn't look up and after a few minutes of reading the green tea bag sachets, I began to take out my honeymoon weekend clothes, disappointed I was going straight into my jeans and t-shirt. I was zipping up the suitcase when she threw the phone across the bed and I saw, to my horror, that it was my mobile and not hers.

"Oh," I said. "You were talking on my phone? Who was it?"

She stared at me, and I could feel the heat trembling inside her, ready to burst from her body. I already knew what she was going to say.

"Your wife," she hissed. I opened my mouth but could only splutter useless noises. "Cheating bastard! Don't even try and defend yourself! Get out! Get out of my room!"

She leapt off the bed and pushed me out of the room, into the hallway and into a lady in a striped sailor dress and a straw hat, wishing with every bone in my body that I'd put my clothes on when I had the chance.

Two hours later, I was still sitting outside the room slumped against the wall. Hotel staff had walked past several times and asked me if I was okay. Thank God, they left me there. It was a quiet weekend and most of the rooms were empty, and they didn't press for details. I had advertised loudly enough that we were a honeymoon couple.

I tapped on the door for the twenty-third time.

"Please, Sophie," I said. "Just one chance. Let me tell you about it." The door opened a fraction and my body stiffened, ready for a pair of shoes to come soaring towards my head.

"Get inside," she said. I stumbled quickly into the room on my knees. She looked at me expectantly.

"Muskaan and I were married seven years ago, in Pakistan," I blabbered. "We had *nikaah* only. Just the ceremony, and then she went back to her house. We haven't lived together, or anything. We never had... private times together. She is my cousin and our elders arranged it. You know how they do things over there, decide our futures when we're still young. I didn't mind at the time, she's a nice girl. But then I realised

I wanted to make a success in the UK. I thought when I've finished my studies, I will call her over here, but I found out it's not easy. I told you my problem. The only way I can stay once my student visa finishes is if I'm married to a British lady or I invest money in a business. Lucky for me you helped."

I wanted to call her darling, but I stopped myself. I didn't want a slap.

"Believe me, Sophie, I wanted to divorce her before me and you got married, but my mother didn't allow it," I said. "She's right in a way. I don't want to hurt anyone. I'm confused."

"Why didn't you tell me?" said Sophie.

"I really liked you. I wanted you to like me too. If I had told you, you might run away miles. I just really really liked you. I'm really really really sorry."

"I should have known it was too good to be true."

"No! It's not, Sophie, it's still good, I promise. Everything will be okay. Yes, our marriage helped me stay in England, but I chose you because I love you. Genuinely, truly." I moved across the carpet gingerly towards where she was sitting on the bed and touched her hand. She shook her head but didn't move away.

"What did you say to her?" I asked. "You were talking for a long time."

"I told her I was a maid," she said. "I gave her the impression that you can afford servants. Just so she doesn't get suspicious. She told me all about herself. She likes talking." Then she laughed, a throaty, gurgling laugh, and my relief was like I'd been pulled back from the edge of a precipice.

We rented a small maisonette on Leeds Road, cosy and perfect for our mini family. Sophie wasn't too happy at first. She wanted to go for something twice the size and tempted me with the hope of a growing family. It did make me fluttery, but I was firm and did what was affordable. She sulked for a few days but soon softened when I announced that we were going on a second honeymoon, on a weekend trip to London.

They were nice, those first few weeks. I really felt well... grown up, complete, part of a smart little unit – me, my wife and our son. I really was thinking he was like my own boy, even though, of course, he wasn't and he met his own disgraceful papa regularly. I just wanted to do what I could to give him a happy life.

I loved us fitting together, not just on the sofa in the evenings. I mean like eating together, brushing teeth, going supermarket shopping. What a thrill it was when we simultaneously went to grab a bag of carrots, bodies colliding. It was boring domesticity for most people, but for me it was the most exciting thing ever. In those days, Sophie was everything I'd hoped for, affectionate and funny. I just wanted to be a kind and perfect husband.

Even Sophie's mum seemed to have changed her mind about me. Sophie had told me that her Mum wasn't very happy about our marriage, but now she was very chatty and friendly, calling me *beta* all the time.

I wanted to end the problem with Muskaan. She was a phantom from my past, a murky threat flitting about in the corners of my sunlit life. But still, I had to be sensitive about the whole thing, and tell her face to face. When we got back from London, I promised myself. Otherwise, if something went wrong it would spoil our weekend.

I could hardly contain myself. It was the ultimate lifetime experience. Being with Sophie, my own private queen, was one thing, but when I thought of how we would also be surrounded by unlimited, magnificent history I was afraid I might pass out. I was jittery with joy just walking down Oxford Street, not least because the face of my beloved Elizabeth Regina beamed out at me from every souvenir stand.

I opted for a budget hotel over luxury, so we could use the saved money to visit maximum attractions. We set out early after leaving our luggage in the room on Friday morning. First stop was the Tower of London, where Sophie was fascinated by the Crown Jewels, her eyes lighting up like the Kohinoor diamond itself. It was lovely to see her animated and having fun, but the enjoyment was slightly soured when she pointed at the Beefeaters and called them dunces. Scandalous.

Next stop was the Natural History Museum. The highlight here was Sophie shrieking and clinging to me when the T-Rex robot roared. Even I knew she was exaggerating her fright, but if it brought her into my arms I wasn't complaining.

"I'm sure you will love this part," I said, leading her into the mammal's section. "Since you're fond of animals."

"Not really," said Sophie. "Who told you that?"

"I thought so because of your cat."

She frowned for a second before speaking.

"Yes, of course, I do love animals," she said. "I just don't get much time for them anymore. So sweet of you to think of it."

I was worried she might get distressed considering all the exhibits were dead creatures, but I assured her they must have led happy lives, and she was quite relaxed as we wandered around the galleries, with their magnificent, soaring arches and intricate stonework, looking at stuffed polar bears, lions and thousands of other specimens.

We finished our tour in Madame Tussauds, and what a good choice it was. Sophie was almost jumping, brimming with excitement as she mingled with waxworks and asked me to take numerous photos of her. I prayed that one day she too would achieve celebrity status in her own right.

Sightseeing done for the day, I was limbering up to rounding off the evening nicely in our hotel room and ordered some nibbles and cold Pepsis.

Of course, the damn phone ruined things again. Sophie seemed to have accepted that I was dealing with it, so I answered it. It wasn't a call though, but a request for a video chat.

"Go on," said Sophie. "Talk to her."

She looked so chubby and delectable, lying there in a hot pink babydoll nightie. I thanked God that I had such an understanding wife.

"Where are you?" said Muskaan peering at the webcam. I could tell see she was trying to work out my surroundings.

"Don't worry about that," I said. "Why have you called, Muskaan? I'm out on a study trip in London, market research." There was no lie. It was educational.

"I want to know what you've decided," said Muskaan. "You're not saying anything about the wedding. When are we going to do it? I keep calling you, but you don't answer."

"Yes, well, I can't say anything about that yet."

Sophie snatched the phone from me.

"Give it back," I said. "What are you doing?"

"Hello, Muskaan," said Sophie.

"Who the hell is she? What's she doing there with you?" said Muskaan. "Are you on a bed?"

"We spoke last week. Remember the maid?"

"Faraz! What's going on here?" screamed Muskaan at the camera.

"Stop it, Sophie! Cover yourself up!" I said, passing her a shawl.

"Well, here's the news. I'm not the maid, I'm his wife," said Sophie. More shrieks from the other side of the screen and suddenly Muskaan was surrounded by her family, including her parents. I wrestled with Sophie to get the phone back and turned it off, blitzing away the image of Muskaan fainting into her father's arms.

I had stupidly left Buckingham Palace till last, the climax of our trip, but now my precious enjoyment of it was spoiled by both Sophie's antics and her rotten mood.

I just wanted to close my eyes and mentally imprint the glory of those regal state rooms, but I could hardly concentrate with

Sophie tutting her way through the guided tour, complaining about the speed of the other group members.

"You enjoy this fancy dress parade," said Sophie, while we were watching the Changing of the Guard. "I'm going for walk." I didn't argue. I was relieved to be left in peace with my camcorder.

"Where shall I meet you?" I called out after her, but she didn't hear me.

Before I realised, half an hour had gone by. I called Sophie's mobile, but she didn't answer. I sent her a text. Then I stood by the statue of Queen Victoria, my back towards her, and rotated 360 degrees, searching for my wife's face amongst the vast crowds of tourists, thousands of faces of every colour and age. No luck.

I checked my location on my London guide app and crossed the road to St James's Park. I had to do something. Perhaps she had come here to enjoy the nature. After a couple of minutes' walk, I breathed freely again. There she was, sitting on a bench next to a big man wearing a light blue suit and a Panama hat. I thought nothing of him, he was just a stranger. I was too far still to call out, and was about to wave instead, when I saw her talk to the man. Then, to my surprise, she took something out of her bag and gave it to him. They spoke for another minute or so, then the man left. Sophie took out her phone and began tapping on it. My phone buzzed. She'd replied to the text I sent her earlier, asking her where she was.

SOPHIE: I'm just having a coffee. I'll meet you back at the Palace in five minutes.

What a liar! I didn't know what to do. Exposing her fib would result in an argument, but at the same time I wanted to know who the man was. I carried on walking in her direction, and she stood up and came towards me, though she still hadn't noticed I was there.

"I told you to wait at the Palace," she said, when she was closer and finally spotted me.

"I was already looking for you in the park when I got your text," I said. "I thought you were having coffee."

"I was, then I came here to get some fresh air."

"Who was that man in the hat?"

"What man?" Her eyes looked definitely sneaky then, sliding from side to side.

"Next to you, on the bench," I said. "I saw you give him something."

"I don't know, he was just some man out for a walk. He asked me if I had a tissue, so I gave him a packet. You know I always keep a stock of them in my bag."

That was true. She did always have tissues in her handbag, both wet and dry.

"Come on, let's go back to the hotel and have an early night," she said, grabbing my hand and rubbing it between her palms. It was a sweet gesture that made my heart melt.

I didn't mention the man again or her earlier moody behaviour, and we did have a pleasantly romantic evening. I didn't realise she was waiting to get back home before making her next move.

I try to be a modern man. Well, what people think of as a modern man. Really my morals are ancient. When our Prophet, peace be upon him, could mend his own clothes and knead dough, who are we to order our wives around like slaves? My mother would think I was a weakling, or as they say in Urdu, I was the one wearing the bangles, but I wasn't going to change my philosophy because of what other people thought of me. Anyway, my point is that I normally made my own breakfast, so having it prepared for me was a luxury. That Monday morning, I had a lecture in the afternoon, so we had a lazy morning. Sophie made me crispy parathas and a chilli and coriander omelette. I munched appreciatively through the meal and when I was leaning back with my tea, she said, casually, "Divorce her."

"What?" I said. "Don't say things like that."

"Why not? You said you intend to do it, so what's the problem?"

"I'm just waiting for the right moment."

"What? I'm not telling you to get married. It's a divorce. Nobody's ever ready for that."

"Well, it's just not nice for her. I feel bad."

"You should have thought about that before."

"Everyone will be mad at me."

"You have to make a choice, Faraz," she said. "Who's more important? Because I'm not putting up with it any longer. We all need to start afresh. It's better for Muskaan too. If you choose not to divorce her, that's understandable, but don't expect me to stay. It's simple."

She said nothing more, but the threat was in the arch of her eyebrow. I'd fallen in love with her, I didn't want her to leave me. Besides that, I knew she could destroy me completely. If she left, there would be no more English future, no business, no empire. A few months down the line I would be back in Pakistan, working for my father, my dreams clapped shut, bitter and gnarled for the rest of my life. This future I couldn't face.

I would be the most hated man in the family for a long time, but it would have to be done.

SOPHIE
2015

Amir's flirtations had been intolerable to me, but they seemed almost insignificant now compared to Faraz's shenanigans. How could he think I'd allow him to keep an extra wife lurking in the background? I couldn't believe I'd saddled myself with another cheat of a man, and that I'd been stupid enough, like my pitiful cousins, to fall for his smooth, innocent-sounding patter. He'd even admitted that he needed a visa, and I'd taken it as a measure of his honesty. It hadn't even crossed my mind that he was using the minor confession as a smokescreen for the major sin.

But the situation wasn't irreparable. I believed there was the beginning of love somewhere in all this mess. Despite the enormity of his lie, I thought his intentions were decent and he wasn't going to just dump me. I wanted to see if we could make it work. But the wife had to go. Faraz had a serious responsibility towards me and thank God he'd decided to fulfil it. He did what he had to on Skype, and I left him to sort out the mess.

Zain had started nursery now, so my days were structured largely around the school run. It wasn't much – three hours – but it was a glorious slice of "me time". The school run itself, though, made me a little anxious. In the first week I was standing in the playground when I noticed a couple of other Pakistani mums looking at me. I tried to ignore them, but they continued to stare. Eventually as I walked past them to get to the classroom, I thought I heard one of them make a comment about "second time". I automatically assumed she was talking about my marriage. I opened my mouth to ask her what she meant but then thought better of it. Perhaps it was a perfectly innocent remark. As far as I knew, they didn't know me. We were in a different area of Bradford now, away from my old neighbourhood. But the incident made me wary and paranoid. I kept myself to myself and let them think Faraz was Zain's father.

"What do you mean, Papa's stopped your allowance?"

Faraz was giving me a foot massage, but not a very good one. He apparently thought his ineffective, irritating pinching of my toes was relaxing enough to ease me into a state so blissful and coma-like that I wouldn't absorb his latest bombshell.

He'd been in touch with his sister in Pakistan. She wasn't happy speaking with him, like the rest of his family, but said she would just convey their messages to him. Firstly, Muskaan had gone into serious depression and was in her third week of fever and flu. Secondly, Faraz's parents wanted nothing more to do with him to the point of cutting off his allowance and disinheriting him.

I disentangled my feet from his hands and sat up on the bed.

"What are we supposed to live on?" I said.

"Don't worry, darling," said Faraz. "Allah will provide for us; you must have faith."

"Yes, I know that, but Allah doesn't send money floating down from the sky. You better sort something out, get a part-time job."

"It might be too much with uni. It's my final year and I'm in the middle of my dissertation. I want to do well so we have a good future together."

"Dissertations and distant dreams don't put food on the table, Faraz."

"I warned you, but you made me divorce Muskaan."

"Don't you dare try and put the blame on me!" I said. Faraz

gave a little one-beat chuckle, short but loaded with scorn. "What? What are you laughing at?"

"Nothing. I was coughing. Yes, I'll try to find a job."

None of this was going to plan. The marriage had been built on Faraz's lie, a despicable act in itself, and now it was having other consequences. I'd dealt with the deception, had no more illusions that it was a crystal relationship with no hidden flaws or secrets. Now that Faraz had no income, everything else was under threat. How would we cope with even basic necessities, and what impact would it have on me reaching my aims? Mum and Dad were going to be proved right that Faraz was far from the perfect partner he'd portrayed himself as. And they didn't even know about the other wife. Thankfully, Faraz's university course fees were paid, but the monthly allowance from his father helped pay the bills. Amir helped towards Zain's expenses, but apart from that there was just the child benefit. I had some savings put away, not much, but I wanted to keep them for Zain, or for only very extreme emergencies.

Friday night was usually my supermarket shopping night. In the first couple of weeks of us being together, Faraz, excited at the thought of the family shop, tagged along too, but I soon convinced him that babysitting Zain was a golden opportunity for them to bond. Life as a full-time mother meant that cruising the supermarket aisles alone felt as wild and adventurous as sailing solo down the Amazon. Well, maybe not quite the Amazon, but the Thames at least. I was thankful to escape the leaden, silent atmosphere that had descended on the flat after the news of Papa's pay cut, even though it meant my shopping trips would have to be less luxurious than what I'd been used to in Amir's day. Gone were the hedonistic hauls of Häagen-Dazs Pralines and Cream and Strawberry Cheesecake, mini crates of luscious black cherries and bags of Tesco's Finest brioche. Disinherited Faraz would have to make do with Value choc ices, Conference pears and toast.

Before heading home, I had to make a detour. I'd controlled

myself since my wedding to Faraz, visiting only once, but tonight I gave in. I felt the overwhelming sense of relief an addict surrendering to his drug. I wanted to see how he looked now that I was with someone else, if there were any traces of sorrow or regret, if he was feeling the pain he'd once afflicted on me.

I parked away from the house, feeling the urge to get out and watch from close range, but as I crept around the edge of the garden to position myself in a safe spot with a good view, I felt an inexplicable need to walk brazenly up to the door and knock. A few seconds later, Amir opened it.

"What are you doing here?" he said, his initial anger quickly melting into worry. "Is Zain okay? Where is he?"

"He's fine," I said. I stared at him, and he stared back.

"What?" he said, eventually.

"Can I come in?"

"Why?"

"I want to talk."

I could see he was thinking about protesting, but then he stepped aside. I stopped in the hallway, awaiting instructions for which room to go in. Amir gestured towards the posh lounge.

"Do you want a cup of tea or anything?" he mumbled, obviously not wanting to make me some.

"I'll make it myself if I do," I said, trying to be helpful.

"No," he said, blocking the entrance to the kitchen.

"What's wrong?" I said. "What have you got in there? A dead body?"

"Don't be silly, Sophie."

"Well? Have you redecorated? I can cope with that, you know."

"No, I haven't. It's like you left it. I just don't want you to... get emotional in there."

I rolled my eyes and went into the lounge and sat down without waiting for him to say it.

"I'm glad you came," he said. "I wanted to speak to you too."

"Really? About what?" It was vague but pleasing news.

"You first. How's Faraz, by the way? He seems like a good bloke."

I grunted in reply.

"Why? What's wrong?" asked Amir.

"He's a double-dealing cheat, that's what," I said. Amir shook his head.

"Don't do it, Sophie."

"What? Do what?"

"Start suspecting him for no reason. Don't spoil it. You're lucky things have worked out for you."

"For God's sake, Amir! I'm not imagining things! You can ask him yourself. He already has a wife in Pakistan."

"What?"

"Yes. It slipped his mind before our wedding."

"And he admitted it?"

I told him about the Skype rigmarole.

"So what happens now?" asked Amir.

"Oh nothing," I said. "I made him divorce her. I wasn't putting up with it."

His eyes widened and I knew he was shocked, but he pretended it was nothing.

"Okay, well, it's sorted then," he said. "Get on with a quiet life."

"I can't trust him, Amir."

"I think you should, Sophie. He's just given up another woman for you."

"Correction. For his passport."

"Still, Sophie. You've got what you wanted. Give it a go."

I was silent for a moment, steeling myself for what I was going to say.

"What if… we gave it a go?" I said it as quietly as I could, like the words were poisoned, deadly.

"What?"

"We both made mistakes. I know I behaved unreasonably. I've learnt my lesson, I promise. We can take things slowly…"

Amir looked at me incredulously.

"What are you saying?" he said. "You're married to someone else now. You shouldn't even think like this."

"But it's not easy to forget everything, is it? I miss you, Amir. Don't say you never think of me."

I rushed to him and threw myself at him, with no thought of dignity or modesty or religion. My face against his, just a perfect inch shorter, where it was always meant to be. He stayed still for a few moments, and I relaxed into him.

"It's too late," he said.

He put his hands on my shoulders, and I slipped deeper into the bliss. He moved me away.

"I'm getting married, Sophie."

It was my turn to be flabbergasted.

"What are you talking about? You can't be!" I said.

"You did. What's so unbelievable about it?" he said.

I reeled away from him, as though he'd attacked me physically. I sat down.

"Who is she?" I said.

"Jannat. She's my mother's second cousin."

I shook my head in impatience.

"So it's all set up for you," I said. "It's not someone you're crazy in love with. Like I'm not crazy about Faraz either."

"You chose Faraz yourself," he said, bitterly. I liked that. It meant he cared. "She's a nice woman. I've grown quite fond of her. You need to go home, Sophie."

"This is my home, not that poky little flat."

"Say *astaghfar*, Sophie, ask God for forgiveness. And go home to your husband."

Enraged at myself, I threw the now mushy, slushy frozen vegetables violently into the freezer drawer.

"Are you okay?" said Faraz, from the corner of the minute kitchen. He was leaning against the sink noisily eating a packet of cheese and onion crisps. I blew a big puff of breath and shut my eyes. I wanted to obliterate everything that had gone wrong over the last few years, slip back to when things had been easy between Amir and I, the mood serene, the decisions we had to make simple and clear cut. Had there ever been such a time? I certainly couldn't go back there now, even in my mind, with Faraz's cacophonous crunching deafening my ears like a drill smashing through concrete.

"Do you mind?" I said. "Can't you eat silently?" He stopped chewing, half a crisp dangling from his mouth. I felt disgusted, maybe irrationally so, but I wasn't thinking straight. "What are you doing? Why don't you just eat it now?" His mouth flapped open and devoured the crinkle cut potato like a guppy gobbling up fish food.

"Don't eat, eat," said Faraz. "You're confusing me. Did you want me to finish or–"

Exasperated, I snatched the bag from him and threw it on to the worktop.

"Just… go inside!" I picked up the packet again and pressed into his hand. "Take it."

"Sophie, I don't need to eat if you don't want me to," said Faraz. "But you can tell me kindly."

Angry as I was, I felt a twinge of guilt. I probably shouldn't have taken it all out on him, even though he was part of my problem, in more ways than just offending my hearing.

"Where's Zain?" I said, softening my tone a little.

"He's in bed," said Faraz. "We had a nice evening. We played that game, Ker-Plunk. It was quite fun."

"Thank you."

I was finding Faraz's habits and mannerisms increasingly annoying, but his concern and affection for Zain was heartfelt. Was he the only hope I had left, a little shimmering sparkle of it in all the rubble around me? I'd spun a diaphanous new life for us but already it seemed full of holes.

* * *

The nursery was part of a new school, and the headmistress had some modern but mostly wacky ideas, such as making the teachers dress as aliens and stand in the stocks to be slimed for charity, and disguising herself as a fir tree every winter, camouflaging herself in the playground, popping out and frightening the life out of unsuspecting parents when they were dropping their kids off.

One of her new ideas was swapping the usual class assembly to which parents were invited for an evening presentation, followed by an immersion experience, where they looked at displays and books and were fed topic-related snacks: Doritos for South American rainforests, shortbread for Macbeth, grapes on toothpicks for Ancient Greece.

Faraz was revising for an exam, so I went to Zain's experience evening, Superhero Night, on my own. Across the hall I noticed a man sitting alone, looking around with a serene expression on his face. I was struck by that. The other mothers were hanging around in pairs or groups of three. If I had to be seen talking to someone, maybe I would go and chat to him. He was wearing jeans with a smart casual jumper over a pale blue shirt. Of the few other fathers there, most were wearing hoodies or t-shirts, with the odd shalwar kameez. He stood out, in a compelling way.

"My superpower is being brave at night-time," announced one of the children on the stage. An appreciative moan went round the room. The man caught my eye and smiled.

We went into the classroom and cooed over exercise books, nibbling on power cookies and raw spinach leaves. I realised the man's son was one of Zain's new little friends, Ayaan, but I didn't want to look over friendly by starting up a conversation, so I tried looking more riveted than I really was in Zain's drawings of Florence Nightingale, one of history's real-life heroes.

"You should visit the museum, if you're really interested in her," he said, over my shoulder.

"Sorry?"

"The Florence Nightingale Museum in London. Or, of course, you could just watch *Ninja Turtles* or whatever the latest cartoon superhero is."

I smiled, and he put his fingers to his lips and laughed.

"Sorry, silly joke," he said. My phone rang. It was Rizwana. There were already two missed calls from her, so I answered it, asking the man to excuse me, and he walked away.

"There's something that might be up your street, an ad in the local paper," said Rizwana. "I'll WhatsApp it to you now. It's in a couple of weeks' time."

Intrigued, I looked at my phone. A new local theatre company was doing a talent search for actors, singers and dancers. No specific roles at the moment, but a chance to get noticed and onto their database for future opportunities. I thanked Rizwana and checked out their website. Although my hopes were still very much alive, I hadn't really taken any practical steps in the last few years. Having a baby, Mumtaz's death, the divorce and then new marriage with all its complexities; recently life had been exhausting and traumatic, my own goals and desires bundled away by the needs and demands of others. I deserved more than that, and now there was an evenness, a lull, and perhaps this was the time and the breakthrough I'd been waiting for.

FARAZ
2015

I could never have predicted my parents would do that to me. I was a good son, and my father was especially fond of me. I knew my mother must have a heavy hand in the disinheriting business. How was I supposed to manage without my allowance? Sophie didn't know it, but I had a frighteningly low bank balance right now. But what could I do? Without Sophie there was no future for me, and I really did mean that in the romantic sense, not just because of my financial calculations. She was beautiful, witty, clever. She could be a bit acidic and temperamental at times, but she was stunning in so many other ways, and I loved her for sure.

Until I finished my course and my visa was sorted out I couldn't get a full-time job either. I could do a few hours a week and I had a job as a delivery boy in Pizza Delite, but it wasn't very lucrative. I managed to borrow a small sum from different friends. Insha Allah, it would get me through the next few months, and in the meantime, I would work on damage control by buttering up my mother.

I was a romantic, but a realistic one. I knew that a happy marriage wasn't just lovey-dovey, like each other and exchange tearful promises, and that's it, sing duets for happily ever after. It required hard work. I was ready for it, and I began to plot my first fun surprise since Buckingham Palace-gate.

I'd always nurtured a love for dance in my youth, and many family members were admirers of my rehearsed routines to medleys of film songs. Sadly, since coming to the UK there was hardly any chance to rock my rumba. I had joined a salsa class before meeting Sophie but got kicked out when my elderly partner complained about my grip. I told them I was only trying to keep her steady, but they asked me to leave.

When Sophie told me that there was a local talent search on, I thought it was my golden chance. I didn't have any ambitions to be a professional dancer, but it would be fun to show my skills to others. Sophie was destined to be an actress, and I really didn't want to steal her limelight. I only wished to be her occasional backing troupe, her support act, if she would let me. Who knew, she might even want to try a bit of boogieing herself. The community centre was offering free dance classes for low-income families. Sophie and I could go together. She would acquire a new skill, and I wouldn't have to worry about flimsy grannies.

SOPHIE
2015

I had to find out about this wedding. Amir was refusing to talk
to me, not even coming over to collect Zain. Instead, Mum was
dropping him off at the house. I thought about putting a stop
to his meetings, but I didn't want Zain or his relationship with
Amir to suffer because of my own selfish motives. I knew Amir
was a wonderful father at heart and Zain loved him, looked
forward to his visits with excitement. Besides, cancelling the
meetings would only anger Amir and cause suspicion, so I let
things carry on as normal. I pretended to be indifferent and
didn't ask Mum about it. She probably knew all the details, but
I didn't trust her, Amir devotee that she was.

The whole thing was dark and covert. I even tried to get
something out of Zain.

"Did Daddy tell you his news?" I said casually, while we
were colouring in a Ninja Turtle.

"He's getting married," he said, looking uninterested.

"Do you know when it is?" He shook his head.

"Can we have jelly after dinner?" he said.

"Yes, you can, but are you sure Daddy didn't say?" Zain
widened his eyes and glared at me.

"No, I said! It's boring!" He threw down his pen and rolled
across the floor to the Lego, the conversation over. I didn't think
he was holding anything back. Amir had been very careful.

None of my contacts came up with anything. I had no way of tracking down where he was going to do the *nikaah*, but the civil ceremony was different. It would have to take place at a registry office or some other approved venue, and the date and intention to marry had to be publicly announced, the paper displayed. I would simply have to visit all the local registry offices until I found Amir's name on it.

There were several in the area. Apart from the main ones in Leeds and Bradford, there was Pudsey, Armley, Dewsbury, the list went on. I took down the addresses from the website and plotted a route.

I dropped Zain off at school, then headed off to my first location, Leeds Civic Hall, the satnav suitably set up. Faraz was safely at university with no idea of what I was up to. Fifteen minutes later I parked in a tight spot on a side road and paid the meter, thanking God I had a little change in my purse. I made a mental note to get some coins before I got back into the car.

After wandering around the building for a few minutes, I eventually found the lists of forthcoming weddings, pinned on a board inside a glass case. Andrew Barton and Laura Higgins, James Blythe and Sarah Shaw, Zoya Malik and Baber Naveed… they went on and on. No Amir, no Jannat. I scrutinised every one of them, then left hopelessly. I bought a packet of crisps and a chocolate bar, just to get change for the next parking meter, then headed back towards my next location.

I visited three more offices before giving up for the day. There was no trace of a marriage taking place between my ex-husband and his mother's second cousin. There was the possibility that they weren't going to do a civil ceremony, but I doubted it. Amir had been so excited about ours that I didn't think he'd pass over an opportunity to do it all over again. He'd treated it like a costume drama, dressing up in top hat and tails, a pocket watch, a bouquet for a buttonhole, hiring a vintage car. He wanted to be a dandy for a day, he said, to contrast with the Islamic wedding day, which was a mind-boggling affair of ostentation and gold and generally just noise, enough to drive any restrained gentleman insane. Not that Amir was a restrained gentleman.

Another alternative was that they'd booked an "approved venue", a hotel or stately home. If this was the case, I was never going to hunt them down. There were too many places it could be.

I mulled over what Mumtaz had told me about her family. Did she ever mention Jannat? I knew she had relations in Glasgow, Peterborough and Manchester. Perhaps Jannat was from one of these cities, and they were going to have the wedding there. I picked up Zain from school and popped into Mum's, praying that Amir had kept his word and not told her about my humiliating outburst. It was my brother's birthday, and I had a present for him, the perfect excuse to stop by. He was still at work, but I made tea for me and Mum, and heated up some leftover paratha for Zain.

"Amir told me his news," I said. "I was surprised, I'll be honest, but I understand, of course. I hope he's really happy."

"Do you mean that?" said Mum.

"Of course I mean it! I don't want him to have a miserable life, while I'm all cosy and shacked up with Faraz!"

"Good. I'm glad you really are moving on. I was a bit worried you still hadn't let go, in spite of Faraz."

I smiled and considered holding my hand out to her, but we never did shows of sentimentality, and the oddness might alert her. I hesitated before my next words. They had to be calculated meticulously. I stole in for a swift kill.

"Well, let me know when it's going to be, I want to buy Zain a little suit," I said.

"I'm not exactly sure of the dates. I'll have to ask Amir."

"Oh, well ask him and tell me, then," I said. Then I took the gamble. "I hope she doesn't find it too strange, moving all the way from Manchester."

"It's only Manchester, Sophie, not Paraguay."

Bingo. My heart lurched but I continued sipping my tea.

"Yeah, I suppose it's not that different to Bradford," I said.

Late that night, lying next to Faraz in bed, I really wondered if I should go ahead with it. Faraz was my husband but lately I was finding him hard work for various reasons, and he was paling in comparison to Amir, who I hadn't yet prised out of my heart completely, even after his rejection. I wasn't going to give up easily. The thought of Amir belonging to another woman was unbearable. And when I remembered that night, what he'd done to me and Zain, thrown us away so mercilessly, I knew I had to go to Manchester, whatever the outcome might be. I owed it to Zain as well as myself to at least try.

I decided to tackle the main office in Manchester first, and I sped off as soon as I'd taken Zain to school. There was traffic on the way, normal for that time in the morning, and it took me an hour and a half to get there. This time I wasn't a hot and flustered crackpot, but a cool, efficient mastermind. I walked into the Town Hall with a confident step, and justifiably so, for as soon as I found the wall of notices, Amir and Jannat were there, left hand side, third one down, 11am next Wednesday morning.

I asked Rizwana to collect Zain from school. Amir hadn't, in the end, made any arrangements for Zain to attend the wedding. My behaviour that night must have scared him. He wasn't taking any chances. If he wanted Zain, he'd have to tell me everything.

Next Wednesday morning, I was in the vicinity by 10.15, and in a safe position to watch their arrival from. 10.30, Amir arrived with a couple of his friends, a few cousins and an aunt and uncle. As predicted, he was wearing another frock coat, pale grey, with a big pink lily buttonhole. He needed to watch out for those pollen stains. His hair was shorter now than it had been when we got married, and a few years of life and wisdom made him look even more attractive. It made me queasy to think of how he'd gone to all this effort to impress another woman. It was intolerable.

The party went into the Town Hall, and after ten minutes or so, the bride arrived with about a million guests. She was wearing a bright pink trouser suit. That said it all. I almost felt like letting him get on with it, if this was what he'd chosen.

I swept into the building. I was dressed in an emerald-green gown, and the guests waiting in the foyer turned to look at me as I walked up to Amir, who was chatting to his friends while they waited for the proceedings to begin.

"Hello, sweetheart," I said, touching his shoulder. All the effort of the last few days was worth it just for the look of shock and terror on his face.

"What are you doing here?" he said.

"I just want to talk," I said. He looked as though he was going to tell me to leave, but then he thought better of it and grabbed my arm roughly and led me into a side room.

"What the hell do you think you're doing?" he said, his voice in a controlled growl.

"Listen to me calmly, Amir," I said. "You haven't thought this through. I'm ready to leave Faraz. It's not working out with him. Let's join our family back together." I placed my hand on his chest, squashing the petals of the lily buttonhole. "You know it makes sense. You know that's how it's meant to be."

"Sophie… You know I'd do anything for Zain…" said Amir. The door opened and Jannat came in. I let her see our little intimate vignette for a few seconds, then I rushed over to her and drew her into the room.

"Come in, dear, this concerns you too," I said.

"What's going on, Amir?" said Jannat.

"It's a shock for you, I know, but it's better that it's happened now than later. Divorces. Messy. Tell me about it." I rolled my eyes comically. Amir and Jannat exchanged a glance. "Anyway, cut a long story short. Amir and I are getting back together." I beamed at them.

"No," said Amir.

"You just said we were, you'll do anything for Zain."

"Yes, I would, but not this. This isn't going to be good for any of us."

"I've changed, Amir. Look at me, how calmly I'm listening to you." I turned to Jannat. "You know he still loves me, don't you? Do you really want to marry him in that condition?"

She looked at me with pity and shook her head. It shocked me more than an outburst would have.

"Amir warned me you might do something to try to ruin our relationship," she said. "But I never imagined this. Let it go, Sophie. Amir's moved on."

"You don't know anything about us," I said. "Tell her, Amir. It's special, isn't it?"

"No, Sophie," he said firmly, then closed his eyes for a moment and sighed. His voice softened. "No."

"Please, Amir," I said, my voice cracking.

I searched his face for a hint, a scintilla of our old, ruined love, but there was no remnant of it anywhere. His countenance was smooth, dapper and hopeful. I bowed my head and walked away.

FARAZ
2015

The rumours reached me before Sophie got home. At least three people rang me to tell me what had happened at Amir's registry office wedding. My brain felt numb with anger and distress. I was ready to give my complete self to her, but maybe I was delusional. While I had been secretly fine-tuning my dance routine over the last week, she had been doing scheming of a very different sort.

I couldn't sit down as I waited for her. How dare she play with my feelings and my reputation like that? My heart was vibrating from my chest to my throat, and I could feel the vein in my forehead throbbing. It crossed my mind to go next door and borrow the neighbour's blood pressure machine to check I wasn't going to have a stroke.

I was still pacing around the flat when she walked in. I faced her, fists on my hips, ready to shout, tell her off, take control, but it all vanished, poof, when she ran into my arms and broke down. There's nothing like a woman weeping into your chest, to make you feel both tender and manly at the same time, and I melted completely.

SOPHIE
2015

"Are you pregnant woman with a trolley?"

I couldn't believe it. I knew I'd put on a bit of weight but to joke about it in such a crude way was cruel and unacceptable. I was in the jam aisle in Morrisons when I heard the remark close to my ear, the man's voice confident and good-humoured. Attractive if it hadn't been so rude. I turned with a scowl. It was the fellow parent from Zain's school, the good-looking man I'd noticed recently. Even worse. I'd have to confront him now, then either ignore him or force myself to smile at him forgivingly every morning for the next seven years.

"Pardon?" I said.

"Pregnant woman with a trolley?" he repeated, oblivious to my clenched fist. "The character in that film? *Monty and the Ghost*?"

Monty and the Ghost. Chunky's horror film.

"Oh my God!" I said. "How do you know about that? It wasn't even finished, let alone released." His face broke into a grin.

"I know the sound technician," he said. "He's an old friend from college. We watched it one bored afternoon. Well, more than one afternoon if I'm honest. It was so bad we found it hilarious."

"I'm so embarrassed!" I said. "Was it really that awful?"

165

"Yes, it was. Sorry. But your scene was good. Very realistic acting."

"It wasn't acting." His eyes widened in shock, we stared at each other for a moment, then both started laughing.

"Ouch!" he said. "I think we met at the school the other day. Are you Zain's mum?"

"Yes. He's in Year One."

"So is Ayaan. Sorry, I should introduce myself. My name's Tariq."

"I'm Sophie. Yes, Zain's always talking about Ayaan. He's mentioned you, too, actually. Said his dad makes the best doughnuts."

"I wish that was true," he said. "Actually, I just buy them from the bakery down the road. Great little Italian place."

"Oh, Zain must have got mixed up. Kids!" I rolled my eyes comically. "But sounds delicious, you must show me where it is some day."

"Yes, definitely," he said, after a moment's hesitation. "Well, I'll let you get on with your shopping then. Hopefully I'll see you at school next week."

I smiled, put the conserve into the trolley, and drifted away down the aisle.

I did see Tariq at school again, but only to pass by in the playground, with a nod and a smile. At home, meanwhile, Faraz was being unnaturally kind, considering what I'd just done at Amir's wedding. We didn't talk about it, but I knew he knew. Yet I'd never seen him angry. Annoyed and impatient, yes, but he never lost his temper. Most men would have been incensed at what I'd done. Faraz bought me a new hot water bottle with an aromatherapy function.

Despite all of these qualities, I was struggling. I'd walked into this blindly. Maybe it had happened too quickly, while I was still reeling from my divorce. Now the frisson of novelty and excitement of being with Faraz had worn off, I was seeing things in a different light. He was good-looking and kind, but what did we really have in common? We made conversation cordially enough, but that real fizz, fluttery and gasp-inducing, was missing. I was dreaming of bigger horizons – I wanted a comfortable, cultured life. Faraz had ambitions, too, but how long would it take him to accomplish them? If he ever did? His idea of culture was his psychotic obsession with the Windsors. Although I wasn't greedy for money, it was becoming a real problem. I was becoming increasingly unsure if Faraz could afford to look after us financially. I could get a part-time job, maybe go back to hairdressing, at least until anything happened on the acting front. But we wouldn't survive on a part-time wage, especially not with the insatiable shadow of Suleiman hanging over my head. He even turned up on that trip to London and I'd had to do some fast talking when Faraz saw me with him.

I could battle through the marriage, try and make it work eventually but, if it didn't, there would be too many regrets later. What if something better was awaiting me beyond the walls of this mucky little flat?

The only speck of hope I had at the moment was the audition. The brief was wide. We had to perform a piece of up to three minutes long that best showcased our talents. I thought the greatest way to show my range was to go classic. If they saw I could do Shakespeare, they'd know I could do anything, and I'd prepared a speech from *Antony and Cleopatra*.

I perfected my look painstakingly. Of course the legendary queen had worn distinctive eye make-up, and I'd discovered that historically she'd used vivid green malachite, flecking it with sparkling gold pyrite. I replicated this with my modern palette and added winged eyeliner. I hovered over whether or not to don a thick black wig with a heavy fringe but decided against it. There was a fine line between the "method" and absurdity. I swept my hair up into a knot and put on a floor-length gold dress. It was stretching the seams a bit too much for my liking, but it would survive the three minutes before the judges. I could keep it covered with a kimono until then.

The community hall in which the auditions were taking place was packed with other hopefuls, some in spectacular garb, some in jeans, variously carrying notes, guitars, hoops, and even a rabbit or two. I didn't look around at them too much. I needed to focus on my own work. We were given big white paper squares with numbers on to hang around our necks. I wanted to argue that the ugly thing would ruin my outfit and affect my performance, but I couldn't risk being disqualified.

It wasn't long before I was on stage with the lights only on me and was relieved that I was feeling an adrenaline rush of excitement instead of nerves, despite so many people watching me.

"Where think'st thou he is now?" I began. I spoke slowly and clearly, infusing every word with emotion. "Stands he, or sits he? Or does he walk? Or is he on his horse…"

As I ended after several more lines, I gazed at a point in the distance, then slowly closed my eyes. It was a moment I'd never experienced before, arresting my audience in thrall, my voice and being commanding the room. I was transported into another realm, ruled by the love of art alone. I was on a world-famous stage trodden by the giants, the Globe or the Lyceum. Even the Kodak Theatre one day, picking up a coveted gold statuette. I held on for a moment and was just about to open my eyes and whisper a breathless "Thank you", before the applause began. But instead of clapping, I heard the introduction to a well-known Indian song play faintly in the background. Surely they would have waited a few minutes for the next act? I spun around and saw the spotlight was now on another figure. His back was towards me, and his shoulders were twitching as he began to dance. Someone in the audience giggled nervously, then others joined in with full blown laughter. I realised who the dancer was, and embarrassed and hot faced, I ran off the stage.

FARAZ
2015

I arrived at the venue shortly before Sophie but waited out of sight in the hallway. Once she'd arrived and got her number tag, I let her go into the main hall before going to speak to the woman at the desk. I explained my concept. We were going to be a husband-and-wife double act, but Sophie didn't know it yet. Luckily the lady was excited by the surprise element of the idea, and thought it showed some originality. She made a note of how my performance was to be set up, straight after Sophie's. My heart felt almost dizzy thinking about the tears of joy that would shine in Sophie's eyes when I proved myself to be the ultimate "supportive" husband.

The audience was made up of all the entrants, with the judges at the front near the stage. I found a seat at the back of the hall, from where I had a clear view of my wife, who was seated nearer the front. I knew she wouldn't notice me. She was absorbed in watching the other performers and, I imagined, rehearsing her own speech in her mind. Even from a distance she looked gorgeous. Hair perfectly arranged, her cute, dimpled face glowing. In that moment I knew why I was able to be so forgiving of whatever she did. Not many men would be able to resist such snares.

After an hour or so, Number 32 took to the stage, an elderly man attempting to do a stand-up comedy routine, telling a joke about his wife's snoring habits. Sophie was number 34, and I could see her getting up to go and stand in line.

She whipped off her black kimono to reveal a gold satin dress. I wasn't too happy about her wearing the figure-hugging gown in public, but I would let it go this time. She began her speech. I thought it was a bit over the top, expression wise, but she still looked like a star. While she was delivering the monologue, I sneaked on to the stage behind her and took up my position, with my back to the audience. I always found this an effective, high-voltage stance to kick things off with.

Sophie finished her speech, and there were a few seconds of silence, then my music began to play softly. I had instructed them to start quietly and get louder gradually. Someone laughed, and then the rest joined in. I ignored them and began my routine. "Do you want to be my *chamak chalo*?" It was a seamless flow from dialogue to dance. I had no trouble with nerves. I wiggled and swayed and twirled my Michael Jackson hat on my finger. The spectators started to cheer me on, and my moves became more confident, almost reckless. Between spins I zoomed in on Sophie. She'd moved to the side of the hall and was staring at me in disbelief.

The song faded out and I finished with an energetic leap in the air. All of a sudden, the audience were giving me a standing ovation. The unexpected reaction made me tremble with happiness, and I felt dazed as the judges told us they would contact us with the results in a few days.

SOPHIE
2015

I didn't wait till the end of the song and ran out while Faraz was attempting to do a back flip. I wanted to leave immediately but I had to go back to the desk to return my number and sign out. The sweltering hall seemed endless, and people were staring at me and whispering to each other as I ran across it to the door. I almost tripped over twice. My burning face was slippery with tears as I gave the card to the woman and scribbled my name. Then I went to the car and drove off. I don't think I'd ever been more incensed in my life. My hands were shaking so instead of going straight home I parked the car down a side road to cool off.

I'd confided my most secret desires to him, and he'd encouraged me to chase them, bring them to life. I'd mapped out everything in my mind, a slow but even ascent, minor roles from local companies to begin with, working up eventually to national shows and television, ending in worldwide fame. This had been a way of possibly getting my first job, but Faraz had made a joke out of my dedication, reduced it with his cringey cheapness. How could he imagine his amateur jig was on par with my classic rendition? It explained the laughter. The audience must have seen him standing there in his glitzy flares. I wasn't the object of their scorn, it was Faraz, but he'd made me look like an idiot too. How was I going to show my face at another audition? I knew from those conversations at Chunky's shoot how stories got passed around. It would be all over the local Asian theatrical network by tomorrow, rumours turning my elegant monologue into a slapstick routine.

Maybe he'd meant well, but it was a savage blow to the little progress I'd begun to make. In that moment of fury, the murkiness of my feelings towards Faraz cleared. The doubts lifted and I could see what I needed to do. I couldn't let Faraz be a hindrance to me.

FARAZ
2015

I reached home before Sophie did. Zain was still at his nan's house so we would get some special couple time together. A fitting end to the most unique day of our lives. A wedding was one thing, but how many couples could boast a relationship like the one we had forged today? We were partners in life and art. Or, in a more on trend way, #couplesgoals.

Sophie had disappeared in the middle of my performance, but I hoped she would be here soon. I lit a few candles and put them on the coffee table, dimming the main light. I made mugs of tea and found some cupcakes in the fridge. When Sophie arrived, I took her coat and sat her down. I tried to slip off the black kimono, but she pulled it tighter around herself. I didn't let this put me off, though, and snuggled up as close to her on the sofa as I dared, which, judging by the look on her face, was at the other end of it. I didn't know what was wrong with her. Nerves, maybe, at the outcome of the audition?

"Come on then," I said. "Tell me what you thought. I didn't want to keep it a secret from you, but I thought the surprise was too priceless."

"I wish you had told me," said Sophie.

"I know. We could have worked on it together." I leaned over and tickled her chin, endearingly. "But don't worry, next time we'll do it properly."

"No. I would have stopped you from coming."

"What do you mean?"

"Why did you do it, Faraz? You knew how important this was to me, didn't you?" She was trying to keep her voice calm but even I could tell she was about to lose it. This wasn't the result I was hoping for at all.

"Yes, yes, darling," I said. "It meant everything to you. I even read the advert. It said we're looking for originality. That's why I did it, to give you an edge. Whoever heard of a Bollywood/Shakespeare combo?"

"No, Faraz! That's not what I want to do! You made a fool of me! If I lose out on this because of you…"

"I just wanted you to win," I said, but she turned away from me, maybe trying to hide her tears. I switched on my phone to make a distraction and checked my emails. There it was, a message from Chapatti Tales Theatre Company.

Dear Faraz,

Thank you for taking the time to attend our audition this afternoon. We were excited to see you today and would love to work with you in the future and will certainly add you to our pool of artists. You have great energy and we feel you might be a great fit for a role in our forthcoming production. We'll be in touch soon with more details.

Kind regards,
Raj

"Here!" I shouted, unable to keep in my delight. "I told you it would work! We're through!"

"What? Really?" said Sophie, sitting up now and taking out her own mobile. I blew out a noisy breath of relief. Sophie was going to see the fruit of my efforts. She tapped on her phone and began scrolling, her face glowing with happiness in a way

I had never seen before. My goodness, it was better than I expected.

But then, within seconds there was an instant transformation.

"What?" she said, her face scrunching up in anger as she read the email. She let out a roar of anger, then threw the mobile on to the floor.

"What's the matter, darling?" I said, picking up the phone.

Dear Sophie,

Thank you for taking the time to attend our audition this afternoon. I'm sorry to say that we won't be taking things forward with you at this time. Unfortunately, we can't give you individual feedback, but please don't let this discourage you. We would advise you to apply again in the future.

Kind regards,
Raj

"How? How? How?" she cried. "You! Over me!"

"Well... they didn't recognise talent, darling," I ventured. "They're morons." Sophie just replied with a series of funny sounds, splutters and gurgles. I thought she was having some sort of attack. "Sophie, are you okay?" I went to the kitchen and got her some water, but when I came back, she was sitting peacefully.

"Sit down, Faraz," she said. "This isn't working."

"I know," I agreed. "It wasn't a good idea; I can see that now. But don't worry, I'll tell them to give you another chance."

"No, thank you. I can fight my own battles. And I didn't mean the double act. I mean this relationship. This marriage."

"Marriage?"

"Yes. It's not working. Faraz... I think... I think we should end it."

"What do you mean? You can't just make these decisions all of a sudden! By yourself!"

"It's not all of a sudden. I've been thinking about it for some time now." She took on a gentler tone. "We're just too different."

"That doesn't matter. Being different is what makes life interesting. And if it's this talent show thing that you're upset about, I won't do it."

"I'm sorry, Faraz. I need someone like me."

"It's not try before you buy!" I piped up. I had to show her I was a robust and assertive man, for once. "You haven't got a twenty-eight days' guarantee on husbands, you know!"

"I've tried my best, Faraz, believe me."

"Is it Amir? Are you going back to him?"

"No, I'm not going back to him. He married someone else, remember?" she said. "But now you mention him, that's what I mean. With him, I had a different relationship. It was more comfortable, he understood me–"

I couldn't take any more. My head burst with pain, and I smashed my fist down on to the table. She jumped and her hand went to her mouth.

"I was just trying to explain," she said hesitantly.

"Don't," I said. "Don't say anything." I was silent for a moment. "We can solve things. Tell each other our problems. Have counselling if we have to."

"I don't believe in counselling."

"Well, I won't do it. I won't give you the divorce. You'll have to get *khulla* through the Shariah Council. You'll have to prove your case with some valid reasons. Not stupid things like you didn't like my *Strictly* number. And you won't find one, because I can say without doubt, and without wishing to blow my own trumpet, that I've been a very proper husband to you."

She considered this a moment.

"I know that," she said. "It's a long process. I don't want Zain or myself to go through that."

I breathed a moment. At last, she was seeing sense.

"So you'd better make things easy for me," she said. "If you don't, I'll have to make things difficult."

"What do you mean?"

"It's going to affect your visa application. If we do things in a civil way, you might be able to find someone else. But if you start messing me around, I'll let everyone know you married me under false pretences."

"But we sorted that out!"

"Not to mention how you can't even afford to support me financially."

"I will, Sophie. It's just a temporary hitch. Listen to me, darling, don't do all this. You'll regret it, I'm telling you." Impulsively I lashed out and grabbed her wrist. She cried out in pain but began wrenching it away and I let her go.

"Don't threaten me, Faraz," she said. "Don't think I won't call the police if I have to. Who do you think they'll believe, all things considered?"

I stared at her. I'd forgotten how much power she had.

She was kind enough to give me time to find somewhere else to stay. I moved in with some friends, and ten days later we sat down with her mother and an imam, and I divorced her. I had no choice. I knew she would be true to her word and carry out her ominous promise. I couldn't afford for her smear campaign to ruin my chances of ever finding happiness, and of living in England long term.

But I still regretted it, because despite everything I really did love Sophie. In the horrible days that followed, I locked myself in my bedroom and wept uncontrollably as I looked at her glorious pictures on my phone, and my friends stood outside the door offering to call a doctor.

It was three weeks before I found the courage to tell my family. My mother still wasn't talking to me, but when I typed a brief summary to her in a Facebook message, she tapped out an instant reply. All was forgiven.

SOPHIE
2015

I was free. Everything I'd said to Faraz was true. Perhaps having experienced true, all-consuming love before, I'd entered the relationship with impossible dreams. Faraz's lies about his other wife hadn't helped and we'd started on fragile, papery foundations. But I'd still been willing to see it through, hoped that we could gradually cobble a harmonious life together out of shreds of love and companionship. It had worked for a short time, but then the gnawing fear that I'd made an awful mistake had grown. My mind wandered, lost itself in thoughts of other possibilities, of a love that I was certain of. It might not be perfect, when I found it, but it would be whole and without compromise.

Everything had been illuminated in sickening clarity on that dance floor, each of Faraz's wiggles inducing a wince and a scream of horror at the realisation. There had been no question of carrying on.

Last time, when I split up with Amir, there had been a paralytic desolation. Now there was air and lightness, joy and zest to go forward. There would be no more haste or rash impulses from now on. This time it would truly be an affair of the heart.

SOPHIE
Present Day

It's been almost four weeks since Tariq vanished. My worst fears haven't come true but neither have we found him. I can't think of what else to do. My mother does her best to comfort me. I know it must take an effort considering the differences we've had in the past. Even now her words are tough, but I know there's only love and concern beneath their easily cracked eggshell surface.

"You can't do this," she says. "Crying and wailing won't get you anywhere. You have to be strong to look after Zain. Tariq will turn up soon, I'm sure of it."

"Yes, dead probably!" I shout at her. "Why are you all pretending everything's going to be alright?" She lets my anger subside a little before speaking.

"Anything could have happened," she says.

"You don't say," I mutter.

"Stop it, Sophie. Do you think I don't care? Tariq's been wonderful for both you and Zain. More than that, he's like a son to me, too. It's unbearable, not knowing where he is, but we can't lose hope." She shuts her eyes for a moment, as if struggling to keep back tears. I go to her and hold her hand, and she pulls me into her arms.

* * *

Later, I get a call from Craig, my friend and ex-tutor from the acting class, and now business associate. When he set up his own film production company recently, I, too invested £8,000, in return for being on the top of his list for leading parts. I was going to be the heroine of his first film, when the time came, and he could afford to make it.

First of all, there was the issue of finding the perfect script. Craig had a pile of them from hopeful writers, but rarely managed to get through more than twenty pages of most of them.

"Good news," says Craig, when I answer the phone. "I think I might have found the story we've been looking for. Women-centred, epic, profoundly emotional. If we can get this, you're going to have an award winner on your hands." Despite my depressed mood, I feel a tingle of excitement.

"What's my part?" I ask.

"A junior doctor who gets kidnapped by a psychotic patient."

I gasp with happy surprise and find myself grinning stupidly. It had everything – a powerful career woman in a suspenseful, thrilling situation. Plenty of opportunity for me to portray an admirable, caring character and perform some high adrenaline action scenes.

"Sophie?" says Craig. "What do you think?"

"It sounds wonderful. I think you should do it. I mean, how does it work now, do you buy the script?"

"I think the best thing to do at this stage is draw up an option agreement. It'll give us a bit of time to raise the rest of the money. The writer's done a couple of kids' TV things, so she's not completely unknown. I don't want to lose out."

"No, no, we don't want to lose out if it's as good as you say."

"Thing is I might need a bit more cash to pay her the first instalment. I don't want to ask you at a time like this, but like I said, I don't want someone else to snap it up."

"Of course… How much would you need?"

"Well, I've got a bit left in the pot, but maybe about five k?

'Course if you can't I'll find another way. But have a think, and I'll send you the script so you can have a read, too."

I put the phone down with a sense of trepidation and worry, but a feeling of adventure too. The promise of the future feels tangible, an elastic, shiny form that I can pluck out of the air and hold safe.

Metaphors and fantasy are all very well, but the future, my life, depend on solid reality and that means only one thing. I've more or less pledged the money to Craig, but I don't know where I'm going to get it from. Before, I'd had resources but now is a very different matter. I'm being stretched in every direction. Unless I think of something soon, another chance will be lost, and my hopes obliterated once more.

My breathing changes when, one evening, the doorbell rings and I see Inspector McKinley standing outside my door. They deliver their horrors in person, as though sympathetic eye contact and a pat on the back will make it any less unbearable. I open the door robotically and offer tea or something cold.

"Nothing, Sophie. Please, just sit down," she says, taking a seat next to me on the sofa. She takes my hand and strokes it comfortingly. "I'm afraid I have some bad news. There was an accident on the motorway. A pile up. Several people were killed." She pauses, gives my hand a soft, clammy squeeze. I want to pull it away from her, but I can't. My body feels heavy, encased in lead.

"We think one of them might be your husband."

I crumple. I fall against the sofa, eyes shut tight. If I keep them closed it'll keep the sickness of her words out.

"I'm really sorry, Sophie. We found a card with his name on at the site."

"A card? It doesn't mean anything," I whisper.

"It's his Marks and Spencer store card, registered to this address."

"No," I say. "It can't be him. I would have felt it if…"

She looks at me pityingly. I think there might even be the faintest touch of impatience.

"I agree instinct can be a very powerful thing," says McKinley. "But sometimes we have to let the rational mind take over."

"It's a mistake."

"Possibly. That's why we need someone to come down and identify him. I'll understand if you don't want to do it. If there's anyone else you can think of…"

"I'll do it."

"I'm sorry to tell you this, Sophie, but the van caught fire. They managed to get the bodies out, but he did suffer some severe burns. There's been some damage to his face. It might be better if you didn't see him."

"No. I have to be sure."

An hour later I ring my mother from the police station. She'd offered to come with me, but I'd told her to stay at home with Zain. There was nothing to worry about. I hadn't really believed that the body they'd found was going to be Tariq.

But now I have to tell her that I've identified the man killed in the accident as my missing husband.

SOPHIE

Even hearing the word is repugnant. Post-mortem. It was bad enough before all this happened, when I had a faint idea what it meant, but then one of my young cousins, a fourteen year-old with a taste for serial killer trash, described the vile process to me in graphic detail. I screamed him down, but not before I heard the words "peel away the face" and "weighing the organs". Now I bat away the gruesome images as I listen to the policewoman summarising the report.

The accident occurred on the M1, going north, when a driver in a Golf, texting last minute arrangements for the stag night he was en-route to, drove into the back of the slow-moving Mini in front. The Mini was overheating and smoking and the driver was obliged to slow down and turn on his hazard lights, a signal that the Golf driver obviously ignored. The Golf and Mini drivers might have survived if the camper van hadn't rammed into the back of them, followed by a couple of lorries.

The police think Tariq had been travelling in the camper van with the elderly couple, Mr and Mrs Cutler, also both dead. Mrs Cutler had phoned her granddaughter, Lily, five minutes before the crash to tell them they'd be arriving at the Lake District in about an hour's time. They were travelling up for a weekend break to celebrate their fiftieth anniversary.

The M&S store card is the only ID they've found, as it was in his pocket. Perhaps he'd been thinking of using it at the next service station? Everything else in the van went down in flames.

They tell me they're looking into the accident, but they don't think there's anything suspicious about it. According to them, Tariq died as a result of the crash and there isn't any reason now to look into where he's been for the last six months. His burial will take place in the Honeysuckle Lane Cemetery tomorrow.

My mother organises the funeral. There's no point in me trying to do it myself when she already knows everybody.

"Who do you want to wash him?" Mum asks me gently. She's probably been avoiding the question, but the ritual cleansing is a necessary part of the burial process, and it must be done.

"Ask the group at the masjid to do it," I say. We're having the funeral prayer at a mosque in Leeds. It's further away and my mother disagrees with me.

"Everyone he knows is in Bradford," she says. "He mostly prayed in the Bradford masjid. Why don't you just have it here? It'll be easier."

"He knows people in Leeds, too," I say. "He worked there. He prayed in the mosque there, too, sometimes. And his parents are buried in that cemetery."

She doesn't argue with this.

Tariq has no family of his own. He was an only child and his parents passed away years ago. He has a few second cousins, but they're in Pakistan. I can't ask his friends – of which he only has a few anyway – to be involved in the final bathing rites. Professionals will wash the body, and then leave the coffin closed. It's not a pleasant sight and I won't put it on display. I don't care about disappointing the gawkers that will inevitably turn up to relish and paw over the pathos of the dead.

The police phone and say the body is ready to be released and I ask the funeral organisers to collect and transport him to the mosque, where he'll lie in the cold room till tomorrow morning. I'll meet them there. My parents argue with me, tell me there's no need for me to go, but I insist.

"Please let me spend our last hours together," I beg. There's nothing they can say to this. My father hugs me again, for the hundredth time since the news. I hug him back, but quickly now. I need to bring out a little fire if I'm to survive this. I stuff a few bags of crisps, a packet of biscuits and bottles of water into a plastic bag, kiss Zain goodbye, and drive to the masjid.

They've laid the body out on the bed already by the time I arrive. It's a small room, the size of a box room, leading off a reception area in the masjid. There's a chair in there, and I sit with a copy of the Surah Yaseen, the chapter of the Quran that's customarily read to the dying, but after a few minutes I'm too cold. I'm still alive, warm, and won't be able to function if I stay in this morbid chamber. I close the door quietly and go into another small room next door. I can see if anyone comes or goes from here.

I settle down on the sofa, open a bottle of water. It smells of incense in here, musky and nauseating. I begin reciting the Quran, trying to use the rise and fall of the rhythmic language to regulate the torrent in my heart, steer me through what I have to do. After a couple of hours my eyes begin to feel heavy. I lie down on the sofa and set my alarm for 5am, in case I drop off. I've checked the prayer timetable. The Fajr *namaaz* will be held at 5.30am, and the masjid will be with filled with members of the congregation. It'll give me enough time to take part in the prayer, then wait till the men arrive to bathe the body, the first of the day's rites. I slip into a heavy, solid sleep shortly after, and don't wake until the alarm goes off.

The men arrive at nine, and I watch as they wheel him into the specially designed bathroom. They ask me if I want to come in, but I refuse. I instruct them to place him in the coffin once they've finished, and seal it shut. I want it to be a dignified ending. Then I ring Amir and ask him to bring some fresh clothes for me. I can't go home and get changed, can't leave anything to chance.

Four hours later, the prayer is read, and he is taken away and buried.

It's late when the doorbell rings. The last of the guests left by the early evening, and I told Mum to go home too, that I'd be fine, even though she wanted to stay to keep me company. Zain is asleep upstairs. It must be someone who couldn't make it to the funeral, dropping by to pay their condolences. I look through the peephole.

It's Suleiman, greasy and smiling as usual, dressed in a white suit and panama hat, with a peach carnation in his buttonhole.

"Hello, dear," he says.

"What are you doing here?" I say.

"I wanted to see if you're okay. Come on, let me in then we can talk."

I don't want to discuss anything on the doorstep, so I step aside.

"I see you're still working on your undercover disguise technique," I remark.

"My, you really have done well this time," says Suleiman, looking the house over.

He goes into the lounge, trampling over our dove grey thick pile carpet with his pointed patent shoes, and settles himself into Tariq's favourite leather armchair.

"What do you want?" I ask.

"A fresh, hot roti would be nice." He throws back his head, shaking it with closed eyes and a grin, delighted with his own joke. Then he straightens himself up and tries putting on a sombre air. "My condolences, dear. I was devastated when I heard about Tariq. So young–"

"Don't waste your breath," I say.

"I really am sorry," he says, standing up and putting his arms around me and drawing me into his chest.

"Get off me!" I shout, pushing him away.

"No need to get so uptight. I'm just trying to be sympathetic," he says. "Well? Do you want to fill me in? What happened?"

"It's none of your business. Just tell me why you're here."

He moves towards the door.

"Where are you going?" I want him out, but not before I know what he's up to.

"You haven't even offered me a drink, despite my very obvious hint," he says, plodding out of the room. He goes into the hall and opens the doors leading off it, turning on all the lights till he finds the kitchen. He lifts the lid off the pot on the cooker.

"Hmmm, *matter keema*. Plate?" He opens a cupboard and finds one. I watch disgustedly as he piles the mince into it and puts it into the microwave. "I don't really expect you to make a roti. A slice of bread will do. In there, is it, or do you keep it in the fridge?" He opens the bread bin and takes out the Warburtons.

"I let you have a nice break," he says. "To be honest I wasn't going to bother you so soon, but what can I do? I'm a bit strapped. Five thousand should do it."

"I haven't got it," I say.

"Don't make me go over all that again. You know what will happen if you don't."

"Do what you want," I say. "Amir means nothing to me."

The microwave pings and Suleiman takes out his dinner. I'm tempted to snatch it from him and tell him to leave again, but he looks at me with suddenly cold eyes.

"Not Amir," he says. "The police."

"They won't believe you."

"There's something you don't know. I've been saving it for a special moment like this." He puts the plate on the bar table and places his hands on my shoulders and starts to rub them in circular movements. "You're tense. Relax." I pull away from him.

"Don't touch me again," I say. He rolls his eyes and perches himself perilously on a kitchen stool. He takes out his mobile on the table next to his plate and presses a button. I hear my own voice, a few years younger, angry, then frightened and jumbled. Snatches of conversation have been chopped and put together to make a damning, murderous monologue that's undeniably incriminating. Horrified, I try to snatch the phone from him but he's too quick and shoves it inside his coat.

"I thought you just said no touching?" he says, zipping up his parka, sealing it, unreachable, inside.

"That poor woman," he says. "She never realised her killer was lurking so close, her own daughter-in-law, no less. It's what old folks like her call *kismet*."

"It didn't happen like that!" I shout. I take a breath and try to talk in a calmer tone. "You know it didn't."

"It's lucky I always keep my finger on the record button. You never know when you might pick up something useful."

"Just give me some time," I say after a moment. "The paperwork will take a few weeks. Tariq's will, I mean."

"Hmm. Okay. Under the circumstances, I can grant you a bit of leeway, in the name of humanity. I'm not a complete ogre. But it's a one off, mind you, don't get too comfortable."

I go into the living room, my head splitting with anger and despair. I sit there until I hear him burp and come out into the hall. He's holding a litre carton of Tropicana orange juice from the fridge.

"I'll be in touch. I might need cash this time. Problems with the bank." He brandishes the drink. "I'll take this one for the road."

SOPHIE

At first, I think it's a bird or maybe just a t-shirt fluttering further down the line, a slight movement in the corner of my eye. I ignore it and carry on hanging up the washing. It's a dull morning, not much sun, the sky coloured grey like old thermals. There's too much on my mind. I have to go shopping before I collect Zain from the Holiday Club, and I mentally go through the cupboards and fridge, listing yogurt and milk and bananas. More seriously there's the question of Suleiman and his threat.

Thank God he's agreed to delay the payment. Tariq was always a generous husband, but now there's not much left in our joint account after all the funeral expenses. Once the inheritance is sorted out, I'll be in a more stable position financially, and it'll be easier to meet Suleiman's repulsive demands. But how long is it going to go on for?

I can't let him go to the police. He was involved too, but he could dress it up any way he wants to, especially with the "evidence" he's presented me with. Over the years he's extorted thousands of pounds from me at varying intervals. It was often almost impossible for me to pay him but there was nothing else I could do. I used my savings, borrowed from the bank, or even sold unwanted knick-knacks and other items on eBay. You'd be surprised what you can make with a collection of tea sets, vases and handbags. Mumtaz's collection of Royal

Doulton figurines fetched particularly good prices, and Amir never noticed the absence of the china ladies.

Above all, it had been vital that Suleiman kept the information from Amir, and then, later, I didn't particularly want Faraz and Tariq to know either. Now, I have no man to lose, but Suleiman has upped his game with this new threat. As I hang up Zain's little jumpers, I'm petrified by the hideous vision of our future, always living in the shade of Suleiman's menace.

There's another movement, more solid this time, at the edge of my vision. I look around just in time to see a figure running away on the other side of the iron gate, long scarf streaking out behind and a blur of blue denim. By the time I unlock the gate and follow her down the alley and into the street, she's nowhere to be seen.

I'm folding up the dry washing when Craig calls me. I realise I haven't even told him what's happened in the last few days.

"I'm so sorry to hear the news, darling," he says. "I literally just heard now."

"I'm sorry too, Craig," I say. "I should have called you. It's just been madness here." He tells me not to apologise and we talk about how surreal everything seems.

"But enough about me," I say. "How's it going with you? What happened about the script?"

"Oh, we can talk about that later. Don't stress about it now."

"No, it's a good distraction for me. I want to know."

"Well, she decided to go with us, and we exchanged contracts. But I just need a bit more cash to pay her the first instalment of her fee."

"I might be able to help. Can you wait a few more weeks?"

"The writer, she's a bit of a nightmare, to be honest. She said she'll go with someone else if we don't keep up with the payments."

I try to keep calm, but a rebellious, frightened gasp escapes my lips. Right now, there could be nothing worse than losing out on that script. I've read it a few times now and I'm sure it's the piece of gold I've been waiting for. A story that has drama, mystery, great characterisation, the kind of tale that could launch a career.

"No, we can't let her do that," I say. "We're going to make the film. I'll find a way."

A bride's jewellery is symbolic in many ways. It's emblematic of her status as a newly married woman, and then, throughout her life, of her husband being alive and well, beside her. It also, to some extent, indicates her wealth and status, in quite a brash and almost distasteful way, with many people choosing to cover themselves in layers of solid gold, clanking like chain mail, to show off exactly how much they could afford. It was so often all about amassing vast amounts of the yellow metal, instead of wearing something intricate and beautiful. The jewellery was worn once or twice, then shut away in a safe forever, because most importantly, it was an investment, a secret treasure to be used as an emergency fund in case of hardship.

Of course, I've never been so unsubtle and showy, and the necklace sets from my mother are delicately chased and engraved. However, the ones Mumtaz bought me are the opposite. Row upon row of ropes and disc pendants; large, ungainly flowers; chunky red and green stones. They're unattractive looking things, and I have no qualms about taking them to the jewellers to exchange for cash. The material value of the gold means more to me at this moment than the sentiment attached to it, and I have no husband to adorn myself with it for.

"Four thousand," says Mr Pratap, when I show him one of the necklaces with its matching earrings and ring. The shop is mirrored all over, walls, ceiling and floor. Mr Pratap wears a garnet-coloured suit with a jet shirt.

"The man next door told me six and a half," I fib. I negotiate with him some more, then settle on a figure. Mumtaz's gift was intended to provide me with security for difficult times, and now it will help to protect the future of her beloved grandson. The money should cover Craig's costs and finally set me on the path to the success that I crave.

I collect Zain from the Summer Holiday Club before going home. He goes there occasionally. It's held at the community centre and the children can go and do crafts and sporty activities. Zain loves it. The other mothers glance at me uneasily, smile and nod, but don't rush over and start talking to me like they once used to. It's still too early for them to judge how well I'm coping with my misery, in which direction to steer the conversation. Chatting with me is no longer a light and carefree discussion about kitchen extensions or *EastEnders* or sales at the Pakistani clothes boutique, seventy-five percent off designer *lawn* and *khaddar*. At least before people could ask me if we were any closer to finding Tariq, criticize the police, offer me some hope that it would be okay.

In addition to the social media sharing everyone took part in so excitedly, they made creative and absurd suggestions on how to hunt him down – hire a detective or a tracker dog, consult a psychic or a mystic, have the house cleansed of evil spirits, announce a please come home message on Punjab Radio.

But now it's a risky passage through tempestuous waters, strewn with dangers. Too frivolous or mundane and I might snap at their callousness. Worse still, go the serious route, ask how I am, mention Tariq and I might break down, have an embarrassing outpouring of tears right there in the playground. Nobody wants to be forced into comforting a frumpy young widow with an awkward hug or pat. I can understand it. And perhaps their fears aren't without reason. The thought of never seeing him again is like a clamp around my brain, a constant pressure. It wouldn't take much to make me cry.

Zain loves to make towers and buildings out of wooden blocks, and we spend the evening making a castle and then a bridge. I love to watch the concentration in his eyes and the delicate movements of his fingers as he carefully creates the structures. When the buildings are finished, we exchange smiles, and he knocks them over. I scoop him up to tickle him and he shrieks with laughter. It's perfect, just what I need to keep my mind off all recent events.

When he's calmer I get him a snack and myself a cup of tea, and settle down on the sofa to watch *Gigglebiz* on the telly. We're laughing at Dina Lady when there's a loud tinkling crash from the conservatory, like someone has tipped a bucket full of cutlery on to the floor. Zain, terrified, jumps up and hugs me.

"It's okay," I say, even though I'm shaking badly myself. I grab his hand and picking up a decorative globe to use as an emergency weapon, force myself towards the conservatory. It's usually my favourite room, bright, filled with gold on a sunny day, and I've decorated it with lots of patterned cushions, plants in colourful pots, mosaic topped tables and a tropical fish tank.

I put out an automatic arm to hold Zain back, before I even take in fully what's happened. It's not a brick through the window, but near enough. A couple of heavy garden tiles have been hurled through the old glass that's never been modernised to keep the character of the building, on the side by the aquarium. The floor is covered in a sparkling, jewelled composition of water, shards of glass, and, beautiful in their tones of vivid pink and blue and iridescent silvers and lilacs, dying fish.

* * *

I'm still trembling, and my mouth is suddenly dry, but I can't let Zain sense my fear. I pick him up and take him back into the living room. It's safer in there. I sit with him on the sofa, my arms wrapped around him tightly.

"Don't worry, darling, it must have been a stormy wind or something," I say. "Will you be brave and watch TV while I tidy up that mess?" He nods. I turn the television back on and tell him not to move from the room.

I get a torch and a hammer for protection from under the stairs and go to the back door in the conservatory, stepping over the wreckage of the aquarium, and step into the garden. I shine the light around but there's nobody. I don't want to go any further out with Zain in the house alone, and I go back inside, and clear up. I put the fish into a small compost bag for the bin collectors to take away. Tariq would probably have buried them in the garden, but I don't have the energy for another funeral. I ring the window company, make an emergency appointment for late evening, then get some thick sheets of card and tape them over the damaged area. I won't bother with contacting the insurance company – I'm not going to report the crime. I don't want the police round again. I've seen too much of them lately and I doubt they'll do much except give me home security advice.

Then I remember the woman I saw in the morning, who ran off when I noticed her. Did she come back and throw the tile through the window? I don't know. I just hope it's a one-off incident, an odd bit of vandalism by a lonely loony.

Now that the well-wishers with their prayers and pots of food have dwindled, Zain and I are finally getting back into our old routine. Mum offered to come and stay again, help me get through these first few days, but I prefer it this way, just the two of us.

In the evening the man from the window company comes

to repair the broken glass. Later, when Zain is in bed, I turn on the laptop and transfer most of the money from the jewellery sale into Craig's account. Then I go to a job-hunting website for actors. It's a constructive distraction. I need to get as much experience as possible if I'm to get anywhere. I note down a few possibilities, realistic projects for a beginner like me, mostly non-speaking parts, then send two or three emails asking for more details.

I take out a pot of cream from the dresser drawer, and scoop some out to slather over my feet. I've been struggling with dermatitis for a couple of years now. The skin on my feet is itchy, flaky and dry, and feels like it's on fire several times a day. The pigment has darkened, and the thick, greyish purple patches make it look like I'm wearing ankle socks made of elephant hide. For a few minutes the massaging soothes the inflammation.

Next, I turn my attention to security cameras. I'm not keen on calling the police but I have to do everything else I can to protect myself and my son. I couldn't forgive myself if anything happened to him because of my carelessness. I'm comparing prices when I hear a rattle at the front door. I stop breathing, listen, ears tuning into the silence. I hear it again. I glance at the clock on the computer. It's ten past ten. Leaving the hallway in darkness, I go to the kitchen and silently take out a knife and the rolling pin and walk to the front door. Dread hammering inside me, I put my eye to the peephole. The lantern is shining over the porch and the path up to the house is dimly lit. There's no one there. I peer closer, my eyes straining to see as wide a panorama as I can, then suddenly a figure comes into view from the left, head moving jerkily, trying to look in, and I gasp with relief. It's Jimmy Manzoor, Tariq's old friend, who lives in the house opposite ours.

I switch on the hall light so he can see it through the window at the top of the front door, then quickly trip back to the kitchen to put my weapons away.

"I hope I'm not disturbing you," says Jimmy, when I open the door. "I didn't want to ring the doorbell in case you were asleep, so I tapped on the window. I just thought I'd pop over and see if you're okay."

"Why don't you come in?" I say. I don't really want him to at this time of night but feel it might be impolite not to offer. He hesitates.

"It's not too late, is it?" he asks, but comes in anyway, and hands me a heavy shopping bag. "Just a few things for little Zain." I know he means well, and I'm touched by his generosity. I'm not the proud sort that misunderstands every little kind gesture following a catastrophe as pity or charity. I put the bag in the kitchen as Jimmy goes into the lounge, then I follow with a glass of orange juice for him. Jimmy's sitting on the edge of an armchair, not looking as comfortable as he normally does.

"I hope you don't mind," he says. "I felt it was my duty to see how you're doing. See if you need anything."

"That's really kind of you, Jimmy," I say. "Thanks. We're fine."

"How has Zain been? Does he say anything... about Tariq?"

"Not really. He has asked where he is a couple of times, but otherwise, not much. He's only six. I think he's still too young to process what's happened."

"He's only a kid. Look at me, even I can't process what's happened," says Jimmy. To my horror, the corner of his mouth wobbles, and a tear rolls down his cheek. He starts to flap his hand in a girly fashion. "I'm sorry. I'm sorry."

Tariq was a quiet, sensitive sort of a man, and although people were drawn to him, he didn't have many close friends. Jimmy was one of them. They'd been at school together and had kept the friendship up over the years despite going their different ways. Tariq had gone to university in Sheffield while Jimmy had done a mechanic engineering apprenticeship, soon turning his hand to buying, repairing and selling old cars. Now he dealt mostly in classic models, restoring them for collectors. Tariq had bought this house first, with Ruby, and when the property opposite had become available he'd encouraged Jimmy to buy it.

I wait politely for Jimmy's little episode to subside. I was expecting him to offer me some support, but he's the one that needs a reassuring hug. I feel awkward, and he senses it.

"I'm sorry. What a baby I am," he says. "I came here to help you out, listen to your feelings, but this is the other way round!" He laughs nervously, his eyes crinkling up. He does have quite an endearing way about him.

"You don't need to worry about me," I say. It seems like this is the only sentence I utter these days. "I pray... I'll get through it. I have my memories. He was a wonderful man."

I can see Jimmy hesitate for a split second, then he reaches across and takes my hand, giving it a little rub, before letting it go. I nod in companionable sorrow and wonder if I should tell him about the woman watching me, the smashed window? Not yet.

"What plans we were making!" says Jimmy. He's referring to the surprise party he and I were arranging for Tariq in the days before his disappearance. "It just goes to show we don't know what Allah has in store for us. What I don't understand is where he was for those weeks before this accident. Are the police doing anything to find out?"

"I don't think so. There wasn't anything suspicious about the accident so it's a fairly straightforward case to them. They won't be making any more enquiries regarding Tariq's movements."

"Don't you want to know the truth?"

Of course, I want to, I'll go mad otherwise, I don't understand anything, but I don't tell him this.

"I'm not sure I do, Jimmy," I say. "What if I can't take the truth?"

* * *

On Friday morning Zain and I go the butchers. It's the first time since the funeral. Mum stocked the freezer with plastic bags filled with portions for two, to save me trips to the shops, but they've run out. To my relief, Mr Ali, who is Turkish, chooses not to treat me any differently once he's offered his condolences, lapsing easily into the relaxed banter that he normally keeps up with his customers. It gives me a brief, refreshing glimpse of the life I might be able to return to, a moment of familiarity and balance in the contradictory world of my mind, that's a whirling chaos and a dead weight at the same time.

We stop off at the park on the way back. Although I'm glancing in every direction for any sign of the denim clad woman, or of any other threatening presence, Zain's bright eyes and loud, uncontrollable laugh as I spin him faster on the roundabout or push him higher on the swing are like a tonic for my anxious state. Looking up at him against the open blue sky, I know that whatever happens in this enormous, mercurial world, he and I will always be together, in a pure, unbreakable bond.

When we reach home, I enter warily as I always do now. I walk around the house quickly, reminding myself to sort out a burglar alarm. Nothing seems out of place. I put the shopping away quickly. I deliberately haven't bought too much so that I can go back to replenish my supplies soon. I need that contact with others, even if they are only shopkeepers and strangers.

I have a cup of tea, then take out Zain's Spiderman suitcase and pack him some pyjamas and three outfits. Amir will be here soon to take him home for the weekend.

He turns up after six, late as usual, tactlessly telling me that his pregnant wife, Jannat, has been uncomfortable and has swollen feet, and he had to spend a couple of hours making sure she was okay to be left alone, even though she'd been alone all day.

"I thought we could go to the museum tomorrow, if Jannat's

feeling okay," he says. "What do you think, little guy?" Zain nods and goes upstairs to get the Buzz Lightyear toy he goes to sleep with.

"Do you really think Jannat should be traipsing around a museum in this condition?" I say. "She might knock an exhibit over."

Amir shakes his head, but he can't help smiling, and I bite my lip, too.

"She's not going," he says. "I meant if she's okay to be at home by herself." He's quiet for a moment. "When are you going to get over it, Sophie? We've all moved on." Then he seems genuinely sad. "I still can't believe what's happened with Tariq. I thought you were happy at last."

"Yeah. Well. I was." I sniff and try to think of a different subject.

"I had a phone call," he says. My head shoots up. Not him, too.

"The police? What did they say?"

"They were just making a few 'routine enquiries'. I think they just want to make sure there was nothing sinister about Tariq's disappearance."

"What did they ask you?" I say. "What did you tell them?"

"They're coming to see me this evening," says Amir. "Don't worry, I won't say anything bad. I'll keep it simple. They don't need to know about our private life."

"Thanks," I say. "I appreciate it."

I hug Zain goodbye and go out to the car with them. It's an excuse to look around for any unwanted visitors, but the light is fading and corners and hiding places are darkening.

Inside, I walk around the house lighting lamps in different rooms, as though they're the atoms of my being stirring into life, alert and aware, waiting for the ambush. I must be vigilant. The plans I've woven are coming loose and I can't let them unravel.

* * *

I begin to think that the house is making me sick. As a new bride I had found it quaint and impossibly romantic. It's full of surprise nooks and crannies, with exposed brickwork and beams, flagged floors, and a landscaped garden with a pond full of koi. For our little family it had been a small paradise. Now, as I wander about alone, it seems hopelessly labyrinthine. Those same little corners have become macabre places for an intruder to hide. Once it surrounded me with warmth and safety and protection, now it swaddles me oppressively. I don't want to stay here any longer than necessary.

Tariq's solicitor rings me on Saturday morning, asking me how I'd like to proceed regarding his will. I say it'll be easier if I just go into his office. I don't want the hassle of him coming to my home. The thought of the will is just something else to make me feel queasy. A document of the dead.

I feel like spending the day in bed, letting myself be engulfed by my feelings, but I resolve to do anything but this. I give the house a quick security check, then I dust the rooms, clean the oven, mop the kitchen floor. When I've finished, I sit down and make a list of positive things that I must do to start rebuilding my life. The main issue is finding out the terms of the will, because this will have an effect on most of the other things, although there are smaller everyday tasks on there that I intend to tackle before then anyway, regardless.

Attend reading of will
Update CV
Send off CV
Search other job possibly?
Haircut
Look at houses and make list
Carwash
Food shopping
Make dentist appointment

Tariq was terrified of the dentist, but I don't mind a good old scrape with the hygienist, and crooked teeth and blotchy gums aren't a good look in my intended line of work. House and mind organised, I drive into town for a leisurely lunch in the coffee shop. Islamically, a new widow, like a newly divorced woman, must stay inside the house for three months unless she needs to go out for something necessary. Coffee shop visits aren't necessary, but I buy some butter and eggs, essential items, to justify the visit to town. The sun is beautiful and for the first time in weeks I feel relaxed as I sit outside with my panini and Aero milkshake, reading a celebrity magazine. It's full of self-promoting, attention-seeking fools but that's what they have to do to gain that measure of wild success. I can't help being fascinated by them, wanting what they have.

For a few minutes I'm lost again in these pleasant, achievable thoughts of a limitless future. I glance into the shop and through the glass I see a woman perched high on a stool like a vulture on a branch, staring at me as though hypnotised. She's wrapped a thin, crinkly scarf around her neck and pulled it up over her mouth and nose, obscuring her features, and is wearing a denim jacket. I think of the person creeping in the garden. Then I take in the large, thick framed sunglasses on her forehead and realise she's also the woman who was watching me in the clothes shop a few weeks ago.

I think about going in to talk to her, but an irrational fear takes hold and I grab my bag and dash down the street. I curse as I realise that I've parked the car in the multi-storey, and have to pay for a ticket to get out. I run to the machine, praying that there won't be a queue, looking behind me several times. There's no one else at the machine, and I scrabble around in my bag for the ticket and change. As I'm waiting for the machine to spit the ticket back out, I see her through the window of the heavy double doors, walking towards me, almost automatically, a veiled cyborg. Now I'm sure she's after me. There's a menacing purpose in her strides. I snatch the ticket and dash in and out of the parked cars till I find my black Renault Clio and drive off.

At home I'm shaking as I pour myself a glass of water and gulp it down, but then I slow my breathing down and tell myself I won't be a weak, quivering coward. It's not easy. The woman has unnerved me. It's too much of a coincidence. Her air of malevolent intent echoes the vindictiveness of the break-in. It must have been her.

Food is the last thing on my mind, but the preparation of it will bring a little order to the storm that's stirring around me. Suddenly I yearn for the comfort of hot buttery daal and rice and soak half a cup of yellow lentils in water. I think of Tariq, who loved daal with sour mango pickle and a blob of Greek yogurt. Others I know (Amir) relegate the humble staple to the bottom of the curry food chain, or even reject it entirely, but Tariq always gave it the respect it deserves. He was different to them, always special.

I can't afford to dwell on my loss again. I banish my memories and open my laptop.

No replies yet to the queries I made. I make a few small changes to my CV, then send off a few applications. "Dusky-skinned waitress for mango juice advert. Young mum in sofa superstore. Presenter for digital Asian channel, astrology programme. Diverse-faced shopper for background in supermarket promotion". Hmm. Been there, done that. I begin to relax, smile even, as I remember Zain's birth in the Tesco staffroom. It feels like a world away. The film never did make it to the big screen. The producers ran out of money before they could release it, and Chunky went back to India.

Applications done, I book an appointment at the hairdressers, and then cross the items off my to-do list. Enough for today. I ring Amir and speak to Zain. He's fine. I turn on the television and flick through the film channels. There's nothing interesting, and a load of weepies on the Hindi ones. I can't bear them. I take out my DVDs, hover between *Gone with the Wind* and *Sunset Boulevard,* and choose the latter. I put the daal on to cook, take out some pine nuts in their sooty black shells, and settle down on the sofa with the blanket. It does me good to escape into someone else's turbulent life for a couple of hours.

AMIR

I'm looking after the kids when the police visit. Jannat, who's suddenly feeling fine, has gone shopping. She doesn't take kindly to reminders of Sophie, and I know all this new attention she's getting won't go down well. I don't blame her, but I just try to keep the peace for Zain's sake.

I ask the police what they want to know.

"Just a general chat about Mrs Shah. Sophie," says the woman. Inspector McKenna, I think, or McKinley. "How long were you married for?"

"Three years."

"Happy?"

"Yes. I'd say happy."

"Yet you got divorced?"

"I didn't say it was perfect," I say. "We had a generally happy life, it was fine, but there were a few little problems, and things ended up getting out of hand."

"Was it an arranged marriage?"

"No. We were at college together."

"Childhood sweethearts."

I'm not really sure what they're up to, what they're investigating. Until I know I don't want to say too much. I wait.

"So, what happened?" she says. "What went wrong?"

"Sophie found it a bit difficult after our son was born, she used to get a bit snappy," I say, choosing my words carefully. "It was normal, but I wasn't the most understanding of husbands. Then my mother passed away and we were both under a lot of stress. One day we had an argument, and in anger I ended up divorcing her."

"You divorced her because of one argument?"

"I was angry. I didn't know what I was doing. It's possible to give an Islamic divorce on the spot, then carry out the paperwork afterwards."

"I'm afraid I don't know much about Islamic divorces. Do you mind explaining how it works?"

"Ideally the process takes place over three months, with the husband pronouncing the words of divorce once each time, in the presence of witnesses. In between each pronouncement the couple have the opportunity to settle their differences and reunite if possible. If there's no reconciliation, then after three months he says he divorces her for the third time, and it becomes final. However, if, like in our case, the husband says the words three times, all at once, usually in a fit of rage, the divorce still stands. There are differences in the opinions of scholars, but this is the most common ruling, and the one we chose to follow."

"So, an otherwise happy couple could have a sudden argument that could end up in a divorce?" asks McKinley.

"I suppose so, yes."

"Was your wife ever violent towards you?"

I'm surprised by the question, but I try to keep my face blank. I don't mention her erratic behaviour before and after the split, and what happened at my wedding to Jannat. Zain's my only concern, and he'll be affected if anything happens to Sophie.

"No," I say. "Sophie's not a violent person."

SOPHIE

I hope this is going to be a fruitful week. The will is going to be read today, and I've had an audition already, with another one lined up. I heard back from both the juice and the sofa advert people.

The sofa audition was a breeze. The role is for a furniture store customer. I thought I'd have at least one line, maybe asking the price, but all I have to do is linger in the background and press a mattress, whilst nodding ecstatically at my screen husband. I can't be fussy. Until the money comes through, I need the cash.

Mum insisted on coming with me to the reading of the will. I protested and said I would be fine, but she doesn't take no for an answer. I'm glad of it now. I'm a little daunted as I wander around the sleek glass building looking for the right office and it's comforting to feel her protective aura around me.

I've met Tariq's solicitor, Robert Morgan, once before, at a party with Tariq. He's friendly enough, a small, bald man with a wonky smile. He murmurs his condolences and asks me to sit down.

"We're just waiting for a couple more people to arrive," he says. It must be Tariq's sister-in-law, Sameena.

"What's the procedure for today, then?" I ask, to make conversation.

"Nothing very formal," says Robert. "I'll read the will and then answer any questions you might have. Can I get you a cup of tea while we wait?" I decline.

"Aah, here she is," he says as the door opens and Inspector McKinley walks in, followed by a man I recognise as one of Tariq's colleagues. My heart lurches. What is McKinley doing here?

"Hello, Sophie," she says. She's smiling but her eyes are ice hard.

"What a surprise," I say. "Is there something wrong?"

"I just wanted to make sure everything was done correctly, in view of what's happened. And to offer you some support, of course."

"Thank you."

"Mr Shah's son, Ayaan, won't be attending today. He'll be represented by Mr Shakeel," says Morgan. Mr Shakeel nods at me and smiles tightly.

Morgan puts on his glasses and looks at the papers in front of him.

"We'll start, then, if everyone's ready," he says. So, the terms of the will are fairly straightforward. First, a few charities and small bequests. A thousand pounds each to Cancer Research, Diabetes UK, and Imran Khan's cancer hospital. Three thousand to the Lone family in Karachi. Do you know about them?" I shake my head.

"Distant relatives, I think," says Morgan. "From his mother's side." I nod. "Hmm. Moving on. A sum of five thousand pounds to his wife, Sophie. The house and the rest of his money, to his son, Ayaan. As his legal guardian, his aunt Sameena has been appointed as his trustee until he turns eighteen."

"Sorry?" The word splutters from my mouth before I can control it.

"Tariq's left you five thousand pounds, Sophie. Everything else goes to Ayaan."

My stomach clenches. I could easily slide off this leather sofa

I'm sitting on and spill on to the floor, but I compose myself.

"Of course," I say. "It's how it should be. Ayaan is his son. It's his right." Mum reaches across and strokes my hand.

"Are you okay?" says McKinley.

"Of course, I'm fine."

My head is dull as Morgan goes over more formalities. It's not the money that cuts me, it's Tariq's deception.

At home Mum makes me tea and finds paracetamol.

"I can't believe Tariq's been so unfair," says Mum, sitting down with a mug too. "He was such a good man. Of course, in the end it was his decision and I respect that. I'm just very surprised. You should speak to Sameena. She might help."

"No," I say. "She hates me. I'm not going to ask her like I'm a pauper. And I don't want the children to be drawn into this. I can't take Ayaan's money."

"Mr Morgan said you should take legal advice; you might be able to prove you've been treated unfairly. And we should speak to an imam. See if the will follows Islamic guidelines."

"What must he have thought of me?" I say. "Not worthy of his money. Not to be trusted. I never realised that he didn't love me." Mum comes over and puts her arms around me.

"Of course he loved you," she says. But a few seconds later she draws away and looks at my face. "Unless there's something you're not telling me. Did something happen between you and Tariq? Something that made him do this?"

"No, Mum, nothing happened," I say. "Nothing that I can think of."

Mum reassures me that everything will work out for the best, and I send her home, telling her I'll be okay. When she's gone, I lie on the sofa, trying to soothe away the terror and the grief. How can Tariq have done this? The truth of our life has become a nebulous, elusive thing. If I'd know what he was thinking, I would never have done what I did.

PART THREE
SOPHIE AND TARIQ

TARIQ
2016

My first wife, Ruby, and I didn't have a flawless relationship. Who does? We squabbled sometimes, irritated each other occasionally, disagreed on politics and films. She was a devoted Shahrukh Khan fan, but I preferred the old actors, Dilip Kumar and Dharmendra. It was because of these irregularities, these mismatches in our characters that we fit together like bits of jigsaw.

We met at a work conference. We were both solicitors, so similar in one way at least. Ruby wasn't the most glamorous or confident woman there, but she had a beautiful luminosity about her face, and emanated a gentle radiance in her manner that drew you to her. We were put together for a group activity, and I couldn't stop staring at her when she was speaking about tax fraud.

I bravely took her contact details, in case I came across any other events she might be interested in. I couldn't believe my luck when another fair came up a month later. I emailed her and she turned up. Soon after she took me to meet her parents, and in six months we were married.

It was shortly after our fourth wedding anniversary, when our son Ayaan was two, that Ruby started experiencing stomach cramps. She put them down to indigestion. She was concentrating on an exam, and we'd been eating takeaways for a week. She'd taken maternity leave before Ayaan was born, planning to go back after a year, but had fallen so wholly into the role of being a mother that she was now thinking of setting up some kind of practice from home.

The doctor also put it down to indigestion. It wasn't until the pain was so bad that she went to A and E that they found the cancer. She died two weeks later.

It was a brutality that racked me to the core. I was in a state of disbelief for at least a year, functioning only to take care of my son and do the minimum at work. Ruby's family were generous with their help and kindness. It was her mother that first suggested that I "find somebody new". Although both her and her husband were bereaved too, their philosophy was to continue embracing life, to learn from the suddenness of Ruby's death. Rather than argue, I nodded and said, "Yes, maybe." The next day she sent me a picture of one of her distant nieces on WhatsApp. I stared at the screen, at the smiling girl, young, exuberant and happy. Pleasant enough. Then I hurled the phone away and cried myself to sleep.

"Please don't do that again," I told my mother-in-law later. Perhaps it was my tone of voice, but after that she never suggested anyone else to me.

The moments that hurt the most were small ones. Ayaan trying to make a tower of bricks, his brow furrowed in concentration. Dragging a chair into the kitchen to wash dishes in secret and getting completely soaked. Looking around sneakily before poking his fingers into the honeypot. Beautiful, everyday fragments of joy that I couldn't share with her, that would have brought out her husky, infectious laughter. I missed her so much.

As a permanently single father, you're the ultimate object of interest in the school playground, especially in our culture, where divorce is less common and extended families are abundant. Your domestic arrangements are open to speculation, inviting a range of madcap theories. So when Ayaan eventually started school, three years after Ruby's death, I preferred to keep quiet, a silence verging on the unfriendly, and no one at the school hazarded an enquiry into my unknown marital status. I offered nods and good mornings, and that was all.

There was one woman I noticed who was in some ways similar to myself. Usually alone, she never made much effort to talk to the others. She seemed forever lost in the depths of her thoughts. Some might accuse her of being haughty and isolating herself, but I considered it rather brave. I had a very brief exchange with her at Ayaan's class presentation evening.

She was pretty, if a little pinched, but I'd seen her laughing a few times with her son, and she seemed transformed, like the time I spoke to her in the supermarket. It was true that I'd seen her in that awful budget movie.

I gathered from Ayaan that Zain's dad had gone away, lived somewhere else. I didn't know what had happened, and there was no one I could really ask. Her enigmatic past, the unusual interest in acting, and her aura of *otherworldliness* all added to her mystique and sparked my curiosity. I could sense she had a story.

She smiled at me in the playground the next time we were waiting outside the boys' classroom. It was a little awkward, yet friendly and intimate at the same time, a secret acknowledgement of our little out of school meeting.

It was almost a month later that I spoke to her. I noticed her car was parked in front of mine as I walked back towards it with Ayaan. I'll admit I slowed my pace then, timing it so we were both unlocking the doors at the same time. A pot of lip balm fell out of her pocket as she took the keys, and it rolled towards me.

"How have you been?" I asked, handing it back to her.

"Fine, thanks," she said. "You?"

"Yeah, you know. You must be looking forward to half term."

"Zain will be with his dad, so I'll have a few days to myself."

"Sorry to hear you're not with his dad." I pause awkwardly. "I don't know, is that the right thing to say?"

"It's fine. It's just one of those things, isn't it?"

"Yeah." She's shared a little of her life and it encourages me to do the same. "My wife... she died. Almost three years ago now."

She gasped ever so slightly.

"Oh..."

"It's okay. And you don't need to say sorry now, too."

We smiled at each other sadly.

I learnt more about her from the only source I was brave enough to question. Ayaan. I realised how desperate I sounded trying to find a love life through my four year-old son, but I didn't really know what I was trying to do. I was still despondent and grieving but I couldn't help becoming intrigued by the new and unknown.

I gleaned dismally little about her from Ayaan, just the roughest scraps of Chinese whispered information.

"So, how's Zain?" I asked innocently.

"Okay," said Ayaan, as he connected the pieces of a toy train track together.

The poor child wouldn't sense the bluntness of me asking about Sophie directly, but I couldn't do it out of self-respect and perhaps a little guilt. I had to make at least some effort at disguising my queries, even if it was only from Ayaan. There was also the smallest possibility that Ayaan might mention my questions to someone else.

"What did he have for lunch today?" Perhaps I would learn something about her from the contents of her son's packed lunch.

"School dinners," said Ayaan.

A few days of this pathetic, fruitless behaviour and I gave up. I don't know why I was drawn to her. She was attractive, yes, but it was more the mystery. She seemed closed, but interesting and, strange though it sounds, it excited me to be able to unlock her thoughts.

Eventually, I plucked up the courage and asked her if she wanted to take the boys out somewhere at the weekend. I could see the hesitation on her face, and I knew what she was worried about. She didn't want to be seen by anyone who knew us, and there was a good chance we would be if we went out.

"We could go out of town if you wanted to," I suggested. "Or you could come to my house. We could sit in the garden." She was weighing it up, probably considering the possibility of being bored out of her mind for a whole day if we went to Flamingo Land and I turned out to be a complete fool. She agreed to the home visit, from where she could make an easy escape if necessary.

SOPHIE
2016

It took a few weeks of me gazing soulfully at trees and clouds before Tariq invited me to his house using the pretext of a play date for the boys. I didn't care where we went as long as I could spend some time with him. Theme parks and bowling alleys were loud and bright, full of teenagers and bawling kids. An afternoon at his house, stretched out on the lawn or on a cosy sofa with a cup to tea would be much more intimate.

I wondered about him. He was one of the only two or three good-looking dads in the playground, always well dressed in discreetly expensive clothes, and I couldn't help noticing he drove a luxurious looking Mercedes S-Class. Above all, I'd picked up on the odd wayward glances that he gave me.

His house, when Zain and I visited, proved to be a big detached property with a huge garden, where we sat with our tea and cake and a plate of pakoras that he confessed to having bought from the takeaway. The boys played and Tariq and I talked about everything.

When he told me about his wife it was touchingly sad. It was evident from his tender manner when he spoke of her that they'd been passionately in love. Her loss had reduced him into a frail being, desperate for the healing touch, something that I was readily available to provide.

I told him about both Amir and Faraz. He'd find out soon

enough, and I preferred him to hear my version of events first. Amir was a rough, unfaithful man and Faraz a liar who had duped me. Tariq added more pathos to his own story by telling me that his parents were killed in a car crash when he was seventeen.

He was even more handsome close up, with an almost studious look. He emanated poise, grace and sensitivity. A gentleman to his bones, with a quiet, witty humour. I felt a familiarity towards him. It was all happening impulsively, but he was so perfect, that there was no room for doubt. A diamond after those dull, lacklustre men.

The boys were playing hide and seek, and I thought it would be nice to show Tariq that I had an affinity with kids, enjoyed messing around with them.

"Can I have a turn hiding too?" I called out to them. "You count, Zain." It would give me an opportunity to be a bit conspiratorial with Ayaan, spark up a friendship. Zain covered his face to count to twenty, and I let Ayaan lead me by the hand to a little space behind the shed that I could squeeze into, whispering and giggling along the way. Zain found me a minute later, and the game turned into one of chasing each other around, laughing and squealing. It was happy and natural, and Tariq joined in too.

He asked me to marry him two months later.

I took a gentler approach to telling Mum and Dad the news this time. Mum was tidying the kitchen and Dad was at the table doing a crossword. I skimmed through the clues, thinking my contribution of an answer might soften him, but I couldn't come up with one.

"I wanted to talk to you about something," I said. "But please, hear me out, and don't get upset." I told them briefly how we'd met at the school and that he was a widower with a son the same age as Zain.

Dad surprised me by showing some enthusiasm. It seemed he already knew of Tariq through a friend of a cousin.

"A sterling fellow!" he gushed. "I've heard he's done a lot of good work with refugees. And getting permanent stays for the elderly. You know, the parents from Pakistan that want to join their children over here." He gave me a hug. "Well done, *beta*, this is more like it. If he can't keep you steady, I don't know what will."

"Are you out of your minds?" shouted Mum. "The ink on her divorce papers isn't even dry yet! She's treating the whole thing like a game." She was almost panting with anger. She muttered under her breath, but we heard her say, "Taking the piss!" Dad and I looked at each other in shock, then supressed a giggle.

"Mum, I admit last time it was a mistake," I said.

"Your behaviour doesn't do much for our reputation, but I don't even care about that. All I'm worried about is Zain. None of this is good for him." She bent over and opened the washing machine and pulled the clothes into the basket. She banged the door shut and stood up.

"Look. I'll support you on one condition," she said. "Let Zain stay here for a while, with us. Just for a few weeks, while you settle down. You can see him whenever you want."

"I don't think that's a good idea, Mum," I said. "More instability and confusion are the last thing he needs." She wasn't happy, but she didn't say anything else.

A week later, Dad forced Mum to invite Tariq over for dinner. It was like watching a bag of peas slowly defrosting. Mum began serving the meal with a cold, solid, blank expression, setting down the kofte and biryani without looking at Tariq directly.

"What is it you like about Sophie?" asked Mum, when we'd started eating.

Tariq broke a piece of naan in half slowly and glanced at me.

"I think it would have to be her courage," he said. "She's not afraid to stand alone, to do what's right for her. I admire that." I smiled, embarrassed and humbled at the compliment, and how he'd seen the truth of who I was.

"Great answer!" said Dad. He pushed a plate of tandoori drumsticks towards Tariq and flashed his eyes at Mum. "Let's enjoy the dinner. We can do the interrogation later." But she wasn't giving up.

"What about Zain?" she said. "How do you feel about that situation? I understand you have a son of your own." Tariq had left Ayaan with his grandparents from his wife's side for the evening.

"Yes, they're the same age," said Tariq. "If I assured you that I'm going to be Zain's perfect father, and it'll be easy, you wouldn't believe me, and you'd be right not to. All I can say at this point is that I'll do my best to make the situation work, to keep Sophie and Zain happy. There will be challenges, of course, but there are in every marriage."

Tariq's honesty and simple straightforwardness worked their magic on Mum, and she ended the evening with a warm smile as she poured him an extra helping of custard with the apple crumble.

SOPHIE
Present Day

Following the reading of the will, a bunch of flowers is delivered later in the afternoon, a fiery mix of oranges and reds. There's a card tucked in amongst them.

"Heartfelt sympathies. Faraz."

Hmm. It's a kind gesture. I take them into the kitchen and arrange them in an enamel jug. Roses and gerberas, romance and fun. Faraz can't know how much he's helped me right now, in this moment, to cheer my mind and stop it from reeling. Today's been a complete shock, but I can't let myself crumble. I'm not only bereft, I'm humiliated and hurt. What can I have done to make Tariq feel like this, to feel so strongly as to deceive me about his will? I don't know what to do.

I'm contemplating all this when the doorbell trills madly, and I'm startled. I look through the peephole and click my tongue. It's Inspector McKinley.

I offer her the customary drinks and she accepts a plain green tea. I don't have the patience to dabble with finicky brews today. I take out some biscuits, ginger nuts and Nice and take them in. McKinley is sitting with a photo album open on her lap.

"Small wedding," she says.

"It was just the family, and a few of Tariq's friends," I say. She lingers over the page, staring at the images hungrily.

"Your tea," I say, but she nods towards the table, so I put the tray there.

"My fiancé's Gujarati," she says. "We're having two ceremonies, one Hindu and one in the church. November. I can't wait."

"That's really nice."

"I love your dress. Is there anywhere you'd recommend? I don't know anything about Asian fashion or weddings or anything." Without realising, my eyes run over her figure.

"I'm not exactly svelte, I know," she says. "Anything that fits! Us fatties need to stick together." Speak for yourself, I feel like saying, but instead I grit my teeth and smile. She suddenly flips the album towards me.

"What happened to the picture?" she says.

It's me, caught unawares there, just as I am now. I'm smiling deliriously, talking to a figure in a dark suit, whose head has been ripped off. Tariq.

"Tariq did it," I say. "He hated having his picture taken. When he saw it, he tore it up."

"Who took the photo?"

"I don't know. Probably my brother. He likes to play pranks on people. He must have taken it without Tariq knowing."

"Why not throw away the whole picture?" She's trying to be clever, and although I'm cautious, she's unsettling me.

"He didn't want to feed me to the shredder," I say.

"I thought you just said he ripped it up."

"He did. It was just a joke, about the shredder."

"A metaphor? I always get mixed up with metaphor and simile."

"Right. Easy mistake," I say, fighting the urge to roll my eyes.

"So, which is it? Metaphor or simile?"

"I don't think it's either, really. Maybe a bit of a metaphor." I can't bear this absurd small talk any longer. "Why did you come?"

"I wanted to see if you were coping," she says.

I sniff.

"God forbid that you ever experience anything like this," I say. "The death of a partner... I can't begin to describe the horror of it."

"I meant the money," she says, watching me.

"Pardon?"

"The situation with the will. Why do you think your husband left you out of the will?"

"He didn't."

"Five thousand pounds? It's nothing for a man like him."

"Well, he's left it to his son. I can understand that, as I'm sure can you."

"Yes, but still," she persists. "There must be a reason."

Suddenly tears begin to puddle in my eyes.

"I don't know," I whisper. "We had the usual arguments, but nothing serious. Do you think it's a mistake? Can anything be done?"

"You'll have to speak to your solicitor. It's a long process, but something might be possible." She puts the book down on the coffee table. "Do you want to tell me anything, Sophie? This is a good time, you know. Before things get too complicated."

So many invitations to divulge secrets. First Mum, now this Inspector. There's nothing I want to tell her, either.

FARAZ

I'm in the middle of a Skype session with Mother when the doorbell rings. Since I split with Sophie my parents have forgiven me, and Mother is once more persuading me to find a wife. She's constantly showing me pictures of girls or recommending I meet daughters of her UK contacts. It's a sore point with her that even Muskaan got married a few months ago to a Pakistani doctor from England and is settled over here now. I don't want to stress about finding a new woman – I have someone in my thoughts already. Besides, I am concentrating on building my business now. Father gave me a large sum after he sold off some land that he'd invested in, and I managed to get the business visa. I'm determined to prove myself a worthy son to him.

The doorbell rings again and I look through the window. It's a sophisticated looking lady, with a smart, professional style. If I was a nitwit with a wild imagination, I might hope she's come to make my dreams come true. But no, there's an unmistakably official air about her. Maybe she's just a spruced-up charity worker. Whatever it is, she must be trying to sell or persuade or recruit, and I don't want to open the door. I hastily say goodbye to Mother and shut the laptop so that the room is flicker free in case she peeps through the window.

My trick of keeping quiet to get rid of the woman at the

door doesn't work, for she presses the buzzer again, loudly. It's so noisy and insistent that I quickly open the door just to shut her up.

"Mr Baig?" says the lady.

"Yes, indeed," I say. I have no reason to deny my identity. "And your good name is?"

"Inspector Lisa McKinley, West Yorkshire Police." Oh my God. I take a sharp breath, then quickly try to disguise it with a cough.

"I'd like to talk to you, please," she says. "Can I come in?"

"What do you want to talk about?" I say. "Do I need a lawyer?"

"It's really nothing to be worried about, Mr Baig," she says. "It's just a few questions about your wife, actually. Ex-wife."

"Sophie? Is she okay? What's happened?"

"She's fine, Mr Baig. There's nothing for you to worry about. May I?"

I lead her into the living room of the flat I'm sharing with a friend. Even though he's a lazy slob I like to keep the place tidy, and I hoovered in here this morning.

"Can I get you a cuppa?" I ask.

"A glass of water will be fine, thank you," says Officer McKinley. She sits down and I pass her a cushion. She accepts it so I pad her with a few more and am just unfolding a blanket for her but she raises her hand.

"It's cosy on the sofa with this," I explain.

"I'm sure it is, Mr Baig, but I'm not here for a slumber party," she says. I get her water and sit down on the armchair.

"You must have heard about Sophie's recent tragedy," she says.

"Yes, yes, of course," I say. "Even though I'm not in contact with her anymore. It was very sad. Poor Sophie." I don't mention that I sent her some flowers yesterday. She wouldn't understand. Instead, I would look like a hopeless and desperate fool. "I thought it was all over."

"Yes, almost. There are just a few things I need to tie up before I can officially close the case."

"Anything I can do, Inspector. In fact, I'm actually feeling quite thrilled to be having this conversation with you. A real lady police. What would you like to know?"

"Let's start with your relationship with Sophie," she says. "When did you meet?"

"It was four years ago last month. We met through a matrimonial service, online."

"Like internet dating?"

"Sort of, for Muslims only. We don't believe in loose relations, so the intention is always to find a person for marriage."

"I see. An admirable intention indeed." She really looks like she means it. "So, Sophie was on this site?"

"Yes."

"So how does it work? Do you meet at the mosque or something?"

Really, the naivety.

"No. Dear me!" I say. "We just went for coffee, like regular daters."

"Alone? Or with her whole family?"

"Alone, Inspector. Ideally, yes, we should have a chaperone, but we're not babies. It was a busy place. I wasn't going to attack her. Or vice versa!"

"That's an amusing thought, Mr Baig. Did the families know you were seeing each other?

"Not at that point. We both knew our families would get upset."

"Why was that?"

Oh dear. Bigamy, in any form, is not something to be confessed to the police.

"My Mother, you know," I say, shrugging my shoulders. "She wanted to find me a bride herself, in Pakistan. I was going to be the first to get married in the family. She had her personal hopes for me."

"And Sophie's family?" she says. "Were they happy with her decision to marry you?"

"Not really. They thought it was too soon after her divorce, especially for little Zain. Plus, they thought I was a fraud, only marrying her for a passport."

"Were you?"

"No!" I'm surprised myself when it comes out like an aggressive shout. "No. I loved Sophie, and I tried my best to treat Zain like my own son. Ask anyone. I'll admit, of course it was an advantage for my visa extension. But I always intended to be loyal to my darling. It just wasn't to be."

I look away from her. I feel like crying but thank God no tears come flooding into my eyes.

"So, what happened?" she asks, a moment later.

"No major thing happened, Inspector. Sophie just didn't think we were suited. She asked me for a divorce."

"And you were happy with that? You agreed?" she says. I can't tell her I hated her decision and wouldn't have done it if she hadn't blackmailed me into it.

"I wasn't happy, no, but I wanted to do what was best for Sophie."

"And what about Tariq? What did you think of him?"

She's caught me off guard with this question and I answer without thinking.

"I never had a chance to meet the deceased, but I've heard good reports." I realise too late the police have ways of checking these things, but I don't want to change my statement. The lady seems satisfied, and says I've been very helpful.

When the Inspector leaves, I go back to the laptop, and open up a page that I've been visiting very frequently lately. It's a house for sale on Rightmove. It's not Sophie and Tariq's house, but it's on the same road, and I think it must be a similar size and layout. I like to look at it, imagine how her life is inside it, how she moves from room to room. The floor plan page is my favourite and helpful for this too. I've been doing a lot of this kind of thing recently. Looking at the house, checking her Facebook and Twitter, even looking at her husband's business website. He's gone now, poor man, and I am sad about that part of it, but I can't help it. I can't stop either. I can't get her out of my head.

SOPHIE

I don't know how long I have. It's true that I'm scared of Sameena, Tariq's sister-in-law. She's never really liked me and once she finds out the power she has now, she'll be itching to get her hands on the house. I should start looking for somewhere else to live straight away. I can't believe I'm in this situation yet again. The telephone rings.

"How did it go?" It's Suleiman. I tell him what happened at the will reading.

"What?" He's incredulous. "He turned out to be a nasty piece of work."

"Please, Suleiman!" I defend Tariq automatically. "He's still my husband. Dead husband. I don't want to hear it."

"You've finally learned to be faithful, eh?" he says. "Bit too late, isn't it? Well, whatever, that's your personal life. We need to talk business. Open the door."

"What?"

"Open the door. I'm outside." The doorbell rings. I turn off the phone and let him in. He's wearing jeans today, with a baseball cap. He walks into the kitchen and gets a plate, then goes into the living room and sits down. He opens the box of Krispy Kreme doughnuts he's brought with him and takes out a salted caramel one.

"Can I tempt you?" he asks me.

"No thank you," I say.

"So. The situation has changed. I need to make a little trip abroad. I got a tip on a Columbian goldmine."

"What's it got to do with me?" I say.

"Stop playing dumb, will you? It doesn't suit you. When can you get the money?"

"I just told you, he's left me with nothing."

"Five thousand, you said."

I want to throw my hands around his fat neck and throttle the nefarious life out of him. I'm speechless at his depraved, blind hunger.

"What do you want, Suleiman?" I say. "You want to put me and Zain out on the street?"

"Why would I want that? I care about you both," he says, chomping on the doughnut. The cake splits and the gooey caramel splatters and dribbles down his chin. I don't think I'll be able to eat Krispy Kremes ever again. "Remember how we said I'm not Amir's real uncle?"

"Yes," I say. "But what's that got to do with anything? And I'm not playing dumb. It's a genuine question."

"Well, I was thinking..." He stops. He actually looks tongue-tied, embarrassed, almost shy.

"What?" I say. "How about you cut to the chase?"

"There's another solution." He pauses. "How about you and me?"

"You and me?" I really don't want to know what he means.

"Look, it's tragic, what's happened to you, I get that. It's going to take a long time for you to get over it. But the fact is you're alone now. You need support, companionship, comfort. You can't spend the rest of your life by yourself. I'm unattached, looking for someone too. I know I'm a bit older than you, but that doesn't matter. This could be the perfect solution to all our problems."

"Don't be ridiculous, Suleiman," I say.

"I know what you think of me, you've heard stories, but I assure eighty percent of them are lies. I admit, yes, I have a chequered past, but really, I'm not a bad man. I'll treat you like a queen. I've changed a lot. I'm even thinking about getting a job."

"You won't find a vacancy for blackmailer in the local newspaper."

"I'm serious, Sophie. Think about it. You'll get some stability, especially for Zain. Accept the offer and I promise to forget you ever bumped into poor Mumtaz on those fatal steps. Otherwise, our present arrangement could go on forever. And catch me on a bad day, well you never know who I might have a little chat to. The police. Your parents. Craig. It'll certainly add a bit of spice to your media profile."

What does he know about Craig? I'm shattering inside but I won't break in front of him. I keep my voice steady.

"You should go," I say.

"Sleep on it and we'll talk about it tomorrow," he says. "Remember, say yes and I press the delete button." He leaves, and I lock the door behind him, double, triple bolts and the chain as a final precaution. I wish I had something more, something that could guarantee absolute safety.

I prowl around the kitchen, flinging spoons and forks into the sink, slamming boxes of leftover dinner into the fridge, seething at what's just happened. Now that he's gone fear has been overtaken by fury, but still a faint, insistent voice tells me to think of things rationally.

I check in on Zain, then go into my own bare, soulless bedroom. The shabby chic postcards smile down at me with gentle, malicious mockery. Staid, not-a-hair-out-of-place ladies that lead respectful, unblemished lives, unlike mine. I can't bear it, I rip them off and throw them into the bin, cracking the glass in one of the frames. I think about going to Homebase tomorrow and looking for some new wallpaper, but then the horrific truth strikes me. This is no longer my home. Borrowed time. I have days to sort myself out, a month at the most.

I lie on top of the bed without changing my clothes, bury my face in the pillows, half hoping they'll swallow me up, suck me out of this warped world gone wrong. Suleiman's offer disgusts me, tarting himself up as my saviour – from himself. It's a sly ruse to gain complete power over me. But I can't ignore his "promise". If he keeps his side of the bargain, at least I won't be forced to make those never-ending payments. Being more or less cut out of Tariq's will means I have nothing. Even though I benefit from the life insurance, I'll need the money to help me with the cost of a flat, and for general living expenses. I can't fritter it all away on making amends for an old mistake.

But the thought of marriage to him makes me queasy. I shudder to think of him at my table at breakfast and dinner – I presume he'll eat lunch at this job he's so confident of getting. I can't even contemplate the idea of him touching me, even with just a fingertip, let alone him sliding into my bed, his large, squelchy bulk pressing up against me.

Most of all, though, is the fact that Suleiman has overstepped the mark this time. Before now the deal had been simple. My money for his silence. But today he hinted that he could let the secret slip at any time if he felt like it, and it's broken the perverse, twisted trust there was between us. If he speaks, everything will be finished for Zain and me, and that I can't allow.

The questions and calculations twitch here and there, something forms and vanishes, my head hammers, hums, fine tunes, then finally, it's left with a single thought.

It's Saturday morning, two days after Suleiman's visit. Zain is at Amir's for the weekend. I'm in two minds about whether or not to pack a picnic for the date I'm orchestrating. Do I really want to go the whole ostentatious hog by making an elaborate ritual out of it? I know I won't even be hungry. These days a bit of Weetabix and a cup of tea in the morning are enough to last me until dinner time. I've lost half a stone in the last month. At least this despondency is doing me some good.

But I have a nice long hike planned for Suleiman, amongst other things, and it can be tiring, so it's best to be well prepared.

"You're right," I say to him on the telephone. "It is worth thinking about. But I'd like to meet your ordinary, moral side first, before deciding on anything, if you don't mind."

"Absolutely," says Suleiman. "No pressure at all." I'm amazed at how he's suddenly transformed, his sharp serpentine tongue softened to whisper a lover's promises.

"Do you want me to speak to your parents?"

"No," I say. "Not them, not yet. They'll only create more obstacles. Let's just get to know each other properly. Why don't we spend some time together today, if you're not busy?"

"Fantastic!" He's almost childish in his excitement. "What time shall I come over? Do you want me to bring anything? It's been a very long time since I did anything like this."

"I thought we could go out," I say. "I need to get out of this house."

"You mean to the cinema? Or go for a Chinese or something?"

"The weather's lovely today. I was thinking somewhere like Bolton Abbey."

"Bolton Abbey?" The puzzled awe in his voice suggests outdoor pursuits are an alien concept to him. He probably hasn't been to a park in decades. "It's not really my cup of tea…"

"I thought I'd bring a picnic."

"But I'm game to try anything once. What time?" The lure of the late lunch has worked.

I tell him to meet me in a couple of hours and go and poke around in the freezer to see if I can find anything to heat up and take with me. I'm not going to fuss around with any foody frippery. There's a packet of shrivelled samosas shivering in the corner of the top shelf. They're probably past their sell by date but it doesn't matter. I don't check. If I don't know I can't be blamed for stomach upsets. I heat up the oil in the deep fryer and toss the possibly expired pastries in. The phone rings again. It's Suleiman.

"I just wanted to ask what the dress code is," he says. "I don't want to look too casual, but a suit might be too much if we're just going for a walk."

I almost feel sorry for him. He really wants this to work. I tell him to wear a suit if he wants and go back to wrapping the samosas in foil. I make a few cheese sandwiches, then take out two packets of crisps and one of chocolate digestives and stuff everything into a nondescript rucksack. I'm not in the mood for hampers and cooler bags. They belong to another era of my life, one of romance and enchantment.

I put on jeans and a top with a maxi length cardigan over it, as well as a baseball cap and a new pair of sunglasses. I've never worn the cap before and hope it'll be an effective disguise. I really don't want anyone to recognise me. They'll only talk. I slip on a pair of flipflops and put some boots into another bag. It's a warm day and the heat will make the skin on my feet itch more if they're shut up in shoes for too long.

I leave the car half a mile from the park and walk. It's a perfect day, warm yet crisp, and the fresh air does me good. I think back to all the long walks I've ever taken. Amir wasn't really one for that sort of thing once the honeymoon period was over, didn't see the point of wandering and ambling aimlessly, unless it was necessary for getting from A to B.

Faraz had made a conscious effort to go on walks, the most concerted being the trip to London, when we'd made a late-night sojourn around Piccadilly and Oxford Street. The breathless exhilaration of the place had averted my attention from the fact that he was continuously tickling my palm and humming Indian songs under his breath.

Tariq, though, had got it right. He'd never taken me out on a special walk, but when we had been side by side, even if it was just out shopping, there'd always been an effortless entwining of fingers, gentle, yet firm and reassuring.

And now here I was, alone once again, on my way to discuss marriage with a man who until now was bent on gathering up all the wretched scraps of my mangled life, not to mend them back together but to gloat over them, like a haul of looted trophies.

I told Suleiman to meet me by the paved barbecue area, which is near the river's edge. I'm not intending to grill anything here, but the spot is good for picnics. There's an older Sikh couple there, cooking something on a camping stove. Now and then the woman twitches her face or moves her head, and the man automatically passes her something from the folding table they've set up, a jar or a bottle or a vegetable, in a silent, mutually instinctive, almost dance-like pattern. The worn in, comfortable expression on her face suggests this is an old routine, evolved from a lifelong relationship.

The woman bothers me. I think I've seen her somewhere before, but I can't place her. I consider moving somewhere else, but I've already laid out the blanket and food, and I'll be even more noticeable if I pack everything up again. Suleiman appears, dressed in cream cords and a brown jumper with a picture of a Yorkshire terrier on it. He has a trench coat over his arm.

"Hello, I'm not late, am I?" he says, not daring to lean over and offer any kind of physical greeting.

"It's fine. I just got here," I say. "Will you be okay sitting on the floor?" He doesn't look happy, but he lowers his bulk on to the rug, wincing as he lands. "Did you drive?"

"Got a cab. Don't drive these days, gives me a headache, all that concentration," he says, helping himself to a sandwich. "Oops! Is it okay to start?"

"Knock yourself out," I say. I slide the box of samosas over and plonk the bottle of tamarind chutney down next to it.

"Yummy," he says. "Now, Sophie, I don't care what you say. Tariq turned out to be a real scoundrel. How could he cut your inheritance like that?"

"Please," I say. "It really is the worst hypocrisy, Suleiman." He has a point, but still.

"Yes, well, at least I'll admit I have a few villainous traits. But I'm not pretending to be anything else. Anyway, we're here to talk about other things. Let's not spoil it." I don't say anything and look at the river instead. It's beautiful today, so shallow that it's skimming over the wide boulders in the bed, bathing them in a glistening sheen. There's a row of steppingstones from this side to the other. Most of the families are on their way out now, but there are still four or five teenagers on the rocks trying to make the crossing, shin deep in water.

"Shall I start?" says Suleiman. "I mean, it's not as though we're strangers, so we can skip the formalities." He sighs and examines a piece of samosa pastry he's broken off. "I wasn't always this... well... bent, you know. I was an ordinary man, once, with morals."

I can't believe it. He wants to philosophise, rationalise, take me on an emotional, psychological journey that explains how he became the damaged individual that he is today. I want to laugh, but I let him talk.

"I married Deeba when I was young, twenty-one. We'd been here in England five or six years, then. My father had brought my mother and the four of us, my brothers and I, from Pakistan. My mother arranged the marriage. Deeba was nice-looking. We didn't look beyond that, in those days. Our parents said the girl was from a good family, and if we liked the look of the photo, that was it. We said yes.

"We had fun at first, for two or three years, but once you're settled it becomes boring, doesn't it? Those everyday pressures, working like a slave to pay the bills, no time for anything else. I had my dreams, and I tried my best to get them. I was thinking of my kids, too. The investments, the gambles, the get rich quick schemes, it was all to achieve something. I never studied properly. My brain wasn't made for that. It was all I knew to do, use my charm and cleverness in a different way. I didn't set out to dupe people, but it just ended up like that. I just wanted one thing to work out, be a success, and I'd go back and fix things, everyone that I'd hurt on the way. Nothing ever did, not in time, anyway. Deeba left me; the kids hate me. Now here I am, all alone. Well, here we are."

"It must be destiny," I say. Despite my sarcasm, I realise they're honest words. I see him for something other than the greedy, smarmy man who usually has desperation dripping off him.

"But don't worry, I've got a bit stashed away, enough to keep us going," says Suleiman. "Some of my gambles did pay off eventually, a couple of them thanks to your donations, I might add. Who knows what else we could do together?"

"Yeah, we're quite the Bonnie and Clyde, aren't we?" I say. He laughs heartily.

"That's what I love about you, Sophie. You're hilarious," says Suleiman. "But seriously, we could do anything, set up a business, anything you like. What about all this acting lark? Are you serious about it?"

I don't really want to tell him, but it's been so long I talked to anyone about my dreams, that I give in.

"Yeah, I am," I say. "Go on, laugh, like everyone else does."

"Why would I laugh? If that's what you really want, you should go for it."

"Well, thanks. For the encouragement."

"It could really work, you know," he says, excited, now. "I know you're working with that Craig, but I've got contacts too. Not Hollywood or anything, but I do know a few production companies. They make those Pakistani dramas. And there's another guy, he's the artistic director for an Asian theatre company. He might be able to give you some tips."

"That would be good, thanks." My adversary, out of all people, is offering to help me achieve my goals. Bizarre.

"I could even be your manager," says Suleiman. I frown at him. "Just a thought." He pauses. "I've always admired you, you know. Ever since we made our little pact together. Not the most auspicious of beginnings, I know. But you were already married to Amir, then there was Faraz. That happened so quickly, I didn't get a chance to make a move. He was a wimp, but he loved you, anyone could see that."

"No, he didn't!" I say. "You don't know the truth! Faraz was a con artist."

Suleiman waves my plea away.

"Then you found Tariq," he says. "He fell for you, too. And he had money. I wasn't only impressed, I really was jealous. You really did have everything. I would sit there, thinking about you sometimes... jealous, angry... sometimes I thought it was bad enough to make me kill someone..."

His words have winded me, given me a sickening feeling in my stomach.

"What did you do?" I say, almost in a whisper.

"What are you talking about?" says Suleiman.

"Tariq. Who else do I care about?" I say, my voice raised now.

The barbecue couple look over at us. They're tucking into naan and chicken and corn on the cob. The woman looks concerned. I smile at her, wave reassuringly.

"Keep your hair on, dear," says Suleiman.

I dig my nails into my palms. I can't let myself touch him. Not now. I lower my tone.

"Tell me what you did to him."

The woman gets up and wanders over.

"How are you?" she says, with a guarded smile. I recognise her now. She was at the audition for the sofa advert I went to a few days earlier, reading for the same part I auditioned for. I bend my head slightly, so the peak of my cap obscures my face.

"Fine, aunty!" sings Suleiman. "Enjoying barbecue?" She ignores him.

"Are you okay? Nice weather, naa?" she says to me.

"Yes, very," I say. "We're fine, thank you." She nods, understanding that I don't need her, and goes back to her husband. Hopefully she hasn't recognised me. I didn't speak to her at the audition, and my face had been fully made up with red lips, contoured cheeks, false eyelashes, and my hair had been long and flowing. Today I'm bare faced, eyes hidden behind sunglasses, hair scraped under the cap.

"You really must think I'm a sick bastard!" says Suleiman, snapping me out of my reverie. He seems genuinely offended. "You think I killed him so I could marry you? Maybe we should forget this whole thing. Let's do the sums and go home."

"No, I'm sorry," I say. "I don't know what I was thinking. Of course you didn't do anything to him. I just don't know what to think, what to feel."

He looks at me for a moment, then leans across. I tense, but to my relief he just pats my hand and backs away. I give him a dismal smile. A bird of prey glides across the turquoise sky. A buzzard, I think, out to kill.

"Shall we go for a walk?" I say.

"I came prepared!" he says. I give him a few biscuits wrapped in kitchen towel to put in his pocket and pack up the rest of the food. He struggles on to his feet in stages, rolling up on to his knees first, then crouching whilst leaning on the floor with his hands, before finally standing up.

We walk along the length of the river for a minute or two till we come to where the steppingstones are.

"Do you fancy having a go?" I ask. He looks doubtful.

"It looks slippery," he says. "To be honest, my balance isn't – as the kids say these days – 'all that'." I laugh. It's the first time I've ever shown amusement at one of his jokes and he seems touched, pleased.

"You don't know how long I've waited for that," he says. We amble along for a few moments before he speaks again. "What do you think? I mean, if we decide to go ahead with it? In terms of the actual event? Would you like something on a grand scale?" He's gone back to behaving strangely, all shy and twee. I cringe inwardly but can't help thawing a little more.

"No, not at all," I say. "It's the last thing I want. How would it look? A widow marrying is enough for people to gossip about, let alone one who's also got two ex-husbands. What do you think they'll say if we have a big do?" I really can't believe the words that are coming out of my own mouth.

"I was thinking the same," he says. "Keep it simple. My God, I never thought I'd be doing this again. And with you of all people! Oh, I didn't mean that in a bad way, just that it's a funny twist of fate."

"Well, let's not get ahead of ourselves," I say. "It's not definite yet, is it?" I take the flip flops off and put them into an outside pocket of the rucksack and put on my boots.

The air is sticky and the damp, green smell of the river is mingled with the remnants of smoke from the barbecues. The sky seems to be slowly darkening, the azure turning to a duller slate blue, yet the light is still golden. We walk past the café and up to the bridge where there's a map on a board. To the right, back the way we came, are the abbey ruins. To the left are the woods, and ahead, over the bridge, is the Valley of Desolation, where the secret waterfall is hidden. It's grouse shooting season and there's a calendar pinned up on the board marking when the Valley will be closed to the public. Today's the last day before they close for two weeks for the hunt. I've already checked the dates online, but I make a show of pointing it out to him.

"It's your lucky day," I say. "It's a magical place."

"Come on then," he says. "You've got me wound round your little finger today. Better not be too much of a trek!" We laugh as we step on to the wide wooden bridge. I love the way it sways slightly as we cross over, with the sound of the water babbling and rushing underneath us. The bank opposite has no buildings, but there are pathways. There's one running along the length of the river, which breaks off into two directions, one leading to another forest, the other to the hidden valley. We set off towards the valley up a slight slope. There aren't many other hikers going the same way. There's a tall man in a purple tracksuit jogging up behind us but, so far, the few others have been going in the opposite direction. We walk in silence, the warmth and humidity wearing us down. The smooth concrete path becomes much gravellier, and we have to jump over pools of mud. I hear Suleiman clicking his tongue as the dirt smears his cream trousers. We're on higher ground now. There are bushes and trees on either side of the path. The river is on our left and although we can hear the soft, whooshing flow of the water below we can't see it anymore because of the vegetation. The woods are on the right, but to the left the grass ends abruptly in a cliff edge. A woodpigeon coos insistently somewhere out of sight and a magpie rattles its creaky song in reply. A small cloud of mosquitoes gathers over my head, and I wave them away, but I begin to feel itchy all over anyway.

"Almost there," I say. I go towards the cliff and peer over. I can see the river and bushes, about twenty feet below, and although the waterfall is there it's not visible unless I literally go and hang over the edge.

"Careful!" says Suleiman, pulling me back by the arm.

"It's down there," I say.

"How are we going to get down? We've seen the spot now, let's leave it."

It's easy to miss if you don't know where it is. Amir and I walked past it on our first trip here and wandered around for ages before giving up. There are two ways down. If you're brave enough there's a kind of ledge that you can get a foothold on if you sit with your legs hanging over. It's a rocky climb down the sheer side of the cliff from there, finding rocks and stones that will take your weight as you go. Amir used to love scrambling down from there, showing off how quick he was, and leaping into the waterfall minutes before I got there via the slow option.

The slower but easier way is to step through a gap in the hedges onto a muddy path that's less than a metre wide and goes down in a curved, gentle slope, hugging the side of the cliff. I go first. It's treacherously slippery. There are brambles spiking out and catching me from the right, where the cliff face is, while about a foot to my left, there's just a drop. A loss of balance is all it would take for me to tumble down on to the rocks. More than once I feel my boots sliding and I straighten myself just in time.

"I am seriously shitting myself," says Suleiman, behind me. I smile but don't turn. "You told me we were going for a walk! Not abseiling! Let's get this clear now. I'm not an adrenaline junkie."

"It'll all be worth it," I assure him. "Almost there."

It takes us a painstaking, step by squidgy step, ten minutes to reach the bottom. The waterfall is before us, a glorious rush of water flowing down over the cliff face, with a drop of about thirty feet. There's nobody else here. We're enclosed on all sides by the rocks, a wonderful, cool dark haven, a cove secret and deep like the heart of a woman. It's lush with the ferns and shines like a mirror where the water sheaths the boulders that are also slippery with algae.

"It looks like Coke," says Suleiman, fascinated. I know what he means. There's a lot of clay in the water, making it muddy.

"Come on," I say, putting the rucksack on a ledge that looks dry and kicking off my shoes.

"Are you crazy?" he laughs. "I'm not freezing myself to death."

"It's warm, I promise." I wade in and splash a handful of water at him.

"Oi!" He takes of his shoes and waddles in hesitantly. I try not to laugh, and instead stand there twirling round and round like I'm advertising adventure parks. The water's only up to my knees. I don't go any further towards the waterfall. I've done it before, and I know it'll be at least waist deep. I don't want to get too wet. There's not enough sun to dry it off.

Suleiman is just standing there as though it's the first time he's ever taken his socks off outdoors. It probably is. I don't mind – at least it's keeping him from thinking of other more unsavoury thoughts.

"Let's go down there," I suggest and walk over to some smooth, flat rocks big enough to sit on. Suleiman wobbles through the water, slipping on pebbles as he moves.

"This feels like a dream," he says, sitting down next to me. "Honestly. I never do stuff like this. My life's a mad race to make money, close the next deal. This is making me feel like giving those things up."

"You should," I say. "You've probably just never tried. It's always possible, you know."

"This is going to sound so cheesy. But you're having some sort of effect on me. Making me wonder if I can be a normal man."

"It's God putting those thoughts in your head. I don't have that power," I say, trying to sound humble. I'm staring at the cascading water when I feel his hand, cold and wetly slimy, closing over mine. I tense but I keep still.

"Is there any better place for me to ask you properly?" he says. "Sophie, will you do me the honour of becoming my wife?"

"I'm broken, Suleiman. I don't think I have anything left. Is it really what you want?"

"We'll heal ourselves together," he says.

I hesitate.

"It won't be easy," I say. "But I'm willing to try."

We put our shoes on to begin the ascent. It's a quarter to six. The car park gate closes at six, but it doesn't matter because neither of us has a car there.

"Ladies first," says Suleiman. But this will ruin my next move.

"No," I say. "You lead the way this time." He looks unsure but starts to clamber up, taking long pauses between each step, nervously checking surfaces for stability. He can check all he wants. It won't be long now. But then again at this rate, we'll be here forever. The air's become cooler and rain begins to plop down in fat drops. Soon Suleiman begins to pant with the effort of the climb. As I suspected, he's unfit and unsteady on his feet, almost swaying with each step.

"That's all we need," he says, as the rain begins to thicken. I put on my leather gloves.

I can't live under this constant fear of being exposed. All I want now is safety for Zain and myself, and a clear road to achieving what I'm capable of. All these husbands have proved nothing but obstacles. Even Tariq interfered in my business, and I wasn't going to stand for that. And now Suleiman thinks he's entangled me with his latest ploy. More fool him.

I wait till we're about halfway up. I'll need a bit of height otherwise it won't work. Suleiman stops and takes out the bit of flowery kitchen towel that I wrapped his cookies in. He ate the biscuits but kept the tissue in his pockets. He uses it to wipe the rain off his face. He's bent over in an awkward, precarious position, on a narrow piece of the path, feet and hands at different levels, his jacket slung over his elbow.

"All this scenery's inspiring," he says, over his shoulder. "What do you think of destination weddings? All the rage now, aren't they?"

"Good idea," I say. "But I'm not sure they have any imams in Vegas." He laughs out loudly, relaxing for a moment, and I take advantage of it. I lunge forward and pull him backwards and to the right with all my strength, keeping one hand on the ledge so I don't topple over with him. His weight helps me. Once he loses balance, it tips him uncontrollably to the side and over the edge of the path. He shouts out as the huge mass of him plunges through the air, his confused face contorting with utter terror. His limbs flail in every direction, but it's useless, and he seems to zoom out of focus as he smashes into the rocky pools below. I cry out myself, instantly horrified, wanting to take my actions back, grabbing at empty space. But it's done. I have to see it through, not lose sight of my reason for doing this. My desperation.

I pull myself together, then scramble down as quickly as I can and wade across to where he's fallen. His neck's twisted and his head is unnaturally bent to one side, as though he's trying to talk on a mobile phone slotted under it, but the angle is too much, almost ninety degrees, and it's grotesque. He's lying on a particularly craggy collection of rocks near the cliff face. Water's running over the stones under him, soaking him through and mingling with the blood that's seeping out steadily from his wounds, most obviously from the back of his head. Although I'm certain he's dead, I take off my gloves and try to find a pulse on his plump, wet, clammy wrist, fighting the nausea as I touch him. I don't really know what I'm doing, but I'm fairly sure there's no heartbeat left to be felt. I've killed him. I'm submerged in a mixture of loathing, fear and relief, as it dawns on me that Suleiman will never have a hold over me again.

I'm going to try and stage it as an accident, but I won't call the police myself, in case they don't believe me. Much safer to leave him for someone else to find. If anyone does turn up, I'll resort to the accident story.

My teeth are chattering with fright, but I force myself to touch him. I put the leather gloves back on. Although he's on the rocks he's still completely soaked now. The dog on his jumper stares at me as I empty his pockets and find a wallet containing forty pounds and a single cash card, but no other ID. His mobile isn't there, either. I can't leave without it, without the evidence that's on there. I press my hands all over his body, trying to find another pocket it could be in. Then I remember his jacket. He was holding it when he fell. I look around and see it floating in the middle of the pool, and I thrash across the water and fish it out. The mobile's there, in an inside pocket, wet, but still functioning. I take it and search the rest of the jacket. There are a couple of Snickers bars and a bottle of blood pressure tablets. I'm in two minds about what to do with his ID. If I take it with me, it might take them longer to identify him. On the other hand, if he's found with no ID it'll suggest someone took it, meaning another person was here. I want them to think it was just an accident that happened while he was out walking alone, so I decide to leave his wallet in his pocket and throw the jacket back into the pool. I leave the body as it is. If I move him, they'll know.

I try to turn the mobile on, but the screen's locked. Luckily it wants a fingerprint and not a password. I'll destroy the phone later, but I have to destroy the evidence now. Gritting my teeth, I dip my hand into the water and pull out Suleiman's squidgy, pasty hand. I feel the vomit rising in my throat, but I swallow it. I dry his fingers on a dry patch of my cardigan. Taking his forefinger, I press it onto the screen of the phone. It bursts into life. It's a "pay as you go". I move over to the rocky wall, concealing myself as much as I can, should anyone pass by from above. First, I delete the voice recording, as well as the video he took the sounds from. It shows the hallway of the house Amir and I lived in, but in the background Mumtaz and I can be heard arguing clearly. Then I quickly scroll through the messages. There aren't many. Mine are the most recent, the conversation about choosing an outfit for our leisurely stroll. There are lots of contact numbers and his email inbox is open. I just give these a rapid glance as they seem irrelevant, and I don't have time to examine them. I put the mobile into my rucksack. I look around the gruesome scene once more. Satisfied I haven't missed anything, I climb back up to the top of the cliff and make my way back to the exit. The place is deserted and even the car park attendant has gone home. I quickly walk the half mile down to the car, despite the sweat pouring off me and the dryness in my mouth, fuelled purely by the survival instinct.

When I reach the car, I gulp down some water, then put

Suleiman's phone under the front wheel of the car. Then I drive and reverse over it, again and again, until it's crushed into smithereens.

He'll stay in the water for a few days now until hunting season is over, and lovestruck couples and intrepid hikers are once again allowed into the Valley of Desolation.

I drive senselessly on the way home, almost skipping two red lights and colliding with a motorcyclist, before forcing myself to concentrate. The last thing I want is to get noticed, remembered. When I see bins lined up outside on the streets, ready to be emptied by the dustmen in the morning, I tie up the sunglasses, baseball cap and the smashed remains of the mobile into separate bags and toss them into bins from two separate houses a couple of miles away from each other.

As I reach home, I can see that the bedroom light is on. I feel my heart beating but then realise I left it on myself. I creep into the house and turn on a few of the lamps downstairs. Not only am I beginning to fear the dark after the break-in, I also need brightness, warmth, a glow to fight this blackness inside me, but I don't want the neighbours to think I'm a paranoid loner who sits in an empty house with every room lit up. I don't think I grasped the enormity and the horror of what I've done in my rush and panic to cover my tracks, but now as I run into the bathroom and fill the tub, I punch the wall in anger and disgust. Then I strip off and sink into the water, my body streaked with tears and Suleiman's blood.

After my bath I go downstairs in my pyjamas. Although I'm feeling sick, I'm also suddenly ravenous. I haven't eaten since the picnic, when I had a miserable cheese and tomato sandwich. I look in the cupboard for a tin of soup but there isn't any, so I take out a packet of Maggi noodles instead. I put them in a pan and pour boiling water from the kettle over them and cook them for the famous two minutes. I slither them into a plate with a blob each of mayonnaise and chilli sauce, then go and sit in front of the TV, as though this is just an ordinary day. *The Chase* is on Challenge, a repeat but I don't mind that. Anything to distract me. I mumble the odd answer while I eat. When Tariq was here, we would compete against each other, keeping strict records of how many questions we answered correctly. Now I just feel self-conscious and stupid.

I've slurped halfway through the noodles when the doorbell rings, and I jump, dropping my fork. My mind flies to McKinley. They can't have found Suleiman already, can they? I move stealthily to the front door and look through the peephole. I breathe a half sigh. It's Faraz. I open the door and say the words without thinking.

"What do you want?"

He looks shocked and dismayed.

"I'm sorry," I say. "I didn't mean it like that. But it's almost eleven o'clock."

"Can I come in?" he says.

"I'm tired, Faraz. I don't think it's a good idea."

"Please. I won't take your time." His pleading usually has an adverse effect on me, but I don't want to create a scene on the doorstep, so I let him in quietly. If he gets upset and starts shouting outside, the neighbours' windows will light up like a cascade of fireworks. He walks down the corridor into the living room. I pause before following him. How does he know his way around my house? He's never been here before.

"Nice house," he says, taking a seat without being offered.

I pick up my noodle plate and take it into the kitchen, bringing him back a glass of apple juice without asking him if he'd prefer a hot drink instead. He always chooses cold drinks when making a social visit. That much I remember.

"I hope you don't mind me coming, but I couldn't help it," he says. "How are you doing?"

I take a moment before answering. I don't trust myself in case I lose control and let something slip, or, even worse, a grisly confession explodes from my lips.

"I'm fine, considering," I say.

"Where's Zain? He must be in bed, I suppose. It's late."

"He's with Amir, actually." Shit. I completely forgot to phone Zain and he'll be asleep now. Neither of us likes going to bed without saying goodnight to each other and I hope he wasn't feeling hurt or sad that I didn't call.

"Will the other little boy be moving back here then?" says Faraz. "Tariq's son?"

"Is that supposed to be funny, Faraz?"

"No, of course not! What do you mean?"

"Haven't you heard? Tariq left all his money and property to 'the little boy'. I only got a few thousand pounds."

"Oh my God!" Faraz exclaims. "What a turd!"

I bite my lip at the profanity.

"Sorry, sorry," he says. "Tariq's gone now. We shouldn't insult him. To be honest, he was a good man. Even though he did steal you away from me." He gulps down the juice. "Anyway, I want to talk to you about something. The thing is... I want to tell you things have changed. You're a widow – no, no," he says, raising his hands when he sees me ready to protest.

"And I'm a self-made man now," he continues. "Before I acted like a mega prat. I can see that now. I just think... me and you, we're made for each other."

This isn't what I expected at all.

"No, please don't, Faraz," I say.

"Come back to me, darling."

"Don't be silly."

"You're in a very vulnerable position. You need looking after. A daddy for Zain. How is he?"

"He's got a dad. Amir. He's fine. You really don't need to worry about us. I'm looking for a job, and once that happens, we'll be fine."

"You know those nice new flats in that development by the tobacco factory?" He isn't giving up that easily. "I bought one of those. You'll never be embarrassed by that ugly old maisonette again. It's not quite as posh as this, but we'll get there one day. Me and you, holding hands through the thick and the thin."

In all honesty, it's not a terrible idea. A peaceful, uncomplicated life with easy-going Faraz. For all his faults, he had loved me. But I have a quick flashback to everything else and of course I know it's not what I want.

"I can't, Faraz. Thank you for being so kind and generous. But it's too soon. I can't even think about a new relationship yet."

"I understand that. I didn't mean tomorrow. I can wait, you take your time," he says. Then, a few seconds later, "Don't make me beg, Sophie. You've already caused me damage once. There's only so much I can take."

Suddenly something glints in his eye, and an angry vein is pulsating in his forehead. I'm frightened. I've never seen him like this before and for once it makes me think about what's been going on in his mind. What's he been stewing over these last few years, since I left him?

"Okay, Faraz," I say. "Give me some time, please. I'll have to think about it. And no promises."

It's like he's been zapped with a remote control. The nastiness vanishes instantly, and his face is all softness and sympathy.

"Of course, darling. I don't want you to rush it. Neither of us is going anywhere."

I can't sleep. I lie in bed for an hour, rolling and twisting. Suleiman's bloody, crushed skull is constantly swimming before my eyes. And now there's the question of Faraz's involvement in what's been happening. I'd initially suspected that woman, the unidentified stalker, of being the vandal. But what if Faraz was the one that broke into the conservatory and slaughtered the tropical fish? Had he been more disturbed by me leaving him than I realised? He was a gentle soul, but it didn't mean he wasn't harbouring a lava-like fury under all that serenity. Heartbreak and humiliation were enough to stoke a violent obsession. I remember his warning when I left him. *You'll regret it...* No, it wasn't true. Even in death Suleiman's playing tricks on me, making me conjure up all kinds of delirious theories.

It's no better when I eventually drift off. I wake up at least five times during the few hours of sleep, imagining all manner of monsters to be standing over me – a stocking-faced assassin, bludgeoned Suleiman, McKinley with a pair of garden shears.

I wake up properly at half past five and turn on my mobile. There are a couple of missed calls from Amir, just before midnight. It must have been just after I fell asleep. I look for the local news, see if any bodies have turned up. There won't be anything this early, even if it has been discovered. It crosses my mind to drive past the park to see if anything's going on. Lunacy. I need to stay away from there. I must wait, sweat it out, but I can't help it. At ten past six I go downstairs and put on the television. Still no corpses in Bolton Abbey. Am I going mad? Why the hell am I desperate for them to find him? I realise I want it to be out in the open so I can measure the risk to me, know what I'm facing, what they know, what I need to do next.

If they catch me, I'll say it was self-defence. I'll tell them his hands were around my neck. He was going to kill me. I gasp as though it's happening to me now. I slap myself, blink it away. I'm losing my hold on reality. I'll have to tell more lies if I want to save Zain from a motherless childhood.

The phone rings. It must be the police this time. Let it ring before my destruction begins. But I can't stand the suspense for long. I pick it up and look at the caller ID. It's Amir.

"Sophie?"

"Amir. Hello," I say. "Is something wrong? Is Zain okay?"

"He's fine. I just wanted to check if you were okay. You didn't speak to Zain last night, so I got worried. I called but you must have been asleep."

"I'm so sorry, Amir. I just did a bit of shopping, and by the time I came home I was exhausted so I had an early night. I don't know how I forgot to call Zain. Was he upset?"

"He was too busy playing. But what about you? You don't sound like your normal self. What's the matter?"

"I don't know," I say. My voice breaks. "I don't know what's wrong with me, Amir. I'm just feeling a bit... depressed... I'm sorry."

"Stop apologising. After what you've been through, it's not surprising. Where's your mum? Why don't you go and stay with her for a few days?"

"No. We'll only argue. You know what it's like."

He sighs. "Do you want me to come over for a while? I can bring Zain home. Save you a trip."

"No. I don't want to cause trouble between you and Jannat."

"You're Zain's mother. She understands that. She can come too, if she wants."

"If you want to help, maybe you could keep Zain for another few days? Keep him busy? He'll enjoy spending another few days with you all. I don't want my horrible mood to rub off on him."

"Of course I can," says Amir. "We'd love to have him for a few more days. But you shouldn't be alone. Meet a friend or something. Get some support."

I tell him I'll drop some more clothes over for Zain tomorrow and we say goodbye.

Meet a friend. I don't really have any.

TARIQ
2016

I don't know what compelled me to do it. I suppose I was drawn to her vulnerability. I honestly thought she was a reflection of me. Life had been difficult for her, but she was trying to navigate it with dignity and patience on her own terms, without being distracted by worldly pressures. As I got to know her, I found her funny and kind. She encouraged me to talk about Ruby, though obviously I tried not to dwell on that topic too much, and she even got along with Ayaan. I thought our shared experiences of heartache in the past would give us a richer understanding of each other and how we could continue on a journey together if we wanted to. The proposal was spontaneous, but maybe romantic for that very reason. The words just spilled out impulsively, but they felt right.

We'd taken the boys to Mega Play, then gone on to Roundhay Park. They were on the climbing frame, shouting and laughing with each other. Like brothers. Sophie and I were sitting on the bench, watching them. Until then I hadn't made any indication that I liked her as anything beyond a good friend, a fellow parent.

"They look happy, don't they?" I said, meaning Zain and Ayaan.

"Yes. It's lovely that they get on so well," said Sophie.

"I hope you don't mind me saying this, but how would you

feel about it becoming something more permanent?" I said quickly. She took a sharp breath. "I know we haven't known each other that long, but I think we get on well enough, wouldn't you say? We could, you know, get married, make a future? Make a proper family?" My speech became tangled and stilted, my tongue tripping over my words.

"You don't have to say anything now, have a think about it, ask your parents."

"Okay. I'll ask everyone else what they think," she said, after a moment. "But I think I know what I want."

I looked at her questioningly and she laughed.

"I'll accept, of course."

I called Sameena, Ruby's sister, and asked her to meet for lunch in the coming week. She doted on Ayaan and, since Ruby's death, had made a point of spending at least one weekend a month with him. We met in Aagra, a big noisy restaurant in Bradford with a statue of an elephant outside.

Normally I would have taken Ayaan with us for a day out with Sameena too, but I deliberately picked a time when he was at school. I wasn't sure what her reaction would be, and I wanted her honest opinion, not the toned-down version that she would give me if Ayaan was there.

Sameena was similar to Ruby in appearance, the same wide eyes and slightly thin lips, but she had a straight-talking, no-nonsense attitude that was completely different to Ruby's sensitive manner. Ruby had been kind to a fault. She was always too easily taken in by a sad face and a sob story.

When Ruby died, Sameena had been like a sister. I had no family of my own, my friends were sparse, and it was Sameena who'd held me when I'd screamed in despair in the first days, and then, as time passed, quietly talked me back to my senses.

"How are the kids?" I asked.

"They're fine," said Ruby. "More opinionated every day.

You should have brought Ayaan. I'm missing him. I won't see him until the Christmas holidays now."

"Yes, we'll come and visit you then."

"Yeah, you must. It's cosy up here in the winter, but you wimps always complain about the cold."

"It was Ruby who used to do that. She even used to wear thermal socks in July."

Sameena shook her head and laughed. I smiled. It was getting a little easier to not break at each memory.

"I wanted to tell you something," I said.

"Ominous," said Sameena.

"I'm getting married." Her eyes opened wider in surprise, but her expression stayed warm.

"That's great, Tariq," she said. "I think the time's right for you, now. Shall I tell Mum to put the feelers out then? I think the girl she showed you last time is married with a baby on the way now."

"I've found someone, Sam," I said.

"Oh. I didn't know you were seeing anyone." I could sense she was a little hurt.

"I'm not, really."

"Well, who is she?"

"Another parent at Ayaan's school."

"Widow?"

"Divorced."

"Okay. Are you sure?"

"Well… not really. It's scary, Sam, I'll admit. It feels strange… I'll never forget Ruby, of course, but I think it's something I have to do now. And she gets on with Ayaan, she's got a boy the same age. I think it could work out well."

"It's great news, T. When can I meet her?"

SOPHIE
2017

Although the wedding was small, Tariq insisted that we do things reasonably. He wanted to keep it low key, but there was no need to skimp to an extreme.

I, for my part, was aware that the occasion was likely to attract gossip, and kept the details refined but chic, refraining from anything too over the top or showy. The theme was winter white to complement the season: pearls, diamante, roses, snowflakes, fur. I arrived at the hotel in a horse and carriage with Dad and Zain. This was my only luxury, and not too excessive, I thought, considering I held back on almost everything else. My thoughts were in a panic from the moment I woke up that day. Had it all come too easily, this latest new beginning? Was something awful about to happen, to bring me back to my dingy reality? But nothing happened, and we were married.

The house was beautiful, a house of dreams, really. Five bedrooms and a spacious, tree lined road in an exclusive area. Ruby had decorated it tastefully, I had to admit, keeping all the original features, wooden beams and ornamental plasterwork, and sticking to traditional prints, mostly stripes and florals. There was a four-poster bed and a great claw-footed bathtub.

But now it was my home. I was Tariq's wife and I wanted to, well, not erase all trace of her, but at least make sure that my influence over the place was stronger than hers. The florid country atmosphere was all very classic, but the chintzy style was just a bit too overblown and outdated for me, and there really was too much brown. I couldn't live in a beige world.

I ordered some beautiful modern rugs, a huge one in grey splashed with parrot green and shocking pink flowers, and a runner for the hall patterned with cute owls. I bought piles of cushions, printed and embroidered with leaves and trees and more hooty characters. I loved this birdy trend, despite cultural beliefs that images of owls and peacocks in the house brought bad luck. I had no faith in these superstitions. I didn't believe a few feathers could cause deaths, infertility or bad exam results.

It was a small step, but already the place was beginning to look more like a home that I could become familiar with, rather than a stranger's house that I was staying in as a guest.

That day I set all the décor up, I made my delicious roast chicken with all the trimmings and my tasty gravy. I fed the boys early and sent them upstairs so Tariq and I could enjoy our evening. I discovered a set of nice china in the dresser and laid the table beautifully, adding new place mats and scented candles, my striking arty new rug underneath it all.

Tariq came in while I was in the kitchen and kissed me, then held my hands in his and smiled.

"What?" I laughed.

"Nothing. I'm just happy," he said. "I'm glad you've made something nice. I'm really hungry today."

"Go and wash up then. It's all ready," I said. "And don't go into the dining room yet."

He laughed and went upstairs, indulging me in my little game. I laid out the food and was just putting a jug of water on the table when Tariq came in and stopped in his tracks.

"What's this?" he said, staring at the rug.

"What do you think? It brightens the place up, doesn't it? I got it off eBay, but don't worry it wasn't like a cheapy seller. It was £100, but I negotiated and for £120 he threw the runner in too."

"It's horrible," said Tariq. I was taken aback but I tried making light of it.

"It just seems that way to you because you're used to old English roses and willow patterns. I think the house needs an injection of colour, something modern to freshen it all up."

"Perhaps I like English roses and willow patterns. And I particularly loved the Moroccan kilim that was under this table. It was an authentic piece Ruby and I bought in Marrakech."

I smiled patiently.

"Don't worry I've just moved it into the conservatory. It goes with all the wooden furniture in there."

"I like it in here!" he snapped. "Why did you mess up my things?"

It was too shocking, the little flare of anger, and I sank down into a chair and started sniffing, not able to hold back the onslaught of tears. It didn't take much. Within minutes of me snatching up a tissue Tariq was apologising.

"I didn't mean it," he said. "Please don't cry. We'll keep the rug. Come on, let's eat. Where are the potatoes?"

I pointed to the kitchen.

"I'll get them. You have a drink. Please, stop crying."

The rug was there to stay.

Tariq always felt so guilty after an argument that he overcompensated later, showering me with affection. Often, he clung to me like he was terrified of letting go. At times it was passionate, but at others it felt suffocating, and it was all I could do not to wrench myself away. After dinner he suggested an early night, as I knew he would, and although I was upset, I knew I had to thaw a bit to keep hold of his sympathy.

We were just getting warmed up under the covers when the

door swung open, and Ayaan was standing there. Tariq quickly disengaged himself and sat up.

"Go back to bed," I said. "Why aren't you asleep?" My tone was sharp, but I was annoyed and embarrassed at this invasion of our privacy.

"What's the matter, son?" Tariq said, putting his glasses on. Ayaan rubbed his eyes and started whining. Tariq leapt up and strode to him, picking him up, soothing him with his voice.

"You should teach him to knock before he comes in," I said, but Tariq paid no attention. I could hear him saying there were no such things as ghosts as he took the boy back to his room. I would ban them from watching Scooby Doo tomorrow. Those banshees and swamp monsters had a lot to answer for. I waited for another fifteen minutes, listening to Tariq still telling stories in hushed tones from across the hall, then I fell asleep.

The rugs were a small triumph. Next, I set about reorganising the cupboards. Thankfully Tariq didn't mind that and even took me to Ikea to buy wire racks and clip-top jars. We bought new duvet covers and vases and a few prints, and as I scattered them around the house, I slowly began to feel less tense and began sinking into a more familiar atmosphere.

The incident made me realise that our life wasn't the beautiful fresh new package that I'd envisaged it was. We both had histories that were inextricably part of us. I knew Tariq had loved his wife and I was comfortable with him talking about her, especially if he found it therapeutic. But we also had to focus on building a happy future. The obstacles to this were always on the periphery of my vision – the photographs, all of them of Ruby. As a bride, in full splendour with layers of make-up and a crimson dress; glowing golden in a summer frock and floppy hat holidaying in Turkey; a happy mother, throwing Ayaan up into the air.

I couldn't stand them. It was like being trapped in a tunnel, crawling towards a spot of light that was my new life, clean and unencumbered, but at every turn or shift I was faced with a Ruby-memory, and the daylight would be filled with tumbling rocks and crumbling soil.

The first two pictures I took down I slipped into the sideboard cupboard without Tariq noticing. Even on display, they were hidden amongst so many other granny objects on the shelves of a dresser that I doubted he realised. Encouraged by his lack of reaction, I gradually got rid of most of them over the course of a few weeks, banishing them to various drawers.

Eventually there was only one left, but it was the main eyesore, a massive portrait that was in the dining room, presiding over every evening as we ate dinner, watching every morsel served and swallowed. Observing, judging, embittering my every night.

I wasn't melodramatic enough to think that she had power over me from beyond the grave, but I'm not ashamed to say I demanded Tariq's full attention. How could I ever have it when she sat there so brazenly, infiltrating his mind with fragments of herself? I wasn't going to have it.

I waited it out. We'd been married for about three months when I finally whipped it off the wall and replaced it with a piece of fashionable high street art, a cluster of teal and black metal daisies, a striking composition against the boring cream walls. As a precaution against any backlash, I put the photo up on the wall of Tariq's study, so he could go in there and look at it if he was desperate.

I was upstairs when Tariq got home that day. The boys were at my mum's, and I'd asked him to bring a takeaway on the way home. When I went down, he was watching television and smiled at me as I went in, but when I picked up the takeaway bags from the kitchen and took them into the dining room, Ruby was reigning once again, looking down at me in a hazy, red triumphant pout. It was like a whack in the face.

I waited till he was settled at the table with his doner kebab and chips. I sometimes ate in front of the telly in the lounge but that was too wild for Tariq. Even eating out of the polystyrene boxes instead of plates was stretching it for him.

"I put a nice piece of art up before," I said, dropping a pickled jalapeno onto his plate. "Did you like it?"

"Not really," he said. "It was trashy."

I drew in a sharp breath. He'd never said anything so nasty to me before.

"Really? I thought it was quite nice," I said. "I spent ages choosing what would coordinate with the décor of the room."

"Certainly too ugly to be replacing my wife's portrait."

I opened and shut my mouth. I had to choose my words carefully. I dipped a chip in chilli sauce and mayonnaise.

"Don't you think… well don't you think you should consider how I feel?" I said. "Now that we're married? I might just want to add a bit of my own personality to our home."

"How do you feel? Is this about you making the house to your taste or getting rid of my wife's memory?"

My hand flew to my mouth. "How can you say that?" I sprang up from the chair and ran from the room, accidentally sloshing a pot of green chutney over Tariq's precision-creased beige trousers.

TARIQ
2017

As Sophie had another fit of wailing, I rubbed my forehead and slowly drank a glass of water. I presented myself always as collected and unruffled, but there were instances when this wasn't the case. My exterior was very good at concealing any unease or alarm that might be flaring inside me. And now, I could feel things beginning to burn.

I let her keep her precious art stuck up there, a badly designed bunch of daisies, ruining my eclectic, moody interior with its cheap vulgarity. Even this I'd put up with, just to keep the peace. In the end Ruby was within me, forever, and it didn't matter if Sophie burned all of Ruby's photos, she'd never be able to erase her spirit. And so, we carried on after that, and things were pleasant. Nobody was perfect, I understood that. I passed over petty, silly issues. Ayaan complained of her shouting at him one day, for not tidying his bedroom, but I told him she must have a rough day.

It was a Thursday afternoon when a case for a business visa turned up at my office. I was a solicitor, dealing with immigration problems. I didn't make claims for crooked clients, instead concentrated on achieving a hundred percent success rate for genuine cases.

The client on that day wanted to establish a business in the UK. Although a more expensive route than a false marriage or pretend political asylum claim, it was a more honest option. He seemed like a nice young man, with a straightforward application and plenty of readily available cash to back it up. I told him I'd have good news for him in seven or eight weeks.

His paperwork sorted into piles, I leaned across the table to shake hands and end the appointment, but he remained seated. I glanced at his cup. Perhaps he wanted to finish his tea.

"I shouldn't have had to do this, you know," he said.

"I know," I said. "You've been here a few years and it must be feeling like home, I suppose. But it's the law of the land, unfortunately."

"I don't mean that. I was married to a girl, a British girl. It should have been enough, but she left me."

"I'm sorry. All for the best, though, eh?"

"I was married to your wife."

I stared at him. I looked at the name on the folder. Faraz Baig. Yes, I remembered. Sophie had mentioned her second husband's first name, but I hadn't made the connection. Anger started to fizzle inside me, but curiosity took over.

"Well, Mr Baig," I said. "I don't know what to say. Why did you come here? Do you expect...? I'm not sure I know what you want."

"Just to warn you, brother," said Faraz. He spoke with an educated Pakistani accent, with an American intonation. "Be careful. She's a poisonous lady."

His words didn't spark the reactions they should have done in me upon hearing my wife insulted. I was ashamed but I couldn't force myself into a rage.

"You're speaking of my wife," I said coldly. He looked at me intently.

"You've seen it already," he said after a moment. "You've seen it already, haven't you? The treachery. The deceit."

"Mr Baig, this is–"

"Did she tell you I beat her, like she told me Amir did? You do know who Amir is, don't you? Or did she tell you I married her under false pretences?"

"She said you needed a visa, yes. Which I can well believe, having read your case file. And she told me you had another wife."

"Sophie forced me to divorce the poor girl, within a week."

"Can you blame her?"

"No. That's why I did it. I wanted her to feel she had her rights, I wanted to show I was serious about keeping her happy. But it didn't make any difference. A few months later, when I didn't satisfy her image of a suitable husband, she got rid of me."

I caught my breath. Was he telling the truth? He'd been honest enough in his visa application, had been quite adamant he wasn't going to use any false information, unlike some of my clients. My mind raced to Sophie's recent removal of Ruby's picture and her reaction when I put it back on the wall. Such a callous regard for my feelings was questionable, but perhaps I was being oversensitive. Then again, what reason would Faraz have for making things up? Jealousy?

"I'm not interested in whatever happened in the past, Mr Baig," I said. "Perhaps you mean well, but I don't wish to discuss my private life with you."

"Thanks for your help," said Faraz, standing up. "I'll make sure I pay your fee for consulting, but I'll find someone else to help me. And I'm sorry for deceiving you, for coming here without telling you who I am."

He picked up his folder.

"Please, Mr Baig. You don't have to do that. I'm still happy to continue working on your case."

He nodded and thanked me again before leaving but took his file with him.

From then on, I couldn't help being wary under the laughter and the loving. I was the consummate actor, hiding it well so that she never guessed that there were fears and doubts simmering under the surface.

I didn't even know what I was scared of. It really didn't seem as though I had much to worry about. We were, by all appearances, happy. There were moments that were like shots to the heart, breath-taking pangs of the love I felt for her. But here was still too much of the unknown and it was all I could do to keep myself a little detached, not let her in entirely, or I would be lost forever.

As weeks went by, I began to think that it was all in my imagination. Faraz was lying about her slyness, and I should have just trusted her. Of course we had the occasional trivial dispute, but that was normal in a marriage. And yes, she was slowly removing more and more of Ruby's things as she bought new household items of her own, but that too was inevitable and healthy, part of the organic process of a new life. It would have been unreasonable of me to expect anything else.

A couple of months after Faraz's warning, I came home one night, early for once, looking forward to a nice dinner. I'd noticed lamb chops in the fridge that morning. The lights of every room in the house were blazing unnecessarily when I opened the door. Wasting electricity was a quibble of mine that I'd mentioned to Sophie before. I shook my head and went into the kitchen. A pan of potatoes was bubbling dangerously, and the pressure cooker was reaching the highest pitch of its whistle. But behind the screech there was another sound, deeper and lower but equally manic. I realised it was Sophie yelling. Who was she shouting at? My instinct was to run upstairs, but instead I crept up without a sound. I wanted to see what was happening for myself. Ayaan's bedroom door was open. The floor was strewn with books, crayons, Lego bricks and hundreds of other small toys, and scattered on top of them were several pictures of Ayaan and Ruby.

"Do you think it's funny? I told you to clear this mess up!" Sophie was shouting.

"Go away!" Ayaan shouted back. "You're not my mum!" I was surprised. I'd never seen him talk like that to anyone. He was always such a good-natured child.

"What did you say?" said Sophie. "Right." She snatched up a handful of Ruby's photos and began to rip them up.

"No! Stop it!" shouted Ayaan, charging at her and punching her leg with his little fists. Before I could do anything, Sophie pushed him away and he fell, crashing into a chest of drawers. I ran into the room and picked him up. He was screaming, and there was blood gushing from a cut on his forehead.

"Ayaan!" cried Sophie. "Oh my God! I'm so sorry, is he okay?" She saw the blood and began shrieking.

"Shut up and get a towel!" I said. I sat on the bed and drew Ayaan closer to me, stroking his back, trying to calm him down. Sophie brought it and I pressed it to the wound.

"Shall I get a plaster?" she said.

"Just go, Sophie. You've done enough."

The cut wasn't deep, thank God, but it still took almost twenty minutes for the bleeding to stop, and ten before Ayaan stopped crying, even though it was probably because of shock rather than pain.

Leaving Ayaan alone with her again was inconceivable. After losing Ruby, I'd become completely possessive over him. I wouldn't take even the tiniest chance of him coming to any harm. When I'd cleaned him up and he was calmer, I asked Ayaan if Sophie had ever hit him, but to my relief he said hadn't.

"But I told you she shouts," he whispered. It was true. He had complained to me a few weeks ago, but I'd just brushed it off as a child's exaggerated perception of a loud-voiced adult. I'd never witnessed Sophie talking to him roughly, but I should have believed him. I hugged him and kissed his head.

"I'm so sorry, son."

I brought him up some of his favourite tomato soup from a can, then put him to bed. I sat watching him, gently patting his shoulder till his eyes closed and he drifted off.

Sophie was sitting in the lounge with just a dim lamp on in the corner, but jumped up when I went in.

"Is he okay? How's his head?" she said.

"He'll be fine," I said. "You're lucky it wasn't worse."

"I know, I know, I'm so sorry, really, I didn't mean to. I was an accident." I was furious with her, but I wanted to hear her explanation.

"What happened?" I said.

"Everything was going wrong. The dinner was taking too long, I dropped a Pyrex bowl and broke it. Then I was on the phone to a director, just having a chat, trying to make a good impression, when the boys started fighting. I had to hang up on him. When I went upstairs the toys were everywhere. I told them off and told them to clear up. Zain was helping but Ayaan just laughed at me. Then he just started beating me up. I was just trying to stop him."

"You pushed him, Sophie. Hard."

"I'm sorry. It won't happen again."

I ate my dinner in a civil manner, then behaved courteously towards her so she wouldn't suspect anything. I even suggested we watch a film, her choice. After half an hour, I went upstairs, leaving her engrossed in mouthing the dialogue to *Maid in Manhattan*, that she'd memorised after seeing it so many times. She paid little attention to me leaving the room. I wanted to get into bed before her, so I could pretend I was asleep when she came and avoid any sort of interaction. Thankfully when she did flop down in bed she was snoring within minutes. There was obviously nothing bothering her about the day's events, then. I, however, didn't want to sleep. I wanted to stay awake, to tear through that bleak, dangerous night in case she had some sort of weird outburst in the middle of it. The morning would bring the safety I needed for Ayaan.

When I turned to face her in bed she was lying on her back, her peaceful, pretty face belying the rough, pushy woman she'd proved herself to be earlier. A shiver went through me when I replayed the scene. Her arm whacking Ayaan and my boy flying into the chest of drawers. I shook it out of my head and turned away from her. I tried to read a book to distract me, but I couldn't concentrate. I lay there, thinking, dozing off in snatches. Sophie slept soundly.

In the morning I said I had a late start in the office and offered to drive the boys to school. Sophie was only too happy to have a lie-in. I dropped the boys off and left strict instructions in the school office that no one was to collect Ayaan except me or his nan, Ruby's mum. Then I sat in the car and rang Sameena. She answered on the second ring, and as usual started accusing me of not keeping in touch, an old habit of hers, although I'd spoken to her only a fortnight before.

"Getting too loved up with your new wife," she said.

"Not now," I said urgently, and she went quiet instantly.

"What's wrong?"

"I need help."

"What is it? Do you need money?"

"It's Sophie."

"Is she okay?"

"She's fine. It's just… I'm not sure I can trust her with Ayaan."

"What's she done?" I could hear the concern in her voice. I gave her a brief account of last night's events.

"I was wondering if you could look after him for a while."

"Of course I can. I'd do anything for him. You know that."

I wasn't going to discuss the situation with the school right now. I'd just move Ayaan in with Sameena and then explain things afterwards. Sameena worked as a teaching assistant in her local primary school and assured me she'd be able to get him a place there. As long as he was attending school, I hoped there wouldn't be a problem.

Sophie was due to collect the boys, but I'd told Ayaan's teacher that he had a dentist's appointment and had to leave an hour early. I picked him up at two o'clock, stopped at Tesco to get some sandwiches and drinks, plus a couple of pairs of jeans and t-shirts for Ayaan, then headed off straight towards Cumbria.

SOPHIE
2017

It was one thing making derogatory comments about my interior design ideas but humiliating me in the public realm was a whole different ball game, something that Tariq was apparently having difficulty in grasping.

I stood outside Purple class and focused my sham smile at Miss Price who was standing at the door summoning the children whose parents had arrived. Zain came out, but she didn't call out Ayaan's name.

"Where's Ayaan, darling?" I asked Zain, but he'd already run off to the climbing frame.

"Just wait there!" I shouted after him.

"How was Ayaan's appointment?" asked Miss Price. I looked at her blankly. "Your husband came and picked him up this afternoon." And said nothing about it to me , I thought.

"Did he?" I said. Then, quickly, my mind added things up. "That's fine, yes, thank you." I thought I heard a hushed snigger behind me, but when I spun around everyone was going about their own business.

I didn't hear from Tariq all day. I phoned him seven times, but it went straight to voicemail. I could have understood, not been so worried, if he'd been by himself. He may have had a meeting or just been generally busy. But why would he have taken Ayaan with him?

Zain kept asking where Ayaan was, but I busied him with a story and then put him to bed, crooning lullabies while expecting the phone to ring and a kidnapper to be on the other end, demanding a ransom.

It was about 11.30 and I was thinking of ringing the police when Tariq finally walked in, still wearing his light grey suit, though he'd taken the tie off. Waiting for him, not knowing anything, had taken the heat off my anger and I rushed straight to him, throwing my arms around him melodramatically.

"What's all this?" He laughed. "Missed me?"

"I love you! I was so worried. Why haven't you been answering your phone? Where have you been?"

"I was on a trip, driving," he said. "Sorry. Reception was bad. Come and sit down." I gave him another squeeze before releasing him. Then I realised he was alone. I'd forgotten Ayaan should have been there too, that he wasn't asleep upstairs like normal.

"Where's Ayaan?" I said.

"Sit down, Sophie."

"Where is he? What's happened?" I began to sob. Tariq pushed me gently on to the sofa. Please God, let him be okay, I should never have pushed him.

"He's fine. Don't worry," said Tariq.

"Thank God. I was scared…"

"I made a decision last night," said Tariq. "I don't think it's a good idea for Ayaan to be here." It took me a few moments to realise the full meaning of what he was saying.

"What?" I said, turning on him. "What are you talking about? I just lost my temper a bit, that was all! It was an accident, how many times do I have to say it?"

"Maybe it was an accident. But how do I know it won't happen again?"

"Are you saying you've never got angry with him?"

"Not like that, no. You were in a rage."

"Or Ruby? Didn't she?"

"Leave her out of this," he said.

I knew I should keep my mouth shut, exit the room, but as usual I ignored that screaming voice of reason inside me.

"No, of course Righteous Ruby never got angry!" I said. "Perhaps if she had, perhaps if she'd applied a bit of discipline, the boy wouldn't be such a spoilt brat!" Tariq's eyes widened but he pursed his lips and turned, stood up, began walking away. Then, because I couldn't help it, couldn't stop myself I was so livid, I lunged at him and pushed him into the wall. He knocked his shoulder, but it didn't have any other effect. Tariq straightened himself, shook his head, and walked out of the room. I heard him go into his study and lock the door.

TARIQ
2017

I unlocked my desk drawer and took out my tablets. I'd first started taking them after Ruby died. The grief, the anxiety for my son, the sleepless nights, not being able to concentrate at work, it had all taken its toll on me, and the doctor had prescribed anti-depressants. If it hadn't been for Ayaan, I might not have taken them, but I needed to be mentally and emotionally stable to take care of him responsibly. The medication helped and I felt more in control, and after a year I stopped taking it.

Recently I'd felt some of those feelings stirring again, ever since I'd started having altercations with Sophie. Sometimes I wasn't sure of what I was doing and what was going on around me, and I'd made a couple of wrong decisions at work, which thankfully had been spotted by a colleague.

The latest episode with Sophie had set off fresh apprehension concerning Ayaan, and although I'd dealt with the issue of his safety, I was still feeling jittery. Tonight, the physical impact of Sophie's anger had added another dimension to my fears. The bodily shock I'd felt as she shoved me had been charged not by brute strength but rage. I kept picturing the moment in my mind over and over again, and my hand was shaking a little as I swallowed a couple of pills. Then I lay back in the recliner and fell asleep.

Surprisingly, the next day I felt better, although my back was hurting from lying in the chair, something that often happened if I slept in an awkward position. Peaceful and a little more level-headed. I almost smiled at how she'd launched herself at me. Sophie's awful behaviour last night hadn't been entirely without reason. I'd taken a huge step that, as my wife, she should have been included in. I couldn't blame her for that. But difficult though it was, I wasn't sorry for taking Ayaan to Sameena's. I accepted that Sophie hadn't deliberately intended to hurt Ayaan, but what if her anger was ignited again, a flame to spilt petrol? Leaving him alone with her was out of the question, for the time being, at least. I'd bring him back home when I could trust her.

I'd first been drawn to Sophie because I thought I'd recognised a spirit close to my own, another lonely soul waiting in the interim between different phases of life. We both had sad, bitter experiences in our past that had made us strong and resilient but had left us drifting along with no sense of the present. She had seemed a warm-hearted woman with a sense of humour and a motherly side to her personality, someone I hoped could forge a future with me. Things weren't turning out as expected, but I thought there still might be a chance we could make the relationship work. When she was happy, Sophie could be a very loving person who would go to great lengths for me.

I was aware that some of Sophie's tantrums were partly due to her insecurity over Ruby. Things between us would only improve if I showed her that I'd truly opened my heart and my life to her now. With this is in mind I decided to make amends the next morning. I washed up in the downstairs shower room, then went to make us both a nice breakfast as it was a Saturday morning, and nobody had to rush off anywhere. Not feeling inspired by the eggs that I ate on most days, I drove down to the local bakery, Pinchitos, where I'd promised to take Sophie in our first conversation. I still hadn't.

It was a beautiful shop. There were glass shelves and domes lettered and swirled in gold, cakes and pastries displayed in pastel coloured paper cases, polished wooden counters. As well as my usual croissants and Sophie's maple and pecan Danish, I picked up apple and custard doughnuts and slices of gateaux. Not particularly healthy breakfast food, but it was a one-time indulgence, an apology.

Back at home I broke a few twigs off the cherry tree in the garden that was just beginning to flower with blossom, and put them in a glass, which I placed on a tray with coffee, orange juice, sliced apples and the pastries.

I crept up the stairs as silently as I could. With a thick pile carpet on our wide staircase, it wasn't too difficult. From halfway up I could see that our bedroom door was open. Maybe Zain had woken up and gone in to check on her like he normally did.

Sophie was awake and texting on her phone when I entered the room, and she turned her back towards me when she saw me. I pulled a small table over and set the tray down on it, then sat on the end of the bed. Then I slid my hand under the duvet and pulled out her foot. She kicked me away at first, but I kept hold of her and began to massage her toes. She wriggled a little but relaxed moments later.

"I'm sorry," I said quietly. "I didn't mean for this to happen."

"You don't trust me," she said. "With your child. How do you think that makes me feel?"

"I think… maybe we need a bit more space for ourselves. And Ayaan will be happy there for a while with his aunt. It's all for the better, really. Think of it like that. We need a bit of time to get to know each other properly, and it's better to do that without too many complications. Ayaan's had a tough time over the last few years, and maybe this change was a bit too much for him."

Sophie looked at me, and although she quickly composed her features to look sympathetic, I caught a sudden flush of excitement, almost greed, on her face for a second.

"I understand what you're saying, and I agree. But I don't want you to think that I don't want him here," she said.

"Of course I don't think that," I said.

"This is his home. And I want you to promise me you'll bring him back to live here soon."

"I'll bring him, soon. Until then, we can visit him. But for now, let's concentrate on us, so he comes back to a happy place."

I smiled and raised a piece of Black Forest gateau to her lips.

It was an unlikely coincidence, me stumbling on Sophie's unfaithfulness. It was a few uneventful weeks after I took Ayaan to live with Sameena. I reached my office in the morning as usual, but realised that I'd left a folder at home, so I went back to collect it. I was approaching the turning into our road, when I saw Sophie pull out and drive away in the opposite direction to me. I followed her, an instinctive whim. It was just after ten o'clock. She must have dropped Zain and come home some time ago. When I'd asked her last night if she had any plans for today, she'd said she was going to spend it in the garden. We'd been to the garden centre the day before and bought a carload of flowers and sacks of compost. She'd already planned where she was going to place her assortment of hydrangeas, lilies and ferns. If she hadn't been so effusive about her planting scheme, I wouldn't have thought anything of it, but I knew she had everything needed, and the grocery shopping was all done, so where was she off to?

The Fisherman was a grimy looking "establishment", an end terrace house made of dark brown brick, with a tatty name board outside claiming it was a B&B. Sophie parked the car outside on the road, instead of in the small driveway, and went inside. I found a spot across the road from where I could watch the house and waited.

SOPHIE
2017

"Come in, come, in," said Suleiman. "Take a seat. It's a very humble abode, but it's just temporary, until my new place gets sorted out."

There was nowhere else to sit apart from the bed in the worn-out room, with its threadbare brown patterned carpet and orange walls. It was stuffy and smelled of damp washing and rotting apples.

"I'd rather stand," I said.

"Oh, come on," said Suleiman. "I don't bite." He winked at me, then propelled me towards the bed, and sat down next to me. He put his hand on my leg and tapped it heavily, smiling. I glared at him, and he removed it.

Suleiman had rung me in the morning, out of the blue, and demanded that I come and meet him there. I opened my handbag and took out an envelope of money and handed it to him. "This is all I had at such short notice. I can give you the rest next week." He took the envelope and counted the notes.

"No can do, I'm afraid," said Suleiman. "It's not even half of what I asked for."

"There's nothing else I can do right now."

"Come, come. You're definitely a lady with means now, so I hear. The sum I asked for is, as they say, paltry to someone like you. By paltry I don't mean chickens–"

"I know what you mean!" I said.

"Good. So, you know our arrangement. Go and get the rest of the money. I'm sure you can make up a good excuse if you have to."

It wouldn't make any difference if I gave it to him now or in a few weeks' time. I had enough in my savings bank to pay him.

"I wouldn't rush you if I didn't have to," said Suleiman, doing his best to look emphatic. "But it's just that there are a few people who won't be too happy if I don't... well, finish off my dealings with them properly. And then I think I might disappear for a little while."

"Fine!" I said. Of course I was upset and incensed by his extortion, but it had become a necessity. I had to do whatever it took to keep my relationship with Tariq intact. I told Suleiman that I would drop the money off to him and then go back to my peaceful and productive morning in the garden, which he had so rudely interrupted. I was about to leave when he stopped me.

"Why don't I just come with you?" he said. "It will save you a trip back. I've got things to do in town anyway."

"No," I said. "I don't want to be seen with you."

"Don't worry, nobody will see me. I'll lie down on the back seat. Don't look at me like that, I've done it lots of times before. I can be quite a contortionist if I have to." I didn't believe that, but if he could stay out of sight, it would save me time.

Suleiman got into the back of the car and lay down, and I flung a blanket and a charity bag of old clothes and shoes that I'd been meaning to take to the recycling centre on top of him, ignoring his groans. Once I'd withdrawn the money from a cashpoint, I drove to a quiet back street, where anyone was unlikely to see us, and let him out. I gave him the money.

"This is a bit far out of town," said Suleiman, as he took in his surroundings.

"It's only a five-minute walk," I said. "Use Google Maps if you get lost." I drove off before he could protest.

TARIQ
2017

After she folded the tall, wide man into the back seat, I followed her as she drove off towards the town centre. I kept a couple of cars behind her black Renault, desperately hoping that she wouldn't spot me. But then, as we reached the traffic lights, she went through the amber and I was left stuck at the red, still a few cars behind. When I eventually managed to get past the lights, it was too late. I couldn't see Sophie's car anywhere. It didn't really matter, though. I had seen enough.

After that I began to notice the change. I would hear her talking loudly on the phone, laughing, then quietening down when she realised I was approaching, and she sent texts furtively, secretly. But I didn't know, because the rest of the time she was loving and attentive to me, perfect. How could she be so duplicitous? Who was he? Was she cheating on me? I was a little surprised at her choice. He was a paunchy, older man, but then it felt like I didn't know her at all now. Perhaps she wasn't even having an affair. They hadn't been behaving like lovers, but that didn't mean anything, I supposed. They could have had an argument. Or perhaps Sophie and this man had more sinister motives. Maybe they were involved in some honey trap scheme together and I was the target.

I didn't want to confront her yet, not until I'd decided what I was going to do. She'd most likely lie about it anyway, and I would have shown my hand for nothing. I had a faint hope that she'd tell me herself, but the days passed without her mentioning it.

I began thinking of it all continuously, my life pulled into a loop that was rotating insanely. There was too much I didn't know, too much uncertainty. There were too many angles she kept hidden, turned away from the light. If she wasn't being unfaithful, then who was the man? And what of her temper? Would she attack me next time it flared up? A turbulent, vicious life was the last thing I wanted, and I certainly wouldn't abide being made a fool of by my wife and her lover/partner in crime. And although it was for his own good, I was finding it impossible being separated from Ayaan. I wanted the marriage to work but at the moment there was too much for my mind to cope with. I needed air.

SOPHIE
2017

For the first time it seemed that our life together was clear of any unnecessary distractions. A placid pool of water without a single ripple on its surface, transparent and glassy to its depths.

Not surprisingly, I didn't hear from the director Craig had put me in touch with. The unfortunate incident with Ayaan while I was talking to him on the phone saw to that. But Craig had another offer for me.

"I'm going to set up my own company," he told me over a coffee at Café Sprinkle. "I just can't find the work. I can't do car ads for the rest of my life."

"You should go for it," I said, wishing I could do the same.

"I've got some savings and I'm going to do a crowd-funding campaign. I'll offer funders memorabilia from the films we'll make. But I'm also open to offers of investment. Any artists that put in money will be first choice for lead roles."

It was such a scintillating, brilliant offer that I was afraid it was too good to be true. At last, I'd have a chance to work with quality material.

The only way I'd have the £8,000 Craig needed from me was if I took it from the school fees fund that Tariq had set up for Zain. We'd talked about possibly sending the boys to private secondary schools and had set up savings accounts for both of them. Tariq had deposited a lump sum of £5,000 into each one, set up a monthly direct debit, then left control of Zain's account to me. There was almost £10,000 saved, just enough to give to Craig and have a bit left over. It was a risky move, but I was certain it would work out. We would make a successful movie and Zain would more than get his money back by the time he started secondary.

It wasn't going to be easy keeping it from Tariq. He'd always been supportive of my acting, but I didn't want to tell him about this venture until I had something concrete to share. How wonderful it would be when I revealed everything to him: the investment, my name heading the credits, how we'd be holding hands on opening night. The thought made me shiver with excitement.

TARIQ
2017

It was just instinct that compelled me to check the bank account. If Sophie was involved with this man, devising some sort of crime, money might be needed. I wasn't sure how much she had put away in her own name, but there should have been a decent sum in Zain's school fund. I'd left Sophie in charge of it, but I still had the online banking passcode written down in the back of my diary. I turned on the laptop in my study and typed it in. Now it was just a question of guessing her password. I knew the bank used a word and number combination. What would she choose? A place, somewhere she longed to visit? We'd talked about going to Morocco one day, Portugal, Mauritius, but she wasn't obsessed with travel. Obsessed… She was obsessed with one thing, something she mentioned more than anything. Her beloved films. As far as I knew, it was likely that she'd picked the name of one of her on screen heroes as her password. I typed in MATTDAMON18. Zain's birthday was on the 18th June. *Your password is incorrect.* I had another go. GERARDBUTLER18. Incorrect again. Another wrong attempt and I'd get locked out.

I sat back and tried to think with a calm, ordered mind. There were too many actors that she idolised. It was impossible to pick the right one. Who stood out? Who did she hold in special esteem? Then I remembered when we met, she'd had a craze for *Gone with the Wind*. I tried CLARKGABLE18. The little circle on the screen whirled and I braced myself for it to banish me from the bank, but then the page changed, and the statement appeared. I was in.

And Sophie had cleaned out the money.

"Where's the money, Sophie?" She was in the living room, flicking through a gardening magazine.

"Which money, darling?" she said.

"Zain's school fund," I said. Her eyes flickered and went from side to side, and her mouth fell open.

"Sit down, dear," she said. "I can explain everything." I ignored her plea to sit and stared at her. "I was going to ask you, but I wanted it to be a surprise. It's Craig. I gave it to him to set up a production company. We're going to make a film. Our own projects, so we can have control over everything, nobody to answer to."

I couldn't believe what I was hearing.

"Have you gone mad? A film company! He only needs to register the name to set up a limited company. It costs less than twenty quid! You've given him eight thousand!"

"Well, office equipment, promotion, all those things?"

I couldn't help it. I shouted at her.

"You stupid woman! You should have asked me."

The colour rose in her face, a raspberry flush washing across her cheeks.

"Tariq, please, don't get angry," she stammered. "I'm going to get it back. Once the film makes money, I'll pay it back with interest."

"What film? What world are you living in? You've thrown away Zain's future for a selfish whim! When are you going to realise you can't act?" Her mouth suddenly went from an imploring pout to a tough, mean pinch.

"What are you saying? I thought you believed in me!"

"I supported your hobby, your interest, yes, but I won't let you be delusional, throw money down the drain."

"Just like the others! And what were you doing snooping around in my affairs anyway, Mr High and Mighty? How did you steal my password?"

I ignored her and turned away.

"Where are you going?" she said. "I won't let anyone get in the way of my dreams, Tariq, let me warn you."

I walked out of the room.

I went into my study for a couple of hours. I tried looking at some work, a case involving a woman who'd been brought over from Sri Lanka as a domestic slave, but I couldn't concentrate. I was nervy, on edge. I took a tablet to stop the jumpiness, then put my headphones on. I'd thought "New Age" ambient music was a pretentious idea, hippy and feminine, when my doctor suggested I try it to help me relax, after Ruby died. But I'd found the sounds of rushing rivers and tinkling wind chimes did help me think of things with more clarity and less turmoil.

Sophie's story was so ridiculous and unbelievable that it had to be true. She must have given the money to Craig and not the other man she was seeing behind my back. But it was still evidence of her erratic, inexplicable behaviour, something that I felt completely ill-equipped to deal with.

I'd have to tell her calmly that she needed to get the money back from him. It wasn't just a small loan that I could overlook. It went without saying that I had no hope that they were going to make a blockbuster hit that was going to rake in millions.

I stayed in my office for as long as I could but eventually, I was hungry and got up to get myself some lunch. I wasn't in the mood to talk yet and wanted to avoid her, so I opened the door quietly. I crept towards the kitchen, glancing into the rooms but she wasn't there. Then I noticed the conservatory door was closed, unusually for this time of the day. As I crept towards it, treading softly on the creaky floorboards, I could hear the murmur of talking. Sophie was on the phone to someone. Craig? Was she doing as I'd asked, and trying to get the money back? I had to know. I got as close to the door as I dared. Although the blinds were pulled down on the other side of the glass door, there was a gap around the edge. Sophie wasn't facing the door, but she might sense a movement, a change in the light and turn and see me. I stopped about half a metre away. I strained my ears to listen to and understand her conversation, over the noise of the fish tank and the loudly ticking clock. The back of my neck was burning hot. Even if she didn't notice me, she might get up suddenly for her own reasons.

"Only three weeks to go now..." Sophie was saying. "My preparations are all done, don't worry about me. You just make sure you're ready... I told you, it was nothing major... he found out about something he wasn't meant to know... I'm so excited... yeah, I know... It took me a while to decide but I went for the gun in the end... We'll get away with it, I promise. He doesn't suspect a thing. Tariq won't know what's hit him."

I felt dizzy, a wave of darkness before my eyes, and stumbled back. I couldn't breathe, couldn't move. But I had to get out of there before she saw me. She was going to kill me. I saw movement in the conservatory as Sophie stood up. *Get out of there now.* I steadied myself by holding on to a chair, then took a gulp of air and slipped away silently from the room.

From the moment I heard her cryptic words, the uncertainty of her lethal intentions began to dominate my every thought and I knew I had to carry out the idea I'd been toying with for some time now. I didn't know why she wanted to kill me, but I assumed it was for my money. Who was her partner, the person she was plotting with on the phone? She'd told them that I had "found out something", referring to the money she'd given Craig, so it was unlikely to be him. I remembered the man from the hotel, another secret she was keeping from me. I had a strong inkling he was the one she was planning this with. It was the only conclusion that made sense. The whole B&B episode had had a dirty, underhand air about it, and now I knew what their intentions were, it only heightened my fear and revulsion. The man looked like the sort who would know "people" who could take care of business – like murder – for him. It sounded so laughable, but perhaps they were going to arrange a "hit"? I would have thought it ridiculous if I hadn't heard the conversation myself. But then again, no. Sophie had bought a gun. She was going to shoot me in cold blood herself.

I'd truly believed that there was love between us, but it had been nothing but a lie, a mirage, a trick of the heart, now dissolved into parched aridity.

I reminded myself that I possessed a cool, rational brain and had to operate in a professional, efficient mode. Every day I relied on evidence and facts for success, and the two vital pieces of information that I'd extracted from the telephone conversation formed the basis of my plan for survival. I knew when and how, and this gave me a huge advantage in my attempt to counter the attack. Sophie was going to make her move in three weeks' time, and her choice of weapon was a gun.

Although I'd had an instinctive response, I realised the police would need something more solid to act on. It was better to leave them out of it for now. They couldn't protect me and involving them would only put Sophie on alert.

The knowledge I had made it easier to try and behave as normal, even though I did find myself jumping at loud noises or when Sophie suddenly appeared in a room. At least I didn't have to fret about being poisoned or knifed or strangled. But still, I had to keep my wits about me, and as a precaution I made sure my meals were served from the same dishes as Sophie's and Zain's. I kept alert while I was driving, in case anyone was following me, and looked out for Sophie's accomplice at all times.

The nights were the trickiest. It was near impossible for me to sleep next to my own killer, not knowing if I would wake up tomorrow. I survived by the days and nights praying and entrusting myself to God, believing that Sophie wouldn't murder me before it was time. My preparation took less than a couple of weeks, well within the time frame I was working against.

Fortunately, I had several bank accounts, most of them business ones, which I had control over, and which Sophie didn't know about. I withdrew a large amount of money from one of them, enough cash to last me a few months if I lived frugally. I could access it later if I needed to. I bought four pay-as-you-go mobile phones and took bits and pieces of clothing from the bottom of the cupboard, things that wouldn't be missed. I bought a new holdall and kept it in the boot of my car to be filled up.

Then, on 9th July, I walked out of the house and didn't come back.

I stayed in a B&B in Devon for a few days, walking coastal paths and exploring coves, a quiet, dawdling existence, purposely distracting myself from trying to make sense of what was happening. But mapping out my next move couldn't be avoided. I had to know what she was doing now that I was gone.

I returned to Bradford to watch Sophie. I followed her in a hired car and staked out the house. Laughably, I bought a few silly wigs and caps, and wore a different one every day, just in case she noticed me, even though I kept enough distance for her not to actually recognise my face. Nothing happened.

Sophie just went about her normal business. The shops, Amir's house to drop off Zain, her mother's place. She looked, I must admit, rather depressed. Was she upset about losing me or because she'd been denied the chance to do the deed herself?

I even spent a morning and the afternoon of different days parked on the road outside the shifty B&B, The Fisherman. I saw the man go out once and get on a bus towards town. There was no sign of Sophie.

Satisfied that Sophie wasn't doing anything untoward for the time being, I went to the Lake District and spent some time in Kendall in a caravan. It was near Sameena and when I was sure nobody was on my tail, I met with her and Ayaan when I could. I hadn't told her what I was planning at first, and when Sophie rang her the day I disappeared, Sameena genuinely hadn't known where I was. I trusted her completely, but I'd still waited a few days before contacting her. It would be easier for her to keep my secret once the initial commotion and enquiries had passed. I never went to the house. I knew Sophie might visit at any time, and she did, on Ayaan's birthday. She even followed Sameena and the children to the café.

I had considered moving Ayaan somewhere else, but I thought a sudden change would only make Sophie suspicious that I was behind it. Sophie didn't have anything to gain from harming Ayaan financially at least, and I considered him to be safe there for now.

I kept an eye on Sophie's Facebook page. I never post anything myself. I only registered on it so I could look up old friends and see their latest news, but I never like or share anything. It's the opposite of everything I am.

I made a new, fake account, just in case anyone was monitoring my old one. Unlike me, though, Sophie was addicted, and checking her social media gave me a better insight into what she was doing than if I'd asked Sameena to make a few discreet phone calls to find out. It looked like she was posting regularly.

16th July 2017 Please! Appeal for help! My darling husband, Tariq, has been missing since last week. He was last seen Thursday morning, leaving for work in a black Mercedes. Please DM if you have any information or call me.

27th July 2017 If you've seen Tariq, you can call the police if you want instead of me, but PLEASE somebody tell me where he is. Somebody must know! Please. I'm begging you.

1st August 2017 Tariq! I'm appealing to you! If you're reading this, please get in touch. Please, my love, tell me if something's upset you. Whatever it is we'll work it out. We just need to talk. I need to hear your voice. Please, just talk to me. Just let me know you're okay.

I nearly gave in. She sounded almost genuine. I was torn. She was so beguiling, an elusive, bewitching creature with her smiles and her tears. But then I remembered that she was plotting to murder me. How could I live with a woman like that? I didn't know what I was going to do. I needed time to think, to let my mind regain its strength.

The time in the caravan was what I needed. I cooked simple meals, took soothing, green walks, and visited the town once or twice. I was good at keeping myself to myself, and nobody asked questions. I had enough to survive, and I knew Ayaan was safe. Nothing else mattered. I didn't want to think about work. The office would be in a hectic state, but I thought they would just about manage without me until I went back.

I would have to return. I hoped my departure had rattled Sophie and that she'd abandoned whatever her scheme had been. From what I'd seen and what Sameena had discreetly learned from different relatives, Sophie seemed to be playing the part of the loyal wife, but I couldn't ignore what I'd seen and heard with my own eyes and ears. All I could do now was go back and confront her with what I knew. After that I could decide what do about our marriage.

I'd dozed off with a book one evening, when the phone rang. It was Sameena.

"Oh my God, Tariq!"

"What's wrong?" I said. "Is Ayaan okay?"

"He's fine. What about you? What happened?"

"I'm fine. What's wrong?"

"I just had a phone call from Sophie's brother, saying they've found you. That you've been killed in a car crash."

"What? What car crash?"

"I'm not sure, some pile up on the motorway."

"When? And where, which motorway?" Of course I knew I haven't been in a car crash, but my heart was thudding loudly.

"He didn't give me all the details. Just that they've found your body."

I couldn't speak for a moment. News of one's own death is enough to flummox anyone.

"Tariq?" said Sameena.

"Yes, Sam, I'm here. I don't understand. Why would they think it was me?"

"They must have some sort of proof. You'll find out when you go back."

"Go back? What do you mean?"

"It's enough, isn't it?" she said. "You have to go back, obviously. You can't put Sophie through something like this."

"You didn't tell them anything, did you?"

"No."

"Who identified the body?"

"I don't know."

"You have to trust me. Don't tell anyone about me yet. Let me find out what's going on first."

"Alright. But don't do anything stupid."

TARIQ
Present Day

I arrive in Leeds the night before the funeral and rent a room in a hotel in the city. I've grown my hair and my beard. Neither is wildly overgrown, but they make enough of a difference to confuse someone who doesn't know me well.

On the morning of the *janaza*, I wait outside the masjid as my own funeral prayers are performed. I can't go in and be part of the deception. After fifteen minutes, four men carry out my coffin and load it into the white van the mosque committee have adapted for the funeral service, and I follow them to the cemetery in my rented car. I hang at the back of the crowd to avoid attention as I watch the burial. Some of the men I know – Sophie's brother, Haroon, a couple of her cousins, a few work acquaintances and Jimmy, who's crying as he twiddles the ropes they've attached to the coffin. I notice one of Sophie's uncles, who I've seen only in pictures as he lives in Cardiff and rarely visits. He's come away to the edge of the cemetery to smoke a cigarette.

"Was it an accident, Uncle?" I put on my best Mirpuri accent, which I've been practising for the last few weeks. It fools him and he doesn't even look at me.

"Yes, it was a very bad accident. The poor guy's face was completely smashed up," he says.

I tut sadly and wait a few seconds before asking my next question. "How did they identify him then?"

"His poor wife had to go in and look at the body. She's a brave girl, that one. Took it all on herself. Didn't want to upset anyone else. She didn't let anyone see him, not even for the bathing."

I bet she didn't. If she knew it wasn't me, of course she wouldn't risk anyone else seeing the body. It was a dangerous ruse. She could have been rumbled at any time if any of my friends, suddenly feeling sentimental, decided to pop into the masjid to take a last loving look at my remains and noticed that something wasn't right.

"Such a devoted wife," continues the uncle. "She even stayed up all night keeping vigil. Reading her surahs next to him, right there in the masjid, so he wasn't alone during his last hours. He was a lucky man. Did you know him well?"

"Not really. I'm a friend of the family." This is one of the most useful phrases in our community, its vagueness providing a way out of so many awkward situations.

We raise our hands for the final *dua*, as earth, "my earth", is piled over the coffin that contains an unknown man, and a plaque bearing my name is placed at the head of my grave.

I don't know, really, why I'm carrying on the pretence. If I'm honest I am rather enjoying the intrigue of it all. And I just want to figure out what's happening in Sophie's head. Has she genuinely made a mistake? It's disquieting to think of her spending the night alone in the mosque, praying for a stranger's corpse, either unwittingly or just to keep up appearances. I think it's the latter. She knows it's not me. A dead and dusted husband is much more convenient and profitable than a missing one. Sophie must have thought things would be transferred over to her smoothly, easily. Little did she know the arrangements I'd made for that side of things. I'd like to have seen her face when she heard the contents of my will. I'm a lawyer with cautious blood running through my veins, and I'd changed it before leaving as a safeguard, just in case she did somehow manage to get rid of me. The life insurance was another matter. We'd taken out a joint policy, and she would eventually receive this if I continue living my ghostly life.

I keep an eye on her for the next few days. I vary the times, popping by in the morning, afternoon or evening, to try and get a better idea of her overall movements. She does nothing much, stays in, apart from taking Zain to the Holiday Club. She looks wretched. Whether or not she thinks I'm dead, she's certainly pining for me. None of this is making any sense. She's conniving and manipulative, but adoring and heartbroken at the same time. A day or two more, and I'll end it. I need to know the truth.

I park in my usual spot, in the latest of my short-term hire cars. I change them every few days, so Sophie doesn't notice me. It's early evening. I've brought some comforting provisions with me – Kettle chips, two baked cheesecake slices in plastic triangles, honey roasted peanuts, a litre of water, prawn mayonnaise sandwiches. I don't know where I've dropped my Marks and Spencer's card. Not that I would use it under these circumstances. Using any sort of electronic card makes it easy to be found, the modern equivalent of leaving a trail of breadcrumbs and footprints, and I'm not going to risk that for any number of loyalty points. I try reading my book, a Jack Reacher novel, but it's difficult to concentrate, so I turn on my mobile phone and log in to my games – chess, Word Feud and Angry Birds. I chomp on the cheesecake and fling birdy bombs through the desert air. Eventually my back gets sore from sitting in one place for so long, and I'm about to leave when I see him. It's the man from the dirty B&B.

I'm suddenly enraged. Despite witnessing her previous sordid meeting myself, I'd held on to the hope that there might be some explanation that would make things clear, some weird but valid reason behind it. But now here he is, in my house, and I don't even want to imagine what they're doing. I feel physically sick. And here I was, just about to try and resolve things.

I don't want to see any more. I go back to the hotel. I think I'm a level-headed, reasonable man, but my emotions have taken over. I want, simply, revenge.

For a couple of days, I'm too upset and foul-tempered to leave the hotel. I get takeaways delivered to the room and eat them in bed. It's a messy habit, but I'm nervy and panicked, and it somehow gives me a sense of safety. When I feel calmer, I go out and get a supply of plain white paper, a pair of scissors, a Pritt Stick and a newspaper. It's all I need to creep her out a little bit. A couple of days later, when I've had time to calm down, I sit in my hotel room and open the newspaper. I flick through the stories without taking anything in, then I take the scissors and snip out words, mixing up fonts and sizes. I arrange them on a sheet of A4.

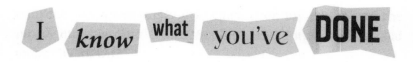

It's such a cliché that I chuckle as I'm doing it. Wearing gloves, I fold it into four and tuck it into an envelope, then stick down the flap with Sellotape. It's a little OCD habit I have. I worry that envelopes will open, so I always add a strip of tape for extra security. But Sophie knows this.

"You're such a fusspot!" she always tells me, laughingly.

She'll know it's me. I remove the tape and put the letter in a fresh envelope, sealing it with a drop of water from a new bottle, spreading it across the gummed strip with a cotton bud. I couldn't bear it if I was tracked down by DNA samples.

The next day, I drive past the house and see her car in the drive. I park around the corner and wait. Ten minutes later she drives past, probably on the way to the Holiday Club to collect Zain. I wait a few moments, then I get out of the car, pulling down my hat and putting on a pair of mirrored sunglasses. I try to walk differently to how I normally do, hunching over a little.

I walk up the path to our house and push the envelope through the letterbox. It's so amusing I can't help smiling to myself. It's so deliciously vague, yet piercingly on target for someone with a guilty conscience.

I repeat the amusing process again the next day. Then I think it's time for the final proceedings.

SOPHIE

The first note arrived yesterday, followed by the second this morning. They're like something from those stuffy TV films with old lady detectives solving crimes committed during the village fete. Hand-delivered letters with messages made from words cut out of a newspaper.

But still, they terrify me. Did someone see what I did to Suleiman? They couldn't have. I made sure there was nobody there. My mind goes to the woman who's been stalking me. She knows where I live. But what does she want? And who the hell is she? I could hardly see her face any of the times I spotted her. The note seems quite infantile, but I'm chilled to think of what she'll do next.

I try to take my mind off her and the note, by thinking of something hopeful. Once the life insurance comes through, I can start finding somewhere else for Zain and me to live, and finally look forward to a more productive, artistic phase of my life. There's nobody left to stop me now. I think briefly about my upcoming role in Craig's film and how a junior doctor would dress, how she'd style her hair. Tied back, I think, minimal but effective make-up.

Before that, though, I have to survive the inevitable investigation into Suleiman's death. It's been two days and though his body hasn't turned up yet, it could do at any time. I go back over the scene yet again. Have I missed anything?

The only possible eyewitnesses are the old couple, but unless the woman remembers me from the audition, which I think is unlikely given my different looks, all she'd be able to give is a vague description.

I decide it's best to be prepared for anything. If I'm forced to run, I will. My eyes fill with tears as I realise that if it comes to that I'll have to leave Zain behind. There's no way I'll make him live a fugitive life. Thank goodness he's still at Amir's in the midst of all this. And my criminal activities aside, it's good for him to spend time with his father. It's also the safest place he can be right now.

Apparently, Ruby and Tariq went camping to the South of France one year. I was bored by the story but it's useful to me now. I go to the garage and find the camping equipment and take a large rucksack. I pack it with clothes, some essential toiletries, and the rest of my gold jewellery. Then I think I might need to take emergency measures and get a tent and a sleeping bag and put them in the boot of the car. I'm not contemplating spending any nights under the stars, not contemplating going anywhere, but I want to be ready for any eventuality.

As it gets dark, I double check the locks and go into the living room. Hesitantly I draw the curtain and look out on to the road, half expecting to see the woman there, watching me. But there's nobody and I come away from the window.

An uncomfortable thought's been niggling at my mind all day. The picnicking witness. I'm reluctant to admit it but I know if I want to ensure complete safety for myself, she'll have to be dealt with. First, I need to find out who she is. I didn't speak to her much when I saw her at the audition and don't remember her name. I Google "older South Asian actresses" and select images. It's a long shot. She might not even be a professional. But after ten minutes I find her, grey haired and serious, a headshot on a page for an acting agency. Shilpa Panesar. She's done a few adverts, some theatre, been an extra on *Casualty* and *Coronation Street*, and there's a link to her website. There's no address on www.shilpsp.com, but there is a telephone number. I search a bit more, and an acupuncture website appears. It's her again – there's a photo of her on the home page. She has another business as a natural healer and has a clinic in Dewsbury.

A mundane series of digits and a dull sounding location that are nevertheless enticing, magnetic and lethal, chameleon pieces of information depending on how I use them. I could just phone her and frighten, threaten or plead with her, but there would no guarantees. And I won't offer a bribe. I know from past experience that the exchange of money in a situation like this is an indefinite entrapment.

I could just stakeout the clinic once Suleiman's body's been discovered, to see if she's visited the police but it's a weak strategy with too many holes. I can't watch the place around the clock, I don't even know how often she goes there, and there are many other ways the police can communicate with her.

An unwelcome but more permanent solution is presenting itself to me. I'm not proud of it, but I do seem to be becoming a specialist in "accidents." A little hit and run outside her office... Or perhaps it would be better to lure her somewhere else, invite her to a meeting about an acting job offer?

I'm getting ahead of myself. Hopefully none of this will be necessary. Perhaps Suleiman's death will be accepted as unsuspicious. I really don't want any harm to come to Shilpa Panesar. Far from doing anything to hurt me, she'd been trying to help when she came over to talk to me at the barbecue area, making sure Suleiman wasn't bothering me. And how do I know if she even has anything to tell the police? I don't want to murder her for no reason. I'm not an evil woman. On the other hand, if I'm forced to, I'll do whatever I have to. I am a mother. Even the humblest of creatures protect their young. I'll remove any threat to the safety and happiness of my son. His future will be at serious risk if I go to jail.

I'm still mulling over all of this when I hear it. The sound of a key turning.

TARIQ

I open the door as quietly as I can, but it creaks, and go down the hall towards the living room. I know she's in there, but she's switched the lights off. There's a grey darkness everywhere and my eyes dart around, eventually settling on a shape in the corner of the living room where the darkness is thicker, heavier. I slide my hand to the wall and fumble for the switch. Light bursts harshly on, and Sophie is illuminated. Her face, filled with fear, instantly transforms into one of consternation. There's no room for fakery here.

"Tariq?" she whispers. She sways, puts her hand on the wall to steady herself. "Tariq? How did you... what...?" She seems lost for words. She drops on to the sofa and I go to her. She throws her arms around my neck and clings to me, sobbing. "Thank God! Thank God you're alive! We thought... Oh my God... thank you!" She kisses my face all over. Then I hold her still for a moment, and for a few seconds it seems I can feel the reconnection of our souls through the warmth of our bodies, and our world is as it should be.

"I can't believe you're here," she says, as we sit holding hands. She's still crying, face soaked. I take out a handkerchief and dab her eyes.

"No more tears now," I say. I get her a glass of water and she gulps it down.

"Where have you been? What happened? Did someone take

you?" Now her eyes are darting around as though expecting to see someone else.

"Nobody took me," I say. "What's the matter, why are you so nervous? I'm here now."

"You frightened me, Tariq," she says. "I thought someone was breaking in. You don't know what's been going on around here." She leans on me, resting her head on my shoulder, her hands gripping my arm.

"Why, what's happened?" I say, doing my best to sound oblivious. "Did someone hurt you?"

"No, it's not that... It's just..." Her voice trails off and she looks at me searchingly. "Never mind that. You still haven't told me. Where have you been all this time?"

I'd expected anger, even fury, but this is concern, love.

"I've been sick with worry," she says. "I know it's dreadful, but I thought you were... well, dead... What happened?"

I let go of her hands, move away slightly on the sofa. The reunion's softened me, but I need to remember what caused all this in the first place.

"I found out you were going to kill me," I say. Again, the look on her face is real. She's utterly shocked.

"How can you say something like that?" she says in a broken voice. I tell her what I overheard, the phone conversation in which she said I wasn't "going to know what hit me". She frowns, puzzled, for a few moments, then her brow clears, and she laughs.

"You left because of that?" she says. "I honestly don't believe this!"

"I think fear of being murdered by your wife is good reason to leave," I say.

"I wasn't going to murder you, you silly man! I was trying to organise a surprise birthday party for you. I was talking to Jimmy. I rented out the community centre and organised a caterer. Jimmy knows all your old friends, people from school and university. He was dealing with that side of things. We were trying to do something memorable for you, and you thought…"

"You bought a gun."

She looks confused again.

"What are you talking about, Tariq?" she says. "Why would I do that?"

"I heard you. You told Jimmy you 'went for the gun'."

"Oh my God!" she says, rolling her eyes. "Yes, a massage gun! For your back. I was going to give you at-home spa sessions. It was your birthday present. I'll show you if you don't believe me."

I feel suddenly hot. Embarrassed, ashamed, cruel. Her explanation rings true. I'd misinterpreted her innocent words and wreaked irreparable damage on our marriage.

"Could you blame me? After you started getting violent with me, I didn't know what you were capable of. And there were other things."

"What other things?"

"The money."

"I explained all of that."

"I know, but after I heard you talking, I thought you might be lying. Then there was Ayaan. I couldn't trust you after you shoved him."

"We talked about that, and I said I was sorry."

"Are you cheating on me?"

"What?" Now there's real shock in her eyes. "How can you even think that?" She bows her head, about to cry again.

"I saw you with a man," I say.

"What man?" she says, her head jerking up sharply to look at me.

"You tell me," I say. "A big man in a white suit and panama hat. He came to the house."

"Oh, him," she says. Her expression's difficult to read, now. Sneaky. "Yes, okay, he did come to the house. But that was only a few days ago. You disappeared long before that."

"I saw him before that, too, when you went to meet him in the B&B."

"How could you have seen me there?" she says. "Were you following me? Spying on me?"

"No, not really. I followed you by accident. Look, I don't think how I found out is the issue here. Just tell me who he is! He's your boyfriend, isn't he?" It sounds childish, "boyfriend", but perhaps accusing her with a different choice of words would make it too painfully real. She pauses for a moment, then laughs.

"Of course not, silly!" she says. "How could you think he was my boyfriend? Why would I do something like that when I have you?"

Now her words seem genuine again, warm and tender. I'm perplexed.

"Then what?" I say.

"He's a relative, a distant cousin of Amir's. He's had some bad luck over the years, most of it his own fault, but I think of it as charity work and help him out sometimes. That's why I met him in the B&B, to give him a few pounds. Then I dropped him off in the town centre. There was nothing dodgy about it, I promise. You can ask Amir about him."

"Why didn't you just tell me?"

"He's not exactly respectable. He's been involved in some unscrupulous things. Not the type you want to introduce to your upstanding husband. He was just an odd relation I saw once in a while out of pity. Like I said, you should have just asked me." She looks at me quizzically. She has an answer for everything, and it's all quite believable, but there's still an aura of deception about her. I don't know what to think.

"I'm sorry," I say. "I shouldn't have gone off like that. I was terrified. And I suppose, in a way, I just wanted to teach you a lesson."

"Teach me a lesson?" she says, sitting bolt upright. "You certainly did that. Tariq, it felt like my world had ended."

"I didn't mean for you to feel like that."

"Is there anything else you did, as part of this 'punishment'?" she asks, after a minute. "Did you break the window?"

"I don't know what you're talking about," I say, but I know I look guilty. I have to tell her. "I didn't break anything."

"But?"

"I did write the anonymous letters," I say. She closes her eyes for a moment but doesn't say anything.

We sit in silence for a moment. I scratch my trouser leg with the key I still have in my hand. The boiler groans loudly from the kitchen. I can't look at her. If all she says is true, that she was being a kind, charitable relative, a devoted, party organising wife and an enterprising but naïve businesswoman, then I'm nothing but the worst kind of man – a suspicious husband.

"You must be hungry," she says at last.

"Not really," I say. "I've been stuffing myself with supermarket sandwiches."

"Have a cup of tea, at least."

"Okay. I've missed your tea." I smile weakly. It's a pathetic thing to say but it's all I have at the moment. She goes to the kitchen. I'm left to think about the irrational way I've behaved over the last few weeks. I'm mortified. All I can say in my defence is that at the time I'd felt cornered and desperate, my head a pandemonium of mistrust when I'd mistakenly thought Sophie was out to kill me.

I'm still in the midst of these speculations when I realise, I haven't even questioned why she identified that man as me. The home telephone rings suddenly. It's an unknown number but I pick it up. In the distraction I'm too slow to notice the figure rushing towards me. Pain crashes down on my head and I go thudding into darkness.

FARAZ

My ex-wife Muskaan had been in England for about six months now, but I hadn't gone to see her. Her doctor husband was also a cousin of ours, Saleem, and despite the tensions between us, I was obliged to visit them in their posh Harrogate mansion. Muskaan looked very well, her hair long and glossy, not hidden under a loose scarf like it used to be. She'd changed her usual cotton *salwar kameez* for skinny jeans and a t-shirt with a cartoon mermaid on it.

It was a very awkward situation to be in, but thankfully her husband is a decent and sober man and started chatting to me very easily about cricket and politics, while Muskaan stared at me coolly with a raised eyebrow.

"Yes, talk to him about games," she said to Saleem. "Faraz is very good at playing games."

I felt very tongue-tied and abashed after that, but Saleem asked her to make some tea and carried on talking as before. Nobody could guess I was his wife's scumbag ex-husband who dumped her for another woman. We could have been back on the roof of our house in Karachi, chatting under a night of stars and mosquitoes.

Encouraged by his friendliness I asked if they had any wedding photos.

"We haven't got the professional ones yet," said Saleem. "But there are quite a few in Muskaan's phone. It's over there, charging." He unplugged it and swiped, then passed it to me. "Scroll left." I went through it, making appreciative noises, muttering "lovely", "handsome", and "food looks yum".

"We had everything fresh," he said. "Live barbecue, ice cream van, chocolate fountain."

"What an extravaganza," I said.

It looked like a very grand wedding, and Muskaan looked rather sweet. Here she was holding a bunch of roses to her face, giving her husband a secret sideways glance, interlocking arms with him to drink Sprite from champagne glasses. I stroked the screen again and here was the next photo, staring at me from a coffee shop table, eating a Danish pastry and reading a sheet of paper. Not Muskaan, but Sophie. I swiped again, and here she was, looking at a dress in Evans, opening her front door, sitting in her car. I was horrified. What had Muskaan been doing?

"That's private!" snapped Muskaan, snatching the phone away from me and slamming down a plate of Jammie Dodgers.

"Private?" I said. "Do you even know anything about privacy? What are these pics? Have you been stalking my wife?"

"She's not your wife anymore!" hissed Muskaan.

"What do you mean?" said Saleem. "You told me those pictures were of your friend."

"What did you do to her?" I said.

"I just watched her." She smiled. "And then I scared her a little bit." She laughed hysterically.

"Why?"

"Do you really have to ask me? After what she did to us? I had so many hopes for us, but you and her – you broke my heart! I wanted my life to finish. And you think I should let her get off free?"

"Muskaan, what are you talking about?" said Saleem. "Can someone please tell me what's been going on?"

Muskaan shoved a mug into his hand in reply.

"I'm sorry about everything," I said. "I'm ashamed. It was my fault."

"Yes, that's true, but she wasn't without blame either," said Muskaan. "And look what's happened to her now. She got what she deserved." This last remark was too spiteful for me to take.

"You're a horrible, disgusting lady!" I shouted, then got up and left the house, leaving Saleem with his mouth wide open, holding tea in one hand and a biscuit in the other.

Since that meeting a few days ago, I've been imagining what exactly Muskaan did to scare her, and mentally rehearsing the words I'm going to say when I explain it all to Sophie. It's going to make her mad, and I've been too frightened to tell her, but it has to be done soon. Tonight.

I need to see she's safe but that's not all. I'll take any excuse to see her. I can't help it. I can't stop thinking about her. She's vulnerable, I know it, and she needs the warm and protective arms of a man around her. Mine.

TARIQ

I'm tied to a dining chair with a long scarf. Sophie is sitting on the sofa. On her lap is a black object that looks like a drill, but instead of the metal bit on the end there's what looks like a black ping pong ball.

"This is the infamous massage gun," she says. "I'd left it all wrapped up in case you came back, but when you mentioned it, I knew it'd be just the thing to knock you out with. Nice and heavy. It was me on the phone, by the way. I rang you from the kitchen so I could catch you off guard." She sighs. "It's a shame because I really do love you. But you're right, darling, with your suspicion. I'm assuming you had suspicions concerning the identification of the body?"

"You knew it wasn't me," I say.

"You don't know how terrified I was when the police told me they'd found a body, but I saw straight away that it wasn't you," she says. "He was just a different shape. He had a round head, not like you, with your beautiful long face. But then it just came to me, a flash of genius. I could just say it was you, and everything would be easier."

"You thought you'd inherit my money?" I ask.

"I needed the money to make everything work. To progress in my career, and so Zain and I had some security, a roof over our heads. I really was losing hope of finding you alive. It was so horrible not knowing. I didn't want you to be dead, but if you were, it was better if we had a body to show for it. Otherwise, we'd be waiting around forever, waiting for yours to turn up. And I've never been one for patience."

"Who was the man you buried?" I ask.

"How do I know? Someone up to no good if he had your Marks and Spencer's card on him."

"Weren't you worried someone might see him and realise what you were up to?" I say. Sophie snorts.

"Do you think I'd be so careless?" she says. She puts the massage gun on the sofa and pulls something out from under a cushion. A knife. "I guarded him like a bulldog until he was safely interred. He got a nice funeral at least, whoever he was. Which, unfortunately, is a lot more than what you're going to get."

"What are you talking about, Sophie?" I try to remain aloof and silent.

"It's all your own fault," she says. "We were happy together, but you spoilt everything by disappearing. Disloyal fool. And now I can't let you go. You saw me with him. You know too much. It's a shame, because I really loved you. I loved you so much."

"Put the knife down, then."

"I can't. I have to work out how to do this."

"Do what?"

"I can't kill you here. Too messy. And I can't take you to the Valley. Imagine all the bodies bobbing to the surface."

"What bodies? Who else have you put there?"

"Keep up, Tariq. Him, of course. My hard luck pretend cousin. Just a loathsome man who was always trying to ruin my life. But if it wasn't for you, I wouldn't have had to do it! If you hadn't gone off like that, I could have just carried on paying him off."

She's relishing giving me the juicy bits of information, tantalising me. She's smiling and her face is rosy, unnaturally bright. My hands are tied behind me. I try to wriggle them, loosen the scarf, but I have to make small movements so she doesn't notice.

"So where is he now?" I say. "Where's this valley?"

"Never mind. Anyway, as I was saying. You should have decided – home or away. You can't have it both ways."

"What are you talking about? Didn't you want me home? Or was that just a lie?"

"Well, I did, until you told me why you stayed away. I wanted you home desperately. I never imagined you were hiding from me out of spite, to punish me. How dare you?"

"It wasn't spite. I was scared."

"And what about your will? Were you scared then? You gave me and Zain a few pounds and made us destitute! We weren't a charity case. We were your family." She has tears in her eyes, but she wipes them away.

"You are my family. I love you both. I was going to come back."

"Too late." She comes towards me with the knife.

FARAZ

I put a little effort into dressing up, smoothing some gel on to my hair and combing it neatly, and taking out my tan-coloured blazer. Sophie liked this one. I hope it will have a positive effect. I splash on some David Beckham aftershave and slip a souvenir tin of mints with Her Majesty's elegantly stern face on them into the inside breast pocket of the jacket.

I'm outside her house in fifteen minutes. I park across the road and gather up my courage. Movement in the window tells me she's inside. I ring the doorbell, but she doesn't come to the door. What if she's in trouble? Bad things have been happening to her recently, and I'm worried.

It won't help to break the door down. It will give any villains inside a warning. Luckily, I watch *Beat the Burglar*, a daytime show about home security. I take out a credit card and insert it into the crack between the door and the jamb. It's an old door, and only takes a few slides up and down before it gives way and opens.

I step inside soundlessly. I know the layout of the house from my research on Rightmove, but I follow the light and the voices down the hall towards the lounge, to where Sophie is standing next to a figure slumped in a chair, a knife in her hand.

"Sophie!" I exclaim, without thinking what effect it might have on her grip. "What's happened? Who's that?" The figure lifts his head and looks at me. "Tariq! Ya Allah! Sophie? What's this?"

"Help me, Faraz. Call the police!" says Tariq.

"No! Don't listen to him, Faraz! He's come back a madman!" says Sophie. "He hid away so he could sneak back and murder me. He just tried it now, he had his hands around my neck."

"Don't believe it, Faraz, please," says Tariq. "Remember what you told me. You can't trust her, you know that, remember what she did to you!"

"Shut up!" cries Sophie, slapping him. "And what's this? How do you two know each other? You tell him something about me?" She's turned to me, glaring at me with shiny maniac eyes.

"No, darling," I say, forgetting that her husband's sitting there. "I just met with him for my visa case." Her face suddenly breaks up and she lets out a whimper.

"Help me, Faraz," she says. "Help me get rid of him then we can be happy together."

The words I've yearned for. I look at their faces, the rumpled cushions, the few drops of blood on the carpet, the memory of Sophie, her sometimes gentle love, her infectious laugh. And, in a flash, I think of her angry with me, not liking my hobbies and my habits, and then the meeting with Tariq, my head a swirling, spiralling time warp, and I make my move.

I bound across the room, going directly to grab the knife from her hand, but she sees what I'm doing, must see it in my face, and raises her arm and aims straight for the heart that's finally abandoned her.

Once more, Sophie Shah v Elizabeth Regina. My eternal queen comes to my rescue, and the knife plunges into the tin of mints in the pocket of my blazer, blocking the blow. Sophie's surprise when her strike fails, and the recoil give me enough time to grab her arm and pull the dagger away with my other hand. I turn to Tariq and try to cut him free, but she throws herself at me like a missile, pushing me to the floor.

She scratches and rips my face as I struggle to get away from her. From the corner of my eye, I see Tariq get to his feet. He's managed to free himself from the bindings and pulls her off me, then both of us try to tame the fire-breathing creature of distorted love and hate.

AMIR

I'm uncomfortable tonight. I've been lying in bed for two hours now, but my eyes aren't the least bit sleepy. I'm worried about Sophie. Things with her feel strange, shifting, and I can't put my finger on what's happening. Jannat isn't helping. She's four weeks away from giving birth and is continuously twitching, groaning and rolling, shaking the bed and disturbing me every time I get anywhere near nodding off.

Eventually I get up. I look in on the boys. Zain has his own little bed in Sameer's room for when he stays over, which is almost every weekend. It's a heart-warming feeling to know that they're like real brothers, unaffected by having different mothers. Jannat can have her moments, and she can't stand Sophie, but she's never shown anything but love towards Zain. The boys are soundly asleep, the room lit peacefully with a string of lights hidden inside stars and planets. I thank God for all my children and thank him that Zain's here with me on this wakeful night.

I go downstairs to have some water. My stomach's rumbling and I take out a packet of Jaffa Cakes. I sit on a kitchen stool and switch on my phone, turn on the "Escape Room" game I installed this morning, and start to work out the coded puzzle, muttering under my breath as I nibble the biscuits. Suddenly it buzzes into life, playing the theme tune to *Rocky*. It's Sophie's mum.

* * *

She's unnaturally quiet as she tells me what's happened, as though the years of struggling with Sophie have finally drained and exhausted her. I'm equally silent. I can't speak from the disbelief.

"Where is she?" I ask in a leaden voice.

"The police took her away, of course," she says. "Where else do you want her to be?"

"And Faraz and Tariq? Are they okay?"

"They're both fine."

"I don't understand it. Sophie…"

"I'm surprised it didn't happen sooner. I've been dreading a day like this for years."

Although I'm in shock, I can relate to the feeling she's describing. Hadn't there always been a small bit of me that was afraid of Sophie's unpredictable moods, of the savagery she might be capable of?

Sophie's mum promises to be here first thing in the morning to be with me and Zain, and head full of foreboding, I finally go upstairs and fall asleep as soon as I drop on to the mattress.

SOPHIE

"So, Sophie," says McKinley, as I sit handcuffed on a chair in the middle of a room. "Let's have another chat, shall we?"

She's already questioned me about the attack on Tariq and Faraz. Last night when they brought me in, they gave me some sort of tranquillisers, so she didn't talk to me until this morning. I told them that Tariq stole into the house and told me that he's been watching me over the last few weeks; very creepy, questionable behaviour. I was scared for my life and that was my reason for acting the way I did. I'm hoping she'll believe me.

"Where were you on Saturday afternoon?" says McKinley. The question is like a needle in my throat, but I manage to keep my breathing even.

"Saturday?" I say. "Let me see. I think I was just at home with several tubs of Haagen-Dazs ice cream. Strawberry Cheesecake and Cookies and Cream. I never can make up my mind, so I buy a variety. I was eating it while I watched crappy talent shows on the TV."

"Was there anyone with you?" she asks.

"No."

"What about your son? Where was he?"

"With his father, my ex-husband, Amir."

"Strange. Your car was seen by cameras on Old Leeds Road at 3.45pm."

"What?" I pretend to think about it, put a worried look on

my brow. "Oh yes, I popped out for some bread and milk. The chocolate was finished too." I smile guiltily.

"Where did you get it from?"

"Najma's Convenience Store on Killinghall Road."

It's true. I did pop in there on the way to Bolton Abbey.

"Where did you go after that?"

"I just went home."

"Your car isn't on Leeds Road again though, driving back."

"Well obviously I took a different route home. I like to have a change. It gets boring otherwise. Especially the school run, but there's not much scope for variety there."

Thank God I didn't come home down Old Leeds Road from Bolton Abbey on Saturday evening. But cameras are everywhere, and they'll find me again. I feel walled in by cameras, feel them closing in from all sides, obliterating me when they reach the centre.

"Do you know this man?" says McKinley. She shows me a picture of Suleiman at a family wedding.

"He seems familiar, but I don't know his name," I say.

"He's a distant relative of Amir."

"I've probably seen him on their party circuit some time."

"His body's been found in the river at Bolton Abbey," she says. "It looks like he fell from the path that leads down to the waterfall."

"Poor man," I say. "How old was he? Did he have any children?"

"Did you tell your husband, Tariq, that you'd killed a man and left him in a river?"

"No! Why would I do that? Do you think I'm crazy?"

She pauses and watches me for a moment. Then she takes another photo out from her folder and holds it up. It's a blurry CCTV picture of me at Bolton Abbey, but my disguise is good. With the cap, the sunglasses and the scarf around my neck pulled up almost over my lips you can hardly see any of my face. There's no way of knowing that it's me for sure.

"We've got this picture of you at Bolton Abbey last Saturday, and we have two witnesses that remember seeing you there."

"Oh, really?" I say. "They're making it up. People are just jealous of me. Everyone wants me gone."

"I think you should call a lawyer, Sophie. I recommended it before I began this interview. One of the witnesses, a woman on a picnic with her husband, recognised you from the audition you went to a few days ago."

I really should have dealt with Shilpa.

"There you go, point proven. I got the job. She's jealous she lost out and now she's trying to pin this random murder on me. It's so obvious."

"She's given us a very detailed description of your appearance."

"Yeah, what? The same as in this photo? A cap and sunglasses? Do you see any of those right now?" I try to look smug.

McKinley smiles. "No, Sophie. She described your feet. And your flip flops, blue, with a lemon print, and the itchy, flaky purplish skin that makes it look like you're wearing ankle socks."

SOPHIE
Six Months Later

I'm a rare breed, don't you think? I've just received an abhorrent third divorce. I'm not around to see the reaction of the gossips and the troublemakers though, cut off from all that hokum as I am, in here.

After all my meticulously formulated ploys and manoeuvres, it came down to my accursed itchy feet in the end. Imagine! My feet were put in a line up and that woman with the camping stove picked them out from amongst seven other dermatitis cases. They must have made quite an impression on her.

I've been in this women's prison for six months now, awaiting trial. My lawyer says I have a good chance of getting away if I act a bit loopy and tell them that the supposed death of Tariq made me do all the things I did. Tariq's poison pen letters and the stalker – who I learned was Muskaan – might work in my favour, as factors that affected my mental stability.

I like to think that my theatrical skills proved useful in orchestrating the whole drama. My performance at the morgue, for example, all that feeling faint, was a masterpiece. It was such a buzz to know they were all taken in by it, like the thrill an actor feels in a live performance, I imagine.

Obviously, my cinematic hopes have been dashed, for now. Craig wrote me a letter saying he'd have to go with a different actress but would make sure I made a good return on my investment. Two months later my lawyer told me the writer was suing him for breach of contract. Craig had failed to pay her anything beyond her first instalment. Sometimes I feel sick to think I was stupid enough to gamble everything I had on his promises.

But perhaps all is not lost. My lawyer told me that *Monty and the Ghost* has gone viral on social media. It wasn't the great work of art I wanted to become famous for, but we all have to start somewhere. I even get fan mail and presents, too, apparently, although I'm not allowed those.

Now, I must use my creativity to help my current circumstances. At night, when the others are sleeping, I practise a deranged giggle as quietly as I can. Then there's the facial tic and the knuckle rubbing. If I start practising now, I might be able to do a convincing job of passing myself off as insane.

Maybe I really did become a bit insane. Yes, I was obsessed with achieving success. But more than that, I was always just a woman who wanted to be in love with a man who loved her too. It's schmaltzy but it really is that simple. The bunch of men that littered my life all let me down with their duplicity or inadequacy. Their affections were lazy, dishonest, and deceitful.

And my latest suitor, Suleiman! It's inconceivable that a man with his wiles was so easily duped. Once I'd recovered from the shock of his revolting proposal, I used it to my advantage, to lure him to the death I knew was becoming more and more inevitable. That, too, was a performance I'm particularly proud of.

I would have done anything for a man who was true.

I feel bad for Zain. I've failed him. But it was for him that I did it. My darling boy. I miss him beyond belief, but I'll have to learn how to live without him now. He's safe, at least I know that. Amir takes care of him, and I'll admit Jannat's not bad when it comes to Zain, though I don't have much time for her otherwise.

I think I'll manage to survive, it's what I do best. Ten years isn't too long. There are some rough women in here – killers, arsonists, thieves. Even getting through breakfast can be a nail-biting experience at times. But I've learned to keep quiet and I'm a strapping girl myself now. I'll cope.

And there's a charming prison officer here that I've been chatting to. He's young, attractive, sympathetic. Looking for a wife.

ACKNOWLEDGEMENTS

Thanks to all the lovely people who took a chance with Sophie- Salma, Abi, Ella and the amazing team at Datura, and my husband and girls, for everything.